I0745839

Perceivers

#4

MIND POWER

by

Jane Killick

Elly Books

Mind Power
Perceivers #4

by

Jane Killick

Published by Elly Books

ISBN: 978-1-908340-25-2

Copyright © Jane Killick 2016

ellybooks.com

ONE

THE teenager's desperation broke into Michael's mind. Her emotions were so strong that they burst through his everyday filters like a gust of wind through netting. There was a craving inside of her body and it had taken over her mind. She needed money, she needed the drugs and she hated herself for it.

Michael — crouched out of sight behind the pre-packaged food aisle of the mini-supermarket — had been planning to pick up a collection of different soups for lunch, but was tempted by a special offer and bent down to take a closer look. The interruption of the teenager's strong emotions made the letters of the advertising sign blur in front of him and he put a hand on the cold, steel shelf to steady himself. He had the power to block out her mind, and he would have already raised his barriers if he hadn't also perceived her thoughts: *When shall I pull out the knife?*

Michael left his shopping basket and paced past the packets of dried pasta and instant mashed potato to the end of the aisle. He put one hand in his pocket and felt for his phone.

His perception was hit by the sudden fear from a second mind, as man a cried out somewhere near the cash desk. Followed by the sound of empty cardboard boxes crashing to the floor.

"Give me the money from the till!" demanded a female voice.

Michael looked out from behind the aisle to see the terrified face of the wizened man who worked in the shop. The warm smile he usually used to greet his customers was gone. In its place was a face as pale as rice paper with two sunken eyes which stared at a kitchen knife pointed at his chest. The blade wavered with the shaking withdrawal symptoms of the drug addict who held it out towards him. Michael couldn't see her face, as it was shaded by the hood of her top which she had pulled up over her head, but he could perceive her desperation as loud as ever. He had no doubt that one false move would cause her to stab her victim.

The cashier must have felt the same, as Michael perceived his thoughts: *Everything will be all right as long as I do as she says, it's not worth risking my life.* It was more like he was trying to convince himself than he actually believed it.

Coins jingled as the cashier opened the till and scooped what few notes there were from the tray.

Michael pulled the phone from his pocket, fumbling as he turned the switch to silent, and dialled 999 for the police.

The young woman snatched the money from the cashier's hands. "Twenty quid?" she said.

"I'm sorry, I'm sorry," cried the man, holding up his hands in a defensive position. He stared, again, at the knife. "Most people pay by card these d—"

"I need more than this!" she screamed. She pushed him back against the stacked shelves with her fist of scrunched up notes. His body banged against a display of alcohol. A bottle of Bell's Scotch wobbled as he struck it with his elbow, then overbalanced and smashed to the ground.

The drug addict didn't seem to notice as the smell of whisky rose into the air. The only thoughts Michael perceived from her was the realisation that twenty lousy quid was only going to buy her one fix.

"Give me more!" She put the knife to the cashier's throat and Michael felt the man's fear turn to terror. The man's eyes looked beyond the robber and out into the shop. They locked on to Michael's gaze. *Help me!* said his thoughts.

The tinny and distant voice of the emergency services operator twittered from the phone in his hand. Michael suddenly realised that he couldn't reply without being overheard. He took a half step out from the end of the aisle and held up the phone screen to show the man that the line was open. Even though he couldn't transmit his thoughts to him because he was a norm, the man seemed to understand.

"Please don't stab me!" The cashier shouted loud enough for his voice to be picked up by the phone. "How about cigarettes? I give you cigarettes. Robbers take cigarettes."

He turned from the knife, grabbed cigarettes from the shelf and stuffed them into a carrier bag.

The young woman, using that strange instinct that non-perceivers have, must have realised something was not right. She swung round without warning and her bloodshot eyes immediately found Michael standing next to the display of tinned baked beans with his mobile phone held out in front of him.

In that moment of shocked silence, the operator called out. "Hello? Which service do you require?"

"What's going on?" said the woman. Michael saw the dark lines of her face for the first time, so sunken that it looked like Halloween make-up.

The phone was in his hand, Michael couldn't deny it, but he could tell a version of the truth. "I called the police. They'll be here any minute to arrest you. You better run while you have the chance."

But he'd mis-judged. Rather than being scared, she was suddenly furious. She turned on the cashier so violently that he dropped the carrier bag of cigarettes and stumbled backwards. She swung the knife at him like a sword and it sliced his arm. He cried out as his other hand grabbed at the wound and blood oozed between his fingers.

"What did you think you were doing?" she screamed, spitting abuse in his face and jabbing him with the point of the knife.

Michael perceived the rage as it burned through her mind. The craving for the drug had taken away her humanity and filled the void with feelings of revenge that threatened to turn to murder.

Without thinking, Michael wrapped his thoughts around the knife. He felt the cold metal of the blade and the hot sweaty plastic of the handle where the drug addict held on to it. As soon as he was sure his thoughts had control of the knife, he willed it away. The blade flew from her hand, as if yanked away by an unseen wire, and clattered to the floor behind her.

Confusion clouded her mind. She looked at her clenched hand where the knife used to be and she blamed the cashier. Without a weapon, she swung her fist at his cheek and it struck his bone with a crack. He slumped to the floor where she kicked him twice before fleeing out of the shop.

Michael dashed behind the counter to find the man doubled over in the foetal position among a scatter of cigarette packets. There was blood on his cheek, blood on his arm and blood on the opposite hand where he had clutched his wound, but he was still conscious.

Michael squatted down next to him. "Are you okay?" he said.

"What happened?" he groaned.

"I don't know," Michael lied. "She went mental and threw away the knife."

"You stopped her," said the man.

"No, I didn't."

"You did! Thank you, thank you."

His phone was still connected to the emergency services. He asked for both police and ambulance, gave the address of the shop and refused to give his name.

"Police and ambulance are coming," he told the man. "You'll be all right."

At that point, another shopper came in who said she used to be a nurse and started doing sensible things like wrapping up her jacket to use as a pillow for the man's head.

Michael took the opportunity to leave. On the walk home, he deleted all the memory from his phone and removed the sim card just to be safe. He deposited one in a public rubbish bin and the other down a drain. He had broken his promise to himself that he would never use his powers in public.

When he got back to his flat, he realised he'd been a bloody idiot.

TWO

MICHAEL sat on a wall by the entrance to the University of Nottingham and looked up at the white of the building reaching into the blue sky. It gleamed as a monument to learning, even if a closer look revealed the cracks in the render and the smear of green where algae grew on the patches of damp. But it didn't matter to him. Against the odds, he had been allowed to study there. He'd chosen an electrical engineering degree course because machines couldn't be perceived. To build or fix a machine he had to be like any other norm and understand its workings. If he'd taken English literature or history, he could have always cheated by reading the lecturer's mind.

The cold of the wall soaked up through Michael's trousers into his buttocks. He didn't know how much longer he could sit there before he stopped being able to feel his bum altogether. The sunshine was warm on his face, but it was halfway through the first term and the air temperature indicated the season was rushing towards winter. Instinctively, he reached into his pocket for his phone to check the time, then remembered half of it was in a bin and the other half was down a drain. He thought of opening up his perception a little bit to hear the thoughts of the passing students, some of whom were clearly rushing for their classes and might have an idea of how late he was. But listening to the unfocussed babble of a crowd thinking all at once about their everyday, insignificant troubles was more uncomfortable than not knowing the time. So he kept his filters high and their thoughts as background chatter.

At last, among the miscellany of passing faces breathing out steam into the crisp morning air, he saw Ian and waved.

Ian was short for a guy, but physically fit beneath the floppy anorak that he wore. They had become friends after meeting at the university running club which Michael had discovered was another place where being a perceiver gave him no advantage. It didn't matter that he could perceive his opponent's plan for winning a race if he couldn't physically run fast enough to catch him.

"Micky!" said Ian, waving back and trotting over to the wall. "I've been texting and texting. Were you out on a bender last night or something?"

"Dropped my phone down the toilet, didn't I?" Michael lied.

"What did you do that for?"

"I didn't do it on purpose," said Michael. He changed the subject. "I wanted to catch you to ask if you're still up for doing some training together — if there's still a spot open on the marathon team."

"Alice's leg isn't going to un-break itself, so I don't see why you couldn't have her spot."

"Good." Michael wasn't a talented runner, not like Ian, but he loved the solitude and the challenge in making his body go further and further each time. At first, he thought that he'd hold Ian back if they went running together, but now he thought it would be the best way to push him to succeed. He didn't mind that he would have to devote hours to it, because it was hours when his mind didn't have to perceive anything.

"So you didn't get my messages, then?" said Ian. His hand dived into his pocket and pulled out his phone. "There was an armed robbery at the end of your road. The police issued the CCTV. Wanna see it?"

The rest of Michael's body turned as cold as his buttocks. He hadn't thought about the shop having cameras. Cameras that were spying on his every move. He hopped off the wall and felt the increased blood flow to his bottom. "Haven't you got labs to go to?"

Ian was studying physics and spent a lot of his time in the university physics labs. "No one cares if I'm a few minutes late," said Ian. "You've got to see this, it's gone viral. They reckon there's a ghost or a poltergeist in the shop."

"A what?"

Ian was already looking up the clip on his phone. "It used to be a house, apparently, and someone got murdered," he went on. "No one wanted to live in it so it was converted into a shop and they say the victim still haunts the place." He gave his last few words a sinister tone like a dramatic TV voice-over artist.

"If it says so on the internet, it has to be true," said Michael, sarcastically.

But Ian was already showing the screen of his phone to Michael. He couldn't help but watch as he recognised the mini-supermarket, even though the camera angle was from high up behind the cash desk. The hooded figure of the robber — her face hidden — was leaning over the cashier who had his back pressed against the display. She jabbed at his chest with the point of the knife. Then the knife suddenly flew out of her hand and out of frame.

"Did you see that?" said Ian.

Michael wished he hadn't. His chest tightened at the realisation that his telekinetic power had been caught on video. "It's a hoax," he said, trying to be dismissive. "Someone probably tied a wire round it and pulled it out of shot."

"It's genuine CCTV footage issued by the police," said Ian. "Look again."

Ian was already hitting the replay button, but Michael had seen enough and backed away from his friend. "I've got a lecture to get to. See you later." He turned and ran to the lecture hall.

But it didn't matter how fast he ran, he knew that there would be no running from the internet.

THE television talked to itself in the living room of Michael's flat. He'd left it on because he liked the background noise and every now and then something interesting came up on the news.

He had escaped to the kitchen where about the only thing he had left to eat was pasta and pesto. He would have gone to the shop to get something else, but after the events of the previous day he daren't show his face in there again, and he couldn't bring himself to go all the way into town just to get something for dinner. So the pan of pasta bubbled away on the top, sending splashes of water onto the hob while he looked into the depths of the pesto jar and tried to work out if it was safe to eat. He'd forgotten to put it in the fridge after the last time he'd used it and there were a couple of small fluffy bits on top. He decided, if he scooped them off with a spoon, the bits underneath would be all right.

The timer on the oven pinged to say the pasta was cooked. He turned off the hob and took the pan to the sieve which sat ready and waiting in the sink. A cloud of steam mushroomed up into his face as he emptied the pan and he breathed in its starchy cooked pasta smell. Using a fresh spoon, he dolloped a heaped serving of pesto into the still-warm pan and stirred. The olive oil began to simmer and release the smell of basil, pine nuts and parmesan. He tipped the pasta back in the pan, gave it another stir and put the result in the bowl he had waiting.

Leaving the washing up for later, he took his meagre dinner through to the living room.

Despite the second-hand furniture, it looked nothing like the student digs some of his friends lived in. He kept it clean and fresh, he hoovered once a week and opened the window to bring in fresh air. He even dusted occasionally.

It was a legacy from his time in the Perceiver Corps and their fastidious army rules. His background of living on an army base meant he had very few possessions to clutter up the place. He'd bought a saggy sofa and armchair with springy cushions from the internet, while the nest of tables he put his dinner on came from a charity shop on the edge of town. The TV was the only thing he had bought new and he'd paid a lot to get one big enough to look like it belonged in a four-bedroomed house instead of a single-bed flat. He didn't care. He liked the way he could watch people on it without having to perceive them.

The springy cushions of the armchair sank around Michael's bottom as he lowered himself onto them. He reached over for the bowl of pasta and pesto and took a wary bite. The richness of the cheese, the nuts and the mild piquancy of the basil filled his mouth. He smiled; there was no earthiness of mould or bitterness to suggest something that had gone off. He ate the second bite with greater confidence, as the woman on the news with perfect hair and a red jacket turned to her next story.

"Government sources have denied reports that perceivers are being used in courtrooms to test the honesty of witnesses in murder trials," she said. "I'm joined by our reporter, Sian Jones, who broke the story. Sian, what you make of this denial?"

The picture on the screen cut to a wide shot to reveal the newsreader with the perfect hair was sitting next to another woman in a black jacket with blonde hair tied back in a ponytail behind her.

In contrast to the newsreader, she looked tired. She had broken the perceiver story the week before and had been all over the news ever since. Michael was fed up of hearing about it.

"What's interesting about this denial, is the government hasn't come out openly to refute the story," said Sian, lifting a stray strand of hair with her middle finger and tucking it back behind her ear. "It's almost as if they're trying to brief against it without having to lay their cards out on the table, which could be embarrassing if they're forced to admit it down the line. As we reported yesterday, a number of people have come forward with compelling evidence that perceivers have been used in at least two murder trials that we know of to read the minds of …"

Michael had heard enough. He looked around for the TV remote control and saw it was on the arm of the sofa where he had thrown it after turning on the TV on the way to the kitchen.

The remote was a familiar object and he only had to glimpse it to hold it with his mind. He willed it across to his hand and caught it with ease.

"… The charity, Victims for Justice, told us they're outraged that this has been allowed to go on and are demanding to know the truth about the use of perceivers in public area—"

Michael changed the channel and the irritating journalist was replaced with an irritating quiz show host. The host was ostensibly harmless, but Michael hated quizzes for the way they exposed his lack of general knowledge caused by the memory wipe he suffered when he was fifteen. So he changed channels again and ended up watching a programme about an overweight English couple who wanted to move to somewhere sunny abroad.

He hardly tasted the rest of his dinner. By the time the bowl was empty, he was wishing he had made the effort to walk into town to buy something that wouldn't have left his stomach bloated and his mouth with a greasy film of olive oil in it. He put the bowl on the nest of tables and debated with himself over the relative merits of watching whether the overweight couple decided to move abroad after all, or going to the kitchen to get the washing up done. Neither sounded particularly appealing.

The doorbell gave him a third choice.

Walking towards the front door, Michael tried to remember if he had ordered anything over the internet recently. Sometimes, if the courier called while he was at university, a neighbour would take in the parcel for him and deliver it in the evening. But, as he got to the door, he perceived the person on the other side of it wasn't one of his neighbours.

There was something familiar about the mind of the person who had rung the bell. But he couldn't place it. He could have tried harder to perceive who it was, but it was easier to simply open the door.

A woman stood in the corridor. She was about the same age as most of the students he hung about with at university and, therefore, a couple of years younger than him. She was dressed all in black with long, black hair which rested on the shoulder of her leather jacket. The only colourful thing about her was the red of her lipstick and lavender of her eye shadow.

She smiled.

Michael didn't smile back. He was too much in shock. It was Pauline: the perceiver he once thought he loved.

THREE

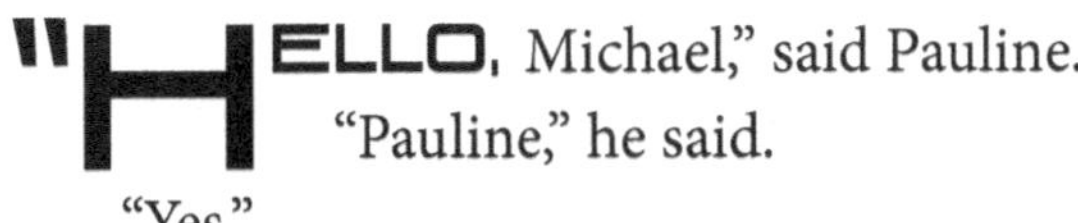

"HELLO, Michael," said Pauline.

"Pauline," he said.

"Yes."

Michael was mesmerised by her face. She looked every bit a woman now, whereas the person he remembered had been a teenager. At the same time as he looked; he perceived. She could have blocked him if she wanted to — he could tell she was as strong as ever — but she let him feel her emotions. She was pleased to see him, a little nervous and also a little surprised to find that he was actually living there.

"Can I come in?" she said.

It was only then that he realised he'd been keeping her standing in the cold of the corridor. "Oh yes, of course." He stepped aside.

Pauline stepped through the doorway and looked around. He self-consciously watched her size up the sofa, armchair, TV and little nest of tables with the bowl that once held his dinner. "Smells nice," she said.

"It was only pasta and pesto," he said.

"Aren't you going to ask me the question I can perceive you want to ask?"

Michael felt himself blush. It had been a long time since his thoughts were overheard by another perceiver. "How did you find me?"

She turned to face him. There was a mischievous smile on her lips. "Micky Page?" she said. "Not a very inspired nom de plume if you didn't want to be found — using your biological mother's surname."

"It seemed to work until now."

"Until a video of you using your powers went flying round the internet."

"I don't know what you mean," he said.

"There's no point lying to me," said Pauline. "I'm a perceiver, remember?"

He felt the heat of embarrassment again. He tried to find out what she was doing at his flat by getting into her mind, but she was skilled enough only to reveal her outer emotions. "How did you know it was me? On the video, I mean."

"You're the only perceiver with telekinesis that we know of. If it wasn't you, then we needed to find out who it was. And if it *was* you, then we needed to find out why you lied about losing your powers."

"I didn't lie," said Michael. "They came back after I left the Perceiver Corps."

She nodded. She had to believe him because he couldn't lie to her without her knowing it. "What do you say about making me a cup of tea and sitting down to talk about it?"

"I don't think I have any tea," said Michael.

"Coffee, then. Looks like you could do with a cup of something."

"Yeah."

He walked into the kitchen and Pauline followed.

She engaged in small talk while he went through the ritual of getting mugs from the cupboard and putting the kettle on. He was glad to have something normal to do, as he was still in shock from seeing her.

"Nice flat," she said.

"Yeah."

"Bit posh for a student, isn't it?"

"My mum helps out with the rent," said Michael.

"Your real mum? The one who brought you up? I thought you didn't speak to her."

"I'm trying to build some sort of relationship with her. What with my dad in jail and everything. It's weird because she remembers bringing me up as a child and I don't remember anything about her, so …"

The kettle came to the boil. He poured the water over a spoonful of granular coffee at the bottom of each mug. They fizzed briefly as the bitter, smoky smell of coffee rose into the kitchen. Out of habit, he went to the fridge. It was only when he opened the door that he remembered there was virtually nothing in it.

"I've got no milk, sorry. Are you okay with black?"

"Black's fine," said Pauline.

He handed her the mug and they went back into the living room. Pauline naturally gravitated towards the sofa and Michael went back to the armchair. But he didn't sink into its springy cushions like he had when he sat down to watch the TV. He sat on the edge and leant forward. He may not have been able to perceive exactly the reason for Pauline being there — not without her feeling him push past her barriers — but he knew it was more than a social call.

Pauline blew across the surface of her drink, sending a mini cloud of steam out into the room. She brought it to her lips, but she must have sensed the liquid was too hot and lowered it to her lap again.

"What happened with your powers?" she said.

"I thought they'd been destroyed by the serum," he said. The serum he had taken to boost his perceiver abilities during the mission which had killed their friend, Alex. Even the passing memory of it was painful and he pushed it away. "I didn't have any perceiver powers at all, not for months. Agent Cooper agreed I couldn't be of any use in the Perceiver Corps, so he let me go. He set me up on a course so I could get up to speed with my education and apply to university. Then my perception started to come back. Just little bits and pieces at first. An overheard thought one week, a perceived emotion the next. By the time a year had gone past, I was as strong as I ever was. Even my telekinesis came back."

"But you didn't tell Agent Cooper?"

"I didn't want to go back there. I still don't want to go back. That's not why you're here is it?"

"No," said Pauline. But there was something in her head that suggested she wasn't telling the entire truth.

"I can tell you didn't come here because you wanted to see me," said Michael.

He perceived she still blamed him for what happened to Alex. It was in her emotions: quieter than it had been in the days after it happened, but still present.

Pauline made another attempt to take a sip of her hot coffee and sat back into the sofa like she was preparing for a long explanation. "You've heard the news, I suppose."

"About perceivers?"

She nodded. "It's all going to come out now. That journalist has pulled down a hornets' nest and now that it's started to swarm, more journalists are piling in on the story. They're going to uncover everything about us and it's happening so fast, I don't know what we're going to do about it."

"What has that got to do with me?"

"We need you, Michael."

Michael shook his head. "I left."

"You lied to get out," said Pauline.

Michael put his mug down on the nest of tables as he felt himself getting animated. He didn't want the damn drink in the first place and he sure as hell didn't want to spill it on his clean carpet. "They let me go," he insisted. "I didn't know I was going to get my perception back and it happened so slowly that by the time it was back to normal, I had a life here. I got accepted to university, I've made friends here — norm friends. I don't want to go back."

"So you're going to leave us to deal with it like it's got nothing to do with you?"

"No, Pauline, it's not like that."

But her disappointment and anger were easily perceptible. She stood up from the sofa. "It was a mistake coming here."

Michael stood up too. It had been a long time since he had seen Pauline and, even though the death of Alex had placed a barrier between them, seeing her again reminded him of how he used to feel.

"Thanks for the coffee," she said, thrusting the mug into Michael's hands. It was still full; she hadn't drunk a drop. "But I think I should go."

"No, Pauline, please stay." He followed her to the door. "At least tell me how you're getting on."

She put her hand on the door handle, but didn't turn it. "I work for the government now," she said.

"Didn't we always work for the government?" he said.

"I mean the actual government. At Westminster where the MPs are. They're worried about this whole perceiver thing. They don't say it to me in so many words, but I can perceive that they're frightened about public unrest much worse than the riots five years ago. Now that people think they were being spied on and lied to by the government, there could be a huge backlash. The Prime Minister was looking for an advisor to help, someone who understands perceivers but who isn't connected to Agent Cooper. I thought you could be that person, but obviously not."

She opened the door. The chill from the corridor spilled into the room as Pauline pulled up her blocks and cut off Michael's access to her disappointed and angry emotions.

"Don't go like this," said Michael. "Come back and sit down. Tell me how the others at Galen House are getting on. Is Norm the Norm still there?"

"What do you care? You left." She stepped out into the corridor and turned to face him one last time. "Have a nice life. Enjoy your university degree and your norm friends and your nice little flat that your mum's paying for. I'm sure it's better than facing up to the truth of what you are."

She strode off down the corridor, the heels of her boots tapping on the hard floor. Michael watched her until she got to the end and disappeared into the stairwell. He pulled back the fringe from his suddenly hot head. It was too late to realise he should have said more to make her stay.

FOUR

MICHAEL ran. The steady beat of his trainers on the streets of Nottingham thumped through his body and joined the beating of his heart. He controlled his breathing to match his feet: forcing the air from his lungs each time his left foot hit the ground. Until he wasn't thinking about it anymore. Until the rhythm of his steps were part of him and his breaths came and went without being told. There was only the road ahead with its occasional roadside tree that he would challenge himself to reach and eventually pass, before targeting a new tree.

If there were other people on the street, he didn't perceive them. The only things in his head were his own thoughts and emotions which pounded through his mind with each step. Pauline still lived in there, along with the things that he should have done and should have said to her. He turned their conversation over and over and tried to outrun his feelings of guilt.

As he turned towards the university, he saw Ian up ahead. His running companion had stopped and gave him a wave before stretching out a leg and leaning over to elongate the muscles in his thigh. Michael slowed as he approached and reached to his right wrist to stop his running watch. He glanced at the figures: five miles in just under forty-five minutes. It was a good time.

"Had a nice stroll?" said Ian. Michael could perceive he was joking, even as his mouth broke into a tell-tale grin.

"We can't all be…" he took a deep breath, "…Superman like you… you know."

"What was your time?"

Michael showed him his watch.

"That's equal your best, isn't it?"

"Nearly," said Michael. He'd had to wait a frustratingly long time to cross a road at one point otherwise he might even have beaten his best time for five miles. Training with Ian was really going to improve his performance.

He stretched out the muscles in his legs like he had been taught in the running club and his breathing soon recovered into a more leisurely pattern. By the time he'd finished, Ian looked like he was getting cold.

"Come on, let's get back to the showers," said Michael.

The two of them headed up Beeston Lane to the university gym. Michael had started to get cold, too, and he knew if he didn't hit the shower soon he might start shivering.

Ahead of them were three young women — students, by the look of their casual dress — one of whom was trying to press leaflets into the hands of passing pedestrians. The other two held clipboards and were casting their eyes about for victims to pounce on. A man with a large sports holdall over one shoulder, and sleeked down wet hair like he'd just come out of the shower, couldn't avoid being stopped by the short blonde one. In less than a minute, he'd put down his bag and was signing up to whatever she was collecting signatures for.

"I wonder what that's all about?" said Ian.

"Let's go round them," said Michael.

"Morning!" said the second girl with a clipboard. She was also not particularly tall and wore a navy blue woollen hat down over her ears with only a few wisps of black hair sticking out of the bottom.

"Morning!" said Ian.

Michael didn't know why he was engaging with her, when everyone knew the trick of avoiding people was to walk quickly by while examining your own shoes. Until he realised Ian wasn't trying to avoid her at all: he was flirting with her.

The third woman thrust a leaflet into Michael's hands. He didn't notice what she looked like because all of his attention was taken by the headline: *Ban Perceiver Spies*.

"We're collecting signatures to demand perceivers be banned," she was telling Ian. "We think it's a breach of our human rights to allow them to spy on our minds. We want the government to come clean over how they've been secretly using perceivers in the police force and the legal system and in business, and take them out of every aspect of public life."

"Yeah, I'll sign," said Ian.

At first Michael thought he was saying it because he was still flirting with the girl. But then he perceived him and realised that he agreed with all the rubbish that she was spouting.

Ian completed his signature and handed the clipboard over to Michael. Michael stepped back from it like it was contaminated with a deadly germ.

"Come on, Micky." He held out the pen.

Michael shook his head. "Perceivers are people."

"I've got nothing against perceivers being people," said Ian. "I knew a couple of perceiver kids when I was at school, but they did the right thing and they got the cure."

Michael would have closed off his perception so he couldn't feel the bitterness his friend had for him and people like him, but he was so shocked, he kept perceiving it. He wanted to ask Ian if he would sign the petition if they wanted to ban people with a different colour skin or people who couldn't run because they were in a wheelchair. But he feared he might give too much away, so he said nothing.

"Look, I'm going to have a shower back at my flat," said Michael.

"That's like a mile in the other direction," said Ian.

"I just remembered I haven't got any shampoo in my locker." He stepped away to indicate he was keen to go.

"You can borrow my shampoo."

"No, it's all right," said Michael. "I have this special stuff, I get dandruff if I don't use it."

The woman took her clipboard and pen back from Ian, apparently realising she wasn't going to get a signature from Michael. "If you change your mind, you can sign our petition online," she said. "All the details are in the leaflet."

Michael looked down at his hand where, he saw, he was still holding their printed piece of propaganda. As he turned away from the man he thought was his friend, he let go of the leaflet and it drifted away in the breeze. He broke into a run and didn't stop until he reached his flat.

MICHAEL rested his head against the window in the back of the taxi and let the rumble of his journey from the train station thump through his skull. The dying green of the English countryside in the throes of autumn blurred past him in a mess of gold, red and brown. The sign on the back of the seat in front of him said that it was a no smoking vehicle, and yet the dirty smell of old smoke was all around him. It seemed to be part of the upholstery. He was beginning to suspect the cabbie was a smoker himself and would occasionally have a crafty cigarette when he didn't have a passenger.

The radio switched from an advert for a local double glazing firm to the news jingle and, without realising it, Michael was suddenly listening to more fallout from the journalist's exposé into the use of perceivers. The newsreader was still using phrases like "reported that" and "according to" to suggest that nothing had been confirmed, but Michael knew that it was all true. He used to be one of those perceivers who used to spy on people. He used to work with the police and look into the minds of suspects to see if they had really committed the crime they were accused of. He thought he was doing his public duty at the time, but it seemed the public thought his actions were reprehensible, immoral, and even inhuman.

"We need to know how deep the spying goes," said a woman in a clip played out in the news. Michael recognised her voice as Claudia Angelheart, the leader of the now defunct campaign group, Action Against Mind Invasion. "If I go to the doctor to say I'm unwell, are they reading my mind to see if I'm really sick or a time waster? If I ask for a loan, are they reading my mind to see if I really intend to pay it back? If I report a crime to the police, are they getting inside my head to see if I'm telling the truth? And, if they're in my head looking for those things, what other private things are they seeing?"

The news, fortunately, was on one of those pop music stations that only bothered with the real world for a minute before launching back into a string of fast beats interspersed with adverts, and so he didn't have to listen to it anymore.

Michael had forgotten he was supposed to give the taxi driver more detailed directions when they got nearer to Mary Ransom's house, but it seemed he didn't need them. The taxi pulled over at the edge of the difficult-to-find cul-de-sac lined with tall trees right next to the driveway. He turned down the radio and the beat of the music faded to almost nothing.

Michael lifted his head from the window. "Are we here?"

"I could go down the drive if you wanted," said the taxi driver. "I just didn't know if I could turn around at the bottom."

"Here is fine," said Michael. He got out of the cab and paid the driver.

Michael threw his overnight bag onto his shoulder and stepped onto the gravel that formed the length of the driveway down to his mother's house. His feet crunched over the stones as he walked down, being careful not to step in the occasional puddle which had formed with the overnight rain.

He had not walked many steps before he could see past the over-hanging branches of the bushes to the front of his mother's impressive, detached and expensive four-bedroomed house. Across the doorway someone had sprayed two words in bright red paint:

PERCEIVER SCUM.

Michael felt the disgust rise in his throat. His mother had been distraught on the phone, but he hadn't really understood why until that moment.

Each crunching step over the gravel brought him closer to the reality of it. The front of the house had once seemed serene, almost charming in its English country setting, but now it was soiled. The paint had done more than leave words on the door, it had left a disgusting message that violated the sanctity of his mother's home.

Michael reached out for the doorbell, but his hand stopped mid-air as he saw the door was ajar. The frame in which it stood — which must have been made from the original wood dating from when the house was built — had been splintered, and the bolts shooting out from the door itself had failed to keep it secure.

"Hello?" he called, as he pushed the door open and stepped inside.

There was no reply. Just a collection of muddy footprints on the doormat and a collection of coats which had been taken from their hooks on the wall and dumped to the floor in a jumble of black and grey. He pushed the door shut behind him and it bumped uselessly against the splintered frame so it remained open just enough to keep the cold of the outside blowing through the crack.

"Hello?"

Only emptiness replied.

He opened his perception enough to take in the whole house. He felt only one presence, close enough to realise someone was in the lounge.

Michael tiptoed over the broken shards of a glass vase that once sat on the shelf above the radiator in the hallway and opened the door to the lounge. What he saw inside was more like a squat frequented by drug addicts than a cherished family home. Across the back wall, sprayed on the cream wallpaper with its delicate powder blue illustrations of flowers, was another disgusting message:

PERCEIVER SCUM.

It looked like the vandals had run out of red paint halfway through because the last two letters had been finished off in green.

The ugly words looked down upon a scene of carnage. There was stuff everywhere. So much that it had ceased to be possessions or important papers and had become merely junk. Someone had taken a knife to an armchair cushion and it lay in the middle of the floor like an old rag while its white fluffy stuffing was strewn around the room like cheap artificial snow in a Christmas shop display.

Sitting on the sofa, among the litter of her life, was Mary Ransom. A small woman with grey hair that had almost replaced her natural blonde, she sat huddled on the edge of the cushion like a homeless person squeezed in on herself to protect her body from the cold of the outside world. Michael perceived that she knew he had walked in, but her body didn't acknowledge him. It hurt to feel her shame at what had happened to her, even though anyone could see *she* was the victim.

"Mary?" he said. He still wasn't able to bring himself to call her 'mum', even though their relationship had got closer ever since he left Galen House.

"Michael," she acknowledged. She shot him a fleeting glance, then went back to stare at her two hands clenched together on her knees. "Why?"

Walking into the destruction of her home was sickening enough, but to perceive his mother's distress was heartbreaking. There was nothing in her mind except despair and the shame of her son having to see her so helpless.

He stepped past her possessions strewn over the carpet and sat next to her. He thought perhaps he should put a comforting arm around her shoulders, but that felt awkward, so he let his hands fall in his lap.

"What happened?" he said.

She held out her hands to indicate the mess that was her house.

Michael chastised himself for asking such a stupid question, but he didn't know what else to say.

"It's because of your father," she said.

"Yes," said Michael.

"He said don't go to the trial. He said, keep myself out of it. But I'll never be out of it, will I? I mean, look — *look!* — I married a perceiver and they're going to make me suffer for it over and over again."

The cracks in her strong, angry words began to show as emotion overtook her. She rested her head on Michael's shoulder and he perceived how the feeling of the warmth from his body made her feel more secure. Even in a house with a busted front door.

He took her hand and held it tightly. They sat like that for a while, her not saying anything and him perceiving that she was trying to keep herself under control, at the same time that she felt she had no control at all.

"Did you tell the police?" said Michael.

"I called them," said Mary. "They came over and took a statement and took photos. They told me they would do their best to catch the people who did it, but you don't always have to be a perceiver to know they're lying."

"What are you going to do now?"

She shrugged.

"You can't stay here with the place like this. Especially not with the door open."

"It's my home, Michael."

"At least get someone in to fix the door," he said. "Then we can get this place cleared up."

"Okay," she said. Quietly, timidly. "Do you want something to eat?"

He wasn't hungry. He was too angry and appalled to be hungry. But he could perceive she wanted to cook something for him. It was something she could do to help which didn't involve dealing with the vandalism in her house.

"Yeah, that would be lovely."

Mary got up from the sofa and headed out to the kitchen.

Michael was left in the mess on his own. There was so much of it, he didn't know where to start.

THE double glazing companies he called said they didn't have someone to spare to fit a door right away and they suggested getting someone in to board up the front entrance until they could come round and measure up properly. So that's what Michael did. He booked a cleaning firm who specialised in removing graffiti and a decorator who could rip off the soiled wallpaper and start again.

By the time he sat down to eat the chicken stir-fry his mum had made for him — apparently from 'leftovers', even though it tasted amazing enough to be fresh — she was worried about how much it was going to cost.

"I thought my father had loads of money."

"Before the vitamin scandal, maybe," said Mary. "How much do you think Ransom Incorporated shares were worth after the trial?"

It was the first time he perceived that she was worried about money. He had always assumed his father was a rich man with money squirrelled away. He hadn't thought that most of it was tied up in the business: the same business that made the 'vitamin' pills that turned so many normal teenagers into perceivers.

After he'd eaten, Michael picked up all the stuffing from the slashed cushion and Mary went back into the kitchen to get a rubbish bag to put it in. It was easier to see what everything else was after some of the mess was out of the way. He found places for the obvious things, like the TV remote control and mantelpiece ornaments. The rest were Mary and his father's personal papers and possessions that he didn't know what to do with. So he gathered those up and put them on the dining table for his mother to sort through.

Among them, he found a couple of those old-fashioned discs that used to have films on. But they weren't commercially produced discs with printed labels, they were plain silver with handwriting on them. One said 'Grand Canyon Tour' and the second said 'Michael's 5th Birthday'.

He put everything down apart from the second disc. He read the writing again.

"What's that?" said Mary.

"It says it's my fifth birthday," said Michael, clutching the gateway to the past with increasingly sweaty fingers.

"I forgot we had that," she said. "Your father got keen on taking videos for all of six months, before he got bored again."

Staring at the disc did nothing to reveal the secrets hidden inside. He looked to his mother. "Does it work?"

"Do you mean, can we play it?"

"I suppose that's what I mean." He was more asking if it was possible than actually wanting to see himself at the age of five.

But she had already removed the disc from his hand and taken it to a cabinet in the corner of the room. She brushed aside some screwed up papers that were in front of it and allowed the piece of machinery to swallow the disc.

"Turn on the TV, Michael."

Michael picked up the remote from the arm of the sofa where he had put it moments before and pressed the on button.

On the wall, beneath the scrawl of PERCEIVER SCUM in red and green paint, light shone out through the cracks in the television screen which it had been smashed by a vandal.

Mary came over to the sofa and tugged at his arm so he would sit next to her.

Together, they watched the image of the same lounge they were sitting in appear in front of them. The same, but different. None of the same furniture was there, there was a long table full of multi-coloured party food. It was almost as bright and colourful as the balloons that hung from the ceiling and the paper hats on the heads of the little boys sitting around it. Michael looked at their faces. All strangers.

"Is one of them me?" he said.

He perceived his mother's surprise. "That's you at the end, look."

The little boy in the yellow hat had the widest eyes it was possible for a human to have. It looked like he was trying to eat the whole spread with his irises. He could perceive his mother's nostalgia for the image, but to him it was just another boy. He looked closer and tried to see the things in the boy's face that he recognised from the mirror, but his features were still young and unformed compared to Michael's stubbled face which he had to shave every day.

A woman he recognised as his mother — thinner, happier, without a hint of grey — leant across the table and held a lit match to five candles sitting atop a cake of bright red, blue and green icing. The video had difficulty in seeing the tiny flames in the daylight of the past, but there was enough flicker every now and again to tell that they were there.

"Make a wish," said the young mother on the screen.

Michael saw the little boy he used to be take a big breath and puff out his cheeks. He blew all across the cake, probably spitting germs onto the top of the icing as he extinguished the little flames with wind from his lungs.

The woman cheered and clapped her hands in an exaggerated childish way that encouraged the other children to do the same. But her smile was real. She was loving it as much as the children.

"Cut the cake," said an adult male voice out of shot and close to the camera. His father?

The younger Mary reached behind and pulled out a large knife. Somewhat like the knife the drug addict had used to threaten the shop assistant.

"Mummy, let me cut the cake! Let me!" squealed the immature voice of the little boy whose birthday it was on the video. Michael still couldn't quite believe it was his own voice.

"You can help me, Michael," said the young mother.

She came right up close to the boy and he put his small hands over the top of hers on the knife handle. They pushed it down into the soft icing of the cake together.

Michael perceived a sadness coming from his mother. His real mother, sitting next to him in the present. A feeling of regret burgeoned inside of her, even though he sensed she was trying to hold it back.

"You don't remember, do you?" she said.

"I was five," said Michael.

"But you wouldn't remember even if it was your tenth birthday, would you?"

"You know what happened to me." His father had tried to destroy his power to stop it being exploited by others, but all it had done was wipe his memories. He couldn't remember anything about his life until he was fifteen.

"All because of perceivers," she said. Michael felt her emotions turning to anger. "Everything in my life has been ruled by perceivers, ever since I met your father. I didn't know what one was back then — no one did. He said it meant that I didn't need to tell him I loved him because he could perceive it. He said feeling my love for him was the most beautiful thing in the world and it made him love me more. I thought it was romantic. I was an idiot."

"No," Michael told her, but she wasn't listening.

"When I couldn't get pregnant he said it was a chance to have a perceiver baby who would grow up to be stronger than anyone else. I thought it would be good for my child — like those foolish, trusting mothers who took the vitamin pills because they thought they were giving their baby the best start in life. Then you were born, and even though you didn't have any of my DNA because I had to use donor eggs, I loved you just the same. More, I think, because I'd tried so hard to have you …"

As she spoke, Michael perceived that love. A love that was split between the little boy trying to eat a slice of birthday cake with one mouthful and getting icing round his mouth on the TV, and the real grown up version of him by her side. It made him embarrassed that he couldn't love her back in the same way.

"… By the time your perceiver powers emerged when you were a teenager, your dad was getting worried. That's when he did that thing that destroyed your memories and I lost you. Then I lost my husband when the authorities caught up with him and locked him up. All I had left was this house."

She looked up at the words PERCEIVER SCUM scrawled across her wall as images of Michael and his friends running round the garden in party hats played on the cracked television screen.

"I'm here now," said Michael. He put a reassuring hand on top of hers and felt how cold her fingers were.

"Yes."

The sound of the doorbell made both of them jump.

"That'll be the repairman," said Michael. He calmed down as soon as he realised what the noise was, but he felt his mother was still shaking beside him.

"Hello?" called a male voice, presumably from the doorstep.

Mary smoothed herself down. "I should put the kettle on."

"Don't be stupid," said Michael. "I'll deal with it."

As he walked out of the lounge, he tuned out Mary's angry, melancholy, regretful thoughts. But he couldn't close his ears and, as he stepped into the corridor, he heard the faint sounds of her starting to cry.

The man at the door was, indeed, the repairman, complete with holdall of tools, overalls and a white van parked in the drive.

He nodded to Michael as he came to meet him. "Nasty business," said the repairman.

"Yeah," said Michael.

"You have access to the house round the back, do you?"

"Um, yeah, I think so." He was trying to remember if there was a back door. He was sure there must be. He didn't visit Mary very often and the conversation they had just had was still living in his head.

"The best thing to do is to board up this opening so the place is secure until you can get someone to fit a new door."

"Right." Michael had little option other than to agree with the expert.

The man walked to the back of his van. From that vantage point, he had a clear view of the damage. "If I were you, when they come to fit a new door, get new locks on the windows too, and an alarm system and CCTV."

"You think these people will come back?" said Michael.

"I can't say, but until someone does something about this perceiver business, there's nothing much else you can do."

Michael had to step out of the doorway as the man came towards him with a length of plywood. He promised to make the man a cup of tea after he had made a quick phone call. He walked up the drive to get some privacy both from him and from his mother.

Michael pulled his phone from his pocket and stood back against the shade of an evergreen bush at the side of the gravel strip. The backup contacts that he had transferred to his new phone included

Pauline's mobile number. It had been a couple of years since he'd dialled it and he wasn't sure if it still worked.

It rang a few times and then Pauline's voice answered. Not her real voice, a recorded voice. She hadn't even changed her message over the two years.

"Hi, Pauline, it's Michael," he told the recording. "I've thought about your offer and I've changed my mind. I'd like to work with the government on the perceiver problem."

FIVE

MICHAEL walked along the corridors of power with his hand on the security badge that hung around his neck to make sure it was facing outwards so people could see that he had the right to be there. If he let it go, he feared it would swing round the other way and someone would challenge him over why he was in the Houses of Parliament. He feared they would realise someone had made a mistake and throw him out.

Except no one seemed to care. The people who walked past him barely gave him a second glance. He checked their passing thoughts just to be certain, but they were too busy thinking how late they were in getting to their next meeting or how much work they had to do. Michael was just another guy in a suit going from one place to another.

The building was a strange place, so steeped in history that he could almost smell it seeping out of the walls. On the outside, the

Houses of Parliament — or Palace of Westminster, as it was also called — rose into the London skyline like a cathedral. Inside, it had the splendour of a castle. Walking into the inner sanctum, the facade of grandeur fell away to reveal the bureaucracy within. Aside from the debating chamber, it was really a series of offices where politicians and civil servants generated mounds of paperwork in their attempt to run the country.

Michael stopped at the oak panelled door which he believed was the office Pauline worked from. He allowed his perception to reach through the wooden panels and detected the signature of Pauline's mind. She was alone. He knocked.

"Come in!" she called from inside.

He opened the door into a cramped office that looked like it was resisting the move into the digital age. A line of metal filing cabinets at the back of the room suggested its work still revolved around paper. On the room's two desks, next to the ageing computers, piles of precariously stacked files rose into the air like models of the Leaning Tower of Pisa.

Pauline had the receiver of a landline telephone clamped to her ear as she stood behind the far desk making gestures for the caller to hurry up while speaking to him in an unhurried way. "Yes, I'll do that no problem." She glanced over at Michael and raised a finger to suggest she would be with him in one moment. "Of course. I'm sure we have the file here somewhere … I will … Yes … Bye."

She put the phone down with a sigh. "Michael! You made it then?"

"Yeah." He lifted up his security badge for her to see. "They let me in. God knows why."

She came out from behind her desk and gave him a hug. He embraced her thin, strong body and felt her warmth soak into his. The last time they had done that, he had also perceived her warm feelings for him, but this time all he perceived was their absence. She released her embrace and stood back. His body grew a little colder without her touch.

"How's your mum?" she asked.

"Fine, I think. She's gone to stay with her sister in Scotland for a few days while workmen are round at the house."

"Sounds sensible."

"How's Galen House?" said Michael.

"Everyone's worried," said Pauline. "You can perceive it. Even when I put up my blocks and everyone else puts up theirs, it sort of lives in the air. Very few of us go out working anymore. So on top of everything else, people are frustrated and angry. Norm the Norm's got them marching all over the base to kill off some nervous energy, but they still bring it back with them."

"You still have a job, though?"

"Yeah, I perceive certain people when they come up before parliamentary committees. They think they're only getting a grilling from the MPs on the committee, but I take a little peak into their minds while they're being questioned so I know exactly what they're not saying. I've been working on the Energy Select Committee recently. It's, um, *fascinating*." She smiled and deliberately allowed Michael to perceive that the dreary business of MPs was anything but fascinating to her.

"I'm supposed to be on a committee," said Michael. "I have no idea what to say to them."

"You need to speak up for perceivers," said Pauline.

"I know. I just wish I had a solution to the whole mess."

"You'll find one. The Prime Minister has faith in you."

"I guess that must be why I sailed through the security checks. As soon as I realised they were doing a background check on me, I thought they'd never let me in this place. I don't go by my father's surname, but that's not going to fool government security. I was at the perceiver riots five years ago, forheavensake! I felt sure that was going to raise a red flag, but it was 'all cleared, Mr Sanderson; here's your security pass, Mr Sanderson; have a nice day, Mr Sanderson.'"

"Like I said," said Pauline. "The Prime Minister wanted you."

"Talking of which, I have a meeting with him. It's in, er ..." Michael pulled out his phone and looked at the diary entry. "... The Disraeli Lounge. Do you know where that is?"

"Yeah, I'll show you."

THERE was a musty smell about the Disraeli Lounge which suggested it had a bit of a damp problem. Even though the radiator was blasting out heat and the nineteenth-century windows had been replaced by replica double glazed versions, the moisture in the walls was not deterred. Michael suspected that the decorators had literally papered over the cracks when they put up the maroon wallpaper which gave the room a darkened tone.

Michael sat on one of two leather sofas facing each other across a small table made of dark wood in the middle of what was effectively a little lounge. There was a desk at one end so someone could work in there if they wanted to, but it had no computer so it seemed unlikely it was used for that purpose very often. It was more like an informal meeting room, although it did little to put Michael at ease.

The movement of the occasional mind past the door was as distant as the sound of the London traffic through the double glazing and Michael paid little attention until he perceived one of the minds come closer.

He stood up as the door opened and a man in a dark grey suit and trademark bright tie of orange and blue stripes walked in. Michael immediately recognised him as the Prime Minister, John Pankhurst. His own nervousness grew into a lump in his throat. He tried to cough it away.

Pankhurst, Michael perceived, was a worried man. In the five years since they had last met he looked like he had aged ten. He had given up disguising his grey hair with brown dye and had let it grow into a thinning pattern on his head. The lines on his face had become more pronounced and his skin had taken on a stressed grey pallor. Pankhurst closed the door behind him with the hurry of a man who didn't want to be observed.

"Sit down. Sit down, please," said Pankhurst in a flurry. "I've got a Cabinet meeting in five minutes."

Michael sat as Pankhurst went round the table to sit on the opposite sofa. He shuffled forward so he perched on the edge of the cushion and glanced at his watch. Michael perceived it wasn't the time he was worried about.

"I wanted to brief you on why you're here," said Pankhurst.

"For the working group on perceivers," said Michael, but even as he said it he perceived that the Prime Minister was talking about something else.

"You will be part of that, of course," said Pankhurst. "But I need you to do something else for me. Something that I don't want other people in this building to know about."

"I don't understand."

"I need you to protect my mind."

Michael sat back. The Prime Minister's skittish behaviour made more sense now. "You're worried that someone's perceiving you?"

"I carry a lot of important information in my head. If someone was to get access to it, it could be very serious. Not just serious for me, but serious for the country. I understand there's things you perceivers do called blocks. Could you block my mind?"

Michael hadn't blocked someone else's mind before, but he had experienced it being done. "Yes, it's possible, but the Perceiver Corps is full people who could do that for you. They effectively work for the government already. I don't."

"Exactly," said Pankhurst. "You're independent. You don't report to Agent Bill Cooper or the army, you can work for me and solely for me. Can you do that?"

"Yes, but I don't understand why," said Michael.

"Think what information a perceiver could discover if they got into my head. When all this started, they were teenagers, they weren't a danger. Now they're older and they're in the police force and the court system — even *we* use them, like your friend Pauline. They're not like normal spies, they don't need to hack into computers or copy documents, they need only to be in the same room as me. If there are any perceivers in Westminster, I need you to identify them."

"I can do that," said Michael as he felt his role at combating the perceiver crisis slip away from him.

"If it were only people with political ambition, I could ride the storm. Politics always was a cut-throat business, but there's been recent intelligence to suggest foreign powers are using perceivers. Whether they have recruited people in Britain, or are possibly growing their own, it's unclear. Either way, I could be vulnerable — the country's secrets could be vulnerable — wherever I go. I'm leaving for the G8 summit tomorrow and I need you to come with me. Do you have a bag packed?"

"No, sir," said Michael.

"Pack one. Someone will pick you up in the morning."

Michael stood as the Prime Minister left the room; taking his paranoia with him.

SIX

MICHAEL didn't think he'd go to Russia again. Ever. If the Russian authorities had known who he was, they would have surely stopped him at the airport. But, as he travelled with diplomatic privilege as part of the Prime Minister's staff, he walked undisturbed off the plane at St Petersburg and got into the second car behind Pankhurst for the journey to the summit venue without anyone stopping him.

Michael kept close enough to Pankhurst to know if any perceiver was trying to read his mind, but Michael was the only perceiver to come anywhere close to him for the whole journey.

Arriving at Constantine Palace in the daylight allowed the full magnificence of the building to express itself. Sat within parkland so vast that the rest of the world lay out of sight, its crisp rendered walls and pillared arches spread themselves as long as a row of Victorian terraced houses, yet infinitely more grand. So many windows looked out onto its acres of lawn and calm man-made lake that it was more like a hotel. Except bigger than a hotel. It was as if the motorcade had driven out of Moscow entirely and arrived at one of the grand stately homes of Versailles or Rome.

The palace was, according to the internet, a remnant of the days when Russia had been ruled by a royal family. When the royals were executed, it had fallen into disrepair and was largely neglected during the rise of communism. After communism collapsed, Russia was ruled by a series of presidents until President Putin came to the building's rescue and had it restored into a presidential palace.

Passing through the entrance of sparkling chandeliers and beautifully painted fresco walls, it was a relief to walk into the meeting room which the architect had had the good sense to paint in plain white. Around it stood the flags of the representative nations of the world's strongest economic powers, all of them hanging from their poles in folds because there was no wind inside.

At the centre was a ring doughnut of a table, much like the round table where King Arthur was said to have held court, except that there was a hole in the centre. Around it, printed onto wooden plaques in front of each chair, were the names of the heads of state and their respective countries. Pankhurst did not immediately sit down, but hovered around by the entrance greeting the other seven most powerful men and women in the world. Like most Englishmen, he had little grasp of other languages, but managed to say hello in French, German, Italian and even Japanese.

Michael stayed out back as much as possible. Far enough away so as not to be noticed, but close enough to detect any perceiver who may come near. He realised, as he stood there, with his back to the wall and his hands clasped behind him, that he had unique access to every head of state in the room. He could unlock their political, their personal and perhaps even their military secrets. If only he could speak their languages. Some might say it made him the most powerful person in the room.

With the informal pleasantries over, the dignitaries sat down at their allotted seats, a few publicity photos were taken and then the extraneous staff were ushered out of the room. Michael had checked them all and there no perceivers among them. He was safe to leave the Prime Minister to his negotiations.

As he was leaving, a strong presence entered his perception: unmistakably the signature of another perceiver.

He looked up to see a Russian soldier approaching. The man was young with a stoic face that hid a tumult of emotions underneath. Like the frenzy of a mind using the serum that can turn a norm into a perceiver; and lead them to the edge of madness.

Michael watched as the soldier walked, almost marching with a determined stride, into the negotiating room. He went over to the wall on the left, turned round to face the room and brought his heavy shoes together to stand to attention. He was one of four soldiers standing likewise against each wall of the room. Outwardly, he looked the same as the others in his military uniform, but inside, his mind was clearly different.

Michael immediately turned and threw his perception around the Prime Minister's mind. He built his barriers to a point where perceivers couldn't break through to read either Michael's thoughts or those of John Pankhurst. Unless they tried hard enough to break through and, even then, Michael was sure he could defend them both.

A hand pulled back on Michael's shoulder. It was the British Chief of Security, a middle-aged man called Barrington. A translucent wire from a communications earpiece curled around the back of his ear while his physical agility and strength were hidden by the cut of his suit. "Time to go," he said into Michael's ear.

"I can't," whispered Michael with as much urgency as he could manage without raising his voice. He glanced over at the sweaty Russian, but Barrington didn't follow his cue and didn't understand what he was trying to say. If only he could think his meaning over to him like he could if it was Pauline standing there. But the man was just a norm.

"Now," insisted Barrington.

"I can't," Michael said again, a bit louder this time. Fortunately, there was still a lot of movement as the dignitaries were gathering their papers and getting settled in their seats and no one seemed to notice.

The hand didn't remove itself from his shoulder.

Pankhurst didn't see any of what was going on behind him. He was pouring himself a glass of water from the jug provided.

"Prime Minister?" called Michael. Louder than he would have liked so it caused the Canadian Prime Minister also to turn round. She gave him a disapproving stare over the top of her reading glasses.

It was her movement that actually attracted Pankhurst's attention. As he turned to see what was going on, still with the glass of water in his hand.

"I need to stay," said Michael, pointedly.

Pankhurst nodded his understanding and shooed Barrington away.

Fortunately, Michael was not the only additional person to stay. As well as the Russian soldiers on security detail, there were translators, diplomatic assistants and someone to make an official record of the proceedings.

Michael took up position against the wall where he hoped to be discreetly out of the way and keep his eyes focussed on Pankhurst.

All the while, he was aware of the soldier's mind. The man was employing no blocks, not even a filter to temper his leaking emotions. They were all out on display for any perceiver to read. Behind the nervousness was an uncertainty, like a growing panic which was making his face turn red like he was struggling to breathe. Michael couldn't understand his thoughts as they were obviously in Russian, but they seemed chaotic. The words rumbled around his head in disjointed segments, sometimes repeated, almost like a person trying to remember a shopping list while in the supermarket.

At the table, President Vodyanov of Russia addressed the meeting in faltering English. "I would like to formally welcome you to Russia," he said, eyeing each world leader in turn. "It has been a long journey for some of you, but we are all busy people and I thought it necessary to get some business under our belts before dinner."

The whisper of translators in the room filled the air with French, German, Italian and Japanese interpretations of his words.

"I think we should put our cards on the table, as you say," continued Vodyanov. "First with regard to the issue of nuclear weapons, I want to make it plain that Russia is not against the principle of reducing its nuclear capability, but only if it is matched by the rest of the world…"

As his president talked, the soldier's perception danced around the room, alighting briefly on the mind of each participant, except for that of his own leader. It was difficult for Michael to monitor closely with his blocks raised around both himself and Pankhurst, but he didn't think the soldier was making much of an attempt to read their thoughts. It was more like a reconnaissance mission in which he assessed the lie of the land before deciding where to strike.

Michael felt the soldier's perception bounce off the block protecting Pankhurst's mind and felt the sting of his surprise. The soldier adjusted his position against the wall slightly and tried again. He pushed harder this time, but his perception didn't get close to penetrating Michael's shield. The flutter of confusion escalated inside the Russian until he turned his attention to easier prey.

The Canadian Prime Minister took off her reading glasses. "Canada, as you know, gave up its nuclear weapons long ago and is a testament to how it is better to use public money for the wellbeing of the people," she told the assembled dignitaries.

"Only because you have the protection of the United States," said Vodyanov. "You even contribute to their nuclear programme!"

The soldier's attention honed in on the Canadian Prime Minister and entered her mind to steal her thoughts as easily as a humming bird steals nectar.

So it continued for a couple of hours. The politicians stated their entrenched positions, everybody listened and no one allowed themselves to be swayed by the others' arguments. The Russian soldier perceived them all as they sat there, gathering up their private thoughts better than any electronic device could. Because, Michael perceived, he could understand it all. Beneath that khaki uniform which suggested a military man trained in the practical skills of weapons and fighting, there was an intellect fluent in French and German and impressively competent in Italian. He struggled with Japanese, but he knew enough to get by.

The strain of being the ultimate fly on the wall turned his mind into a frenzy of thoughts. The more the politicians droned on about state security and the principle of mutually assured destruction, the more the soldier's mind fragmented. The sheen of sweat had spread to his forehead and he had begun to physically shake like a man forced to stand there for hours on punishment duty.

By the end of two hours, Michael was also beginning to tire, so he was glad when President Vodyanov adjourned the meeting. "Dinner will be served in an hour, so we have time to 'freshen up', I believe is the expression, and then I see shall see you there."

A collective mumble filled the room as the heads of state spoke to their aides and people shuffled away their papers. Michael was relieved and began counting down the moments to when he could retreat to the shell of his own mind again.

The soldier had understood every English word spoken by his president. He knew that the meeting was over, but still he did not relax. He remained standing to attention at the side of the room, shaking slightly as French, German, Italian, English, Japanese and Russian thoughts whirled around his head like odd socks in a washing machine.

Pankhurst was on his feet and chatting to the President of the United States whose eye he had managed to catch as she headed towards the door. Despite having journeyed all the way from Washington that morning and having sat in a dull meeting for two hours, she looked immaculate in the spotless white jacket she wore over navy blue blouse and trousers. "Perhaps we can have a few words tonight during dinner," suggested Pankhurst.

"Of course," she said with a smile which indicated that she knew she was the one with the upper hand in the relationship. "I hope they don't serve meatballs again. I mean, I like garlic, but you can have too much of a good thing, you know what I mean?"

At any other time, Michael would have been excited to be standing so close to the President of the United States, but he was too preoccupied by the spin cycle of the Russian soldier's thoughts. The end of the meeting should have brought some sort of relief to the spy — as it had for Michael and the politicians — but instead it had inflated his anxiety. Michael glanced over to see the sheen of sweat on his face. It was more than anxiety; he was *scared*.

The soldier reached down to the gun holster on his belt.

Michael suddenly realised where he had felt those sort of intense frightened and desperate thoughts before. It was right before the businessman Benjamin Conte had thrown himself out of his office window and plunged to his death.

The soldier pulled out his pistol.

"Prime Minister!" Michael yelled and threw himself at Pankhurst. The Prime Minister was larger than him, but the momentum was enough to knock him off his feet and the pair of them went sprawling to the ground.

Michael looked back to see the soldier had the gun to his head. Tears were now streaming down his face. "Ya ne mogu bolshe!"

He closed his eyes and pulled the trigger. A gunshot pierced the air and the soldier's chaotic thoughts were gone in an instant.

Screams erupted all around him as panicked people dropped their papers and started running.

Pankhurst looked up at Michael who was lying half on top of him. As he understood what had just happened, Michael perceived his growing gratitude.

Next to them, the President of the United States stood in shock as the red splatter of the soldier's brains ran down her white jacket.

SEVEN

PANKHURST sat perched on the edge of the sofa in one of the guest suites of Constantine Palace and brushed his hands through his thinning hair.

The room was pristine with a glass table centrepiece surrounded by two upright armchairs and the sofa which the Prime Minister was sitting on, all upholstered in spotless cream fabric. Soft light from half a dozen spot bulbs in the ceiling gave the room a serene atmosphere, while the spongy carpet underfoot suggested very few people had had the privilege to stay there.

Pankhurst, however, was a mess. He had loosened his bright tie and thrown off his jacket to reveal a creased shirt which had lost its crisp whiteness to the grime of the day.

"Does someone want to tell me what the hell happened?" said Pankhurst.

He shouted out his question to the room in general, but the only two other people in it were Barrington, the British security chief, and Michael.

Barrington kept an outer appearance of calm as he stood as if on guard duty by the door which led out into the rest of the palace, but inside Michael could perceive that he was panicking. He was a proud man who considered the safety of the Prime Minister his top priority, and yet it had been some inexperienced twenty-year-old — which was how he regarded Michael — who had pushed Pankhurst out of the way when a crazy man pulled a gun.

"A Russian soldier shot himself, sir," said Barrington.

"I *know* that, Barrington," said Pankhurst, running his fingers through his hair a second time. "He splattered his brains across half the leaders of the free world. I was not asking you to state the bloody obvious. What I want to know is why was a suicidal man allowed into the heart of the G8 summit with a loaded pistol?"

"It was agreed with the Russians that they would have armed personnel stationed around the dignitaries at all times for protection. They were all loyal soldiers, vetted by the Russian Federal Security Service. If it's any consolation, sir, the Russians seem as shocked by the whole incident as the rest of us."

Michael stepped forward from his position standing against the side wall. "The man who shot himself was a perceiver."

Barrington swivelled to give Michael the most vicious stare possible, which he matched with a feeling of irritation that he didn't realise Michael could perceive. "What are you talking about?"

"He was perceiving everyone at the meeting," said Michael. "The Russians on the ground may not have known why he blew his brains out, but I bet someone high up put him there to read minds."

Barrington turned back to the Prime Minister while pointing an accusing finger at Michael. "With respect, sir, what's he doing here? I understand you wanted to bring your intern to the summit for experience, but I have to object to him interfering in security matters."

"If interfering means pushing me to the ground when someone pulls a loaded gun, I'm all for it," said Pankhurst.

Barrington kept his face steady while his ire was provoked in his mind. Michael couldn't blame him. If he had been in Barrington's position, he would have felt the same.

"Is it okay if I sit down, Prime Minister?" said Michael. "I don't feel comfortable talking about this stuff at a volume people might overhear."

"Take a pew," said Pankhurst, indicating the upright armchair on his left. "You better sit down too, Barrington. You're making the place untidy."

"Sir." Barrington undid the button of his jacket and took up position in the other armchair, opposite Michael. "But I don't buy this perceiver theory. The perceiver outbreak was a British phenomenon and, anyway, the soldier was too old. Even back home the oldest perceiver can't be any more than nineteen by now."

Michael sighed. The man was so ignorant. "I don't think the soldier was born to be a perceiver. His power was too strong, too indiscriminate and he didn't seem to be able to control it like someone who has lived with it since he was a teenager."

Barrington stared across the glass table at him. "Where did you get all this information?"

"I got it by perceiving him," said Michael. "I'm a perceiver too."

Michael felt Barrington's disbelief only for a moment before it morphed into understanding and then turned to anger.

"You knew this?" Barrington asked the Prime Minister.

"I didn't want to tell you unless it was necessary," said Pankhurst.

"Didn't you think it was necessary *before* a crazy man pulled out a loaded gun in front of you?" Barrington checked his anger. He took a breath and smoothed his tie down across his lean torso. "I'm sorry, sir, but you might have been killed. So, for that matter, could the leaders of America, Russia, Germany and the other four countries round the table."

"Well, you know now," said Pankhurst.

"Next time, I'd appreciate being fully briefed. I can't be expected to do my job if I'm not given half the information." Barrington averted his eyes as his attention was taken by something coming through his earpiece. He put his finger to his ear. "Excuse me," he said. "I'm getting details of arrangements for getting everyone out of here." He stood from the armchair and walked over to his previous position by the door and carried out a whispered conversation with whoever was speaking in his ear.

Michael looked at Pankhurst who had given up his anxious pose for a more exhausted one leaning against the back of the sofa. "You knew, didn't you?" said Michael.

"I didn't know anything," said Pankhurst.

"With respect, sir, you can't lie to a perceiver."

"I suspected the Russians might put a perceiver spy in with the G8, but I didn't know for sure."

"Did you also suspect they might be using the perceiver serum?" said Michael.

Pankhurst's thoughts suggested he did, but he wasn't about to openly admit it. "You think that's what the soldier was taking?"

"Almost certainly," said Michael. "I saw into the mind of someone on the serum when the Russians were testing it out on British businessmen. Just before one of the businessmen killed himself, his mind was as messed up as the soldier's. The serum can turn a norm into a perceiver, but if they take too much of it, it sends them mad."

"The Russians must have known that, surely," said Pankhurst. "Why put someone like that into the G8? If he hadn't killed himself and I hadn't brought a perceiver with me, no one would have been the wiser."

"They must have thought it worth the risk," said Michael. "The soldier was an intelligent man who could speak almost every language native to the people in that room. There can't be many people like that in the Russian military. Perhaps they used him one too many times."

"Evidently."

Barrington left his position by the door and came over to them. "The cars are ready to take us back to the airport, Prime Minister," he said.

"We're leaving now?" said Pankhurst.

"Now, sir, yes," said Barrington with an urgent nod.

"At least I'll be spared the garlic meatballs."

A quizzical expression formed over Barrington's face as he ushered them out of the door.

EIGHT

MICHAEL stood with his back to the wall of the famous Victorian terrace called Downing Street and looked out at the press scrum ahead. They were one alien mass of microphones and camera lenses that all lifted and turned in unison, like the eyes of a single organism, to point towards the Prime Minister as he stepped up to a wooden podium his press secretary had placed in front of the iconic black door of Number Ten.

In a fresh suit, after a recent shave and a comb run through his hair, the dishevelled man Michael had seen in the Russian presidential palace had been swept away and replaced with a neat version suitable for the cameras. Even if underneath, Michael perceived, he remained unnerved and struggling to keep that side of him hidden from the public.

"I am disappointed that the important work that I, and other world leaders, were due to conduct at the G8 summit had to be cut short," Pankhurst told the alien mass.

Michael allowed his perception to reach out to the journalists and their supporting camera crews and found not one perceiver among them. Satisfied, he returned his attention to protecting Pankhurst's mind.

"It is the belief of the Russian authorities that this was the lone action of a man suffering from an undiagnosed case of PTSD. I am inclined to agree. Therefore, our thoughts go out to his family at what must be a very difficult time. The Russian authorities will, of course, carry out a full investigation into the circumstances surrounding the incident and we will be reviewing security arrangements for future international summits. Thank you."

A man called out from the press scrum. "How are you?"

Pankhurst had half-turned from the podium when the question called him back. "I am unhurt, as were all the other leaders of the G8. Shaken, but not stirred, as James Bond would say."

A chuckle rippled through the alien.

"Is it true the soldier who shot himself was on an experimental drug?" called a woman's voice. The owner of the question peered out from her colleagues, allowing her blonde hair to be visible among the dark coats and suits of the others. Michael recognised her as Sian Jones, the reporter who had broken the perceiver story.

He perceived Pankhurst falter inside, while outwardly he maintained his smile. "Miss Jones, where did you get that idea?" He dismissed the question with a raised eyebrow, turned from the alien and walked towards the house.

Calls of "Prime Minister! Prime Minister!" from the journalists who hadn't been quick enough to shout their questions went unheeded.

Someone inside, who must have been watching proceedings, opened the door to Number Ten and Pankhurst stepped inside. Michael followed.

Michael wasn't entirely sure what he had expected to see inside the famous official residence of the Prime Minister, but he hadn't expected the entranceway to be like someone's lounge. It was probably the fireplace that made it feel that way, set into the wall of the sizeable square room with a checked pattern of black and white tiles on the floor. As more of the Prime Minister's staff joined them inside, it felt less roomy, until the policeman who stood dutifully waiting, closed the door behind them.

Pankhurst turned to his press secretary who had a computer tablet clutched to her chest like it was her most treasured possession. "Find out what that Jones woman was doing there," he told her.

"My understanding is their political correspondent is ill with the flu that's going round," she replied.

"So they get one of their investigative reporters to fill in?" said Pankhurst. "What happened to that annoying Carlisle man they usually use? Find out, will you."

"Yes, Prime Minister."

The woman took the tablet from her chest and tapped at the screen with her finger as Pankhurst walked past her.

Michael followed him up a set of sweeping stairs with pictures of all the past prime ministers on the wall. It was like walking through the history of British politics in a matter of moments.

The building had nowhere near the magnificence of the Russian presidential palace, but its grand interior was still a surprise considering the modest front door they had just walked through.

At the top of the stairs, Barrington greeted Michael with a nod to indicate he should walk over to him. So Michael turned right to meet the head of security while Pankhurst turned left to go to the Cabinet Room.

Barrington did not have a curly wire leading from his ear that morning, but he otherwise looked the same as he had in Russia, in his dark suit which caused him to blend in with the politicians as if he were part of the furniture. Which, presumably, was the point.

Barrington bent over to mutter a clandestine question in Michael's ear. "All clear?"

"Yes."

"Ready to check on the Cabinet?"

"Yes," said Michael.

By this, Barrington meant to subtly perceive each member of the government as they joined the Prime Minister for a meeting. He found Michael a place to stand that was both out of the way and close enough to mentally touch their minds.

In ones and twos they arrived: the Home Secretary, the Defence Secretary, the Foreign Secretary … All of them norms, all of them wrapped up in their political thoughts which Michael wasn't interested in and had no business in perceiving. Pankhurst's paranoia in suspecting his colleagues were perceivers spying on him appeared unfounded.

Once the last of the Cabinet members had disappeared through the double oak doors of the meeting room, Barrington leant forward to speak in Michael's ear for a second time.

"All clear?"

"Yes," said Michael.

"Let's move on to the staff."

They descended the grand staircase past old and mostly deceased prime ministers, going back in time with each step from Tony Blair, to Winston Churchill and Benjamin Disraeli.

Michael had already brushed at the mind of the police officer inside the front door and found that he was a norm, but it was confirmed as he got closer. The man's thoughts were docile — it had to be boring standing there all day doing nothing — but were alerted when someone knocked on the front door.

The officer opened it to reveal a flustered man in a grey suit whose wispy hair had been blown by the wind outside and uncovered his bald patch. He carried a cardboard file stuffed with papers. "Have they started yet?" he asked.

The officer said that he thought they had, but the man probably didn't hear him. His attention was stolen by something that had touched his mind and he turned his head to look up the stairs.

Michael felt it too. The man was a perceiver.

Their gaze locked. Michael perceived the man raise barriers around his mind. Weak barriers belonging to a natural born who must have met very few other perceivers in his life and had little occasion to use them.

The door was still open and the draught from outside was blowing in. The flustered man turned away from Michael and looked around the entranceway like someone who had just realised they'd got out at the wrong train station.

"If it's urgent," said the police officer, "I'm sure they can be interrupted, they've only just sat down."

"What?" said the flustered man. He turned to the officer like he had only just remembered he was there. "No, it's fine. Not urgent. I can leave this with you, can't I?" He held out the report.

"Not really, sir."

"When there's a break, just see that Anne Wintershall gets it."

Barrington jogged down the last remaining steps to rescue the police officer from the report being thrust in his face. "I'll do that for you," he said.

Michael perceived the man's relief as he finally managed to offload the file and head for the door.

Before he turned to go, the man glanced up the stairs to where Michael stood. *Don't say anything*, his thoughts begged, knowing that Michael could hear him. *If you keep quiet, I promise not to say anything about you.*

PANKHURST sat on the same brown leather sofa where he had briefed Michael on his new job barely a week before. On a china plate in front of him were two halves of an anaemic white bread sandwich with a bite taken out of one of them. The discarded packet on the table revealed that it contained ham and mayonnaise.

Michael sat opposite while Barrington took up his customary stance by the door with his hands clasped behind his back.

"Are you sure?" said Pankhurst.

"I'm sure," said Michael.

"Peter Wauluds is one of my most capable ministers," Pankhurst went on. "I was going to promote him next reshuffle."

Wauluds was a latecomer to the political arena, according to his Wikipedia page. Michael had looked him up after their encounter in Downing Street. He had risen through the party with the shrewdness of a capable political operator. He was soon selected to stand as an MP in a safe seat and given a junior ministerial role in the Ministry of Justice. The smart money was on him becoming party leader sooner rather than later. They put his skill down to a background in business, where he had been successful in pharmaceutical research. Michael put it down to his ability to perceive the people around him so he knew how to ingratiate himself with the right people and manipulate them to his own ends.

Pankhurst took another bite out of his sandwich. Mayonnaise oozed out between the two slices of bread and dropped in a creamy-white blob, like bird poo, on his tie.

"Could my day get any worse?" With the sandwich in one hand, he used the other to fish in his trouser pocket.

Barrington came to the rescue with a pristine folded handkerchief. Pankhurst took it and brushed at his tie so the blob of mayonnaise turned into a greasy mark.

There was a knock on the door.

Pankhurst looked across the table to Michael. "Make yourself scarce. But not too scarce. I need to know for sure before I sack the bastard."

Michael removed himself from the sofa and went to stand at the back of the room where it was darker.

Pankhurst nodded to Barrington.

Barrington opened the door. Wauluds walked in. He was no longer flustered, Michael perceived, but angry and confused. He also realised that Michael was in the room. The darkness in which he stood was no protection from a perceiver's senses. Wauluds didn't even have to turn around to look.

"Take a seat, Pete," said Pankhurst.

Wauluds did as he was asked. Michael kept perceiving him.

"How are you doing, Pete?"

"Fine. Busy."

"And your wife?"

"She's fine too." He paused. "What's this about?"

Pankhurst looked up and beyond his shoulder to where Michael was standing. There was one question in his mind.

Michael stepped forward into the light. He nodded to indicate that, yes, Wauluds was a perceiver.

Barrington was the only person in the room who was not able to feel the Prime Minister's disappointment.

"I'll be honest with you, Pete," said Pankhurst. "I've had some news about you which has made me unhappy. Very unhappy indeed."

"I've always been loyal to the party," said Wauluds. "And to you, John, you know that."

"I thought it until I found out you were hiding something from me. Until I found out that you have probably been spying on me and other Members of Parliament ever since you were elected."

"No!" protested Wauluds. "That's not true."

Michael perceived he was being honest. More or less. Honest in the sense that any information he had gleaned from his colleagues had remained private. He hadn't read their minds and passed that knowledge on to any third party. At least, not very often.

"You're a perceiver, aren't you?" said Pankhurst.

"Perceivers are teenagers," said Wauluds. "I know I look young, Prime Minister, but I'm actually fifty-five."

His little attempt at a joke fell flat and did nothing to lighten the mood.

"They call people like you 'natural borns'," Pankhurst continued. "Your mother didn't take a pill like the mothers of the teenagers. You were born with the perceiver mutation which would have lain dormant until your teenage years. Back when you were a teenager, no one knew about perceivers, which is why you were able to keep it a secret. Or so I've been told."

"Who told you? Him?" Wauluds turned and pointed an accusing finger at Michael. He was so angry that his arm was shaking.

"Forget him," said Pankhurst.

"What's he even doing here? If you're going to sack me, at least have the decency to do it without an audience."

"So you are able to perceive that my intention is to sack you?"

"What? No! I … Jesus!" He brushed back the wisps of his hair with his fingers. "How long have you known?"

"About you?" said Pankhurst. "Just today. About the possibility that perceivers could have infiltrated my inner circle? I've suspected for a while."

"So you're going to get rid of *me* and keep *him*?" Wauluds didn't even turn to look at Michael this time, he just gestured behind him. "You're swapping a perceiver you already know and trust with a perceiver you don't."

"If that were true, you would have told me, long ago, what you are. But you've hidden it from me all these years. How can I trust you?"

Wauluds sat back against the sofa with the slump of a defeated man. "Will I have to stand down as an MP?"

"No, that would cause too much fuss. With our ratings in the polls, we could do without a by-election. Just give me your resignation as a minister and issue something bland to the press. You need to spend more time with your family, that sort of thing."

Wauluds stood up. "I think you're making a mistake."

Barrington opened the door and allowed Wauluds to walk through it.

"I hope not," said the Prime Minister, as the door closed behind him.

He picked up his sandwich and bit into it like it was the sandwich's fault. With his other hand, he pulled out his phone and checked his schedule. Talking with his mouth full, he asked Barrington to get in touch with his PA to bring him a clean tie.

Michael waited long enough for Wauluds to have walked far enough away and he made his excuses to leave.

As he left the Disraeli Lounge, he sensed another perceiver waiting for him. In the tiniest of moments, he thought it might be Wauluds wanting to ambush him. But that brief thought was extinguished when he recognised the signature of Pauline's mind. Her thoughts were full of anxiety and she wasn't making any attempt to hide it.

She stood, tucked into the edge of the corridor, like a timid mouse.

Michael walked up to her. "What's happened?"

"Galen House," she said. "They've found out about us."

NINE

SIAN *Jones stood on a stretch of grass with the wire perimeter fence of a military base behind her. Visible behind her left shoulder was the entrance. Two armed soldiers in camouflage paced backwards and forwards in front of the barrier as if they didn't know a camera crew was filming them.*

Jones, with her black lapel microphone obvious against her blue coat, tucked a few strands of hair back behind her ear to stop them being blown about by the wind. "This is where some of the strongest perceivers in Britain have been living for the past five years as part of a secret government project to develop young people into spies for the country," she told the camera. "Known as the Perceiver Corps, they have been training with the army as an elite squad able to use their mind-reading powers in any situation."

The shot cut back to a comfortable breeze-less studio where the news presenter with a perfectly shaped bobbed hairstyle was watching Sian Jones on a television screen. "Is this where the perceivers you've been telling us about have come from? The ones which have been placed inside police forces and courtrooms across the country?"

Sian was full screen again. A few spots of light rain fell onto the camera lens and created little blurry specks on the picture. "That's my understanding," she said. "Officially, according to the Ministry of Defence, this army base trains soldiers to serve in the infantry divisions of the army. Unofficially, according to some of the local people I've been speaking to, a significant number of young people have been seen coming and going from this base in recent years. It only serves to confirm my information that this is a secret base for perceivers."

Pauline's mind filled with anger as she watched the news report on Michael's television. Michael wanted to put a comforting arm around her as she sat next to him on his sofa, but he knew their relationship hadn't been that intimate for some time and kept his hands tucked between his knees.

His flat was small, being just a tube ride from Westminster and, therefore in an extremely expensive part of London. It was about half the size of his flat in Nottingham and quadruple the price. He was lucky the Prime Minister's office was paying for it, otherwise he would have had to live far out of town.

The landlord who had furnished the place obviously had a thing about red. Up one end, the cupboards of the kitchenette gleamed with bright, shiny red doors; while the only sofa up the other end was covered in a red fabric. It was one of those sofas with a small back rest and a wide seat which meant leaning back was difficult. So they sat on the edge as they watched the news report. Which they probably would have done regardless of the design of the sofa: it wasn't the sort of news that perceivers could relax to.

"I should go back," said Pauline.

"You can't," said Michael. "There's a camera crew watching the front gate."

"They will have gone by the time I get there. It's not right for me to be here while all the other perceivers are dealing with this." She stood up.

"You're not leaving now? I thought we agreed, you're safer here."

"I'm just going to make a phone call," she said. She reached for her handbag which she left on the floor and pulled out her phone. "Is there somewhere that's a bit quieter?"

Somewhere private, she meant. But other than the room they were in, the flat only had a bathroom and a bedroom.

"You stay here," said Michael. As he got up, he turned off the TV — the news had moved on to something else anyway — and chucked the remote control back on the sofa. "I'll go sort out a bed for you."

Michael left Pauline alone and went to the bedroom where he stripped the bed of its week-old bedclothes and replaced them with fresh. He returned to the living room carrying the bundle of used sheets clasped to his chest.

He heard Pauline say goodbye to whoever she was talking to and hang up the call. Both her face and her emotions revealed she wasn't happy.

"Norm the Norm wants me to stay here," she said. "Apparently more journalists have been arriving to chase the story and the whole base is on lockdown. The norm soldiers, not to mention the army brass outside of the Perceiver Corps, are livid."

"That's settled, then," said Michael. "You stay here tonight. I've put clean sheets on the bed for you."

"I'm fine with the sofa."

"Even so, you're my guest and I insist."

She must have perceived there was no changing his mind and so she shrugged off the argument. "Okay."

Michael was going to put the used sheets on the sofa for him to sleep on, but now they were all bundled up in a ball in his arms, he could smell how stale they were. So he took them into the kitchenette instead and stuffed them in the washing machine.

Pauline followed him in. "What do we do now?"

"I was thinking we could order in pizza," said Michael. "Or Indian. There's a great place I found round the corner that does deliveries. It tends to stink out the flat, though."

Even as he was speaking, he perceived that wasn't what she meant. "What are we going to do about the journalist, Sian Jones, putting all our secrets out there out in public?"

"I have the first meeting of that working group on perceivers tomorrow," said Michael. "Maybe something will come out of that."

"Maybe," said Pauline.

"So," said Michael. "Pizza or Indian? Or anything you like, this is central London, after all."

Pauline turned her nose up. "I'm not that hungry."

"Or I can cook something. Well, I say 'cook', I can put something in a pan and give it a stir."

"What have you got?"

"Hmm." He opened the shiny red door of the cupboard next to him. Inside was a packet of dried pasta and two tins of soup: one chicken and mushroom, the other cream of tomato. He tried the fridge next, even though he knew there was only a carton of milk, a two-litre bottle of fizzy water and a jar of pesto in it. "I got pretty good at pasta and pesto when I was a student."

"That sounds nice."

He perceived that she was only saying that to be polite. But that was okay. Cooking gave him something to do and if she enjoyed it, it would be a bonus.

Michael made far too much pasta and pesto for the both of them and brought two steaming bowls over to the sofa with an apology. "You don't have to eat it all."

"Smells lovely," she said. This time, she meant it.

They ate without saying much. As Michael got to about halfway through his mound of food, he realised that Pauline had closed her mind off to him. Not that he was looking, he just sensed that whatever thoughts she was having, she wanted to keep them to herself.

"Thanks for letting me stay," she said eventually.

"You couldn't have gone back to Galen House, not tonight."

"I could have got a hotel room."

"On the salary you get from the Perceiver Corps?"

"Or I think the woman in my office has a spare room. She keeps talking about her son having just gone to university."

"It's nice to have you here," he said.

He got the sense that it wasn't the thing she had been thinking about behind her blocks. She put her fork down and placed the bowl of pasta on the floor. "I'm sorry I didn't speak to you after Alex died."

So that was it. The reason for her shutting him out.

"It was a shock," said Michael.

"You did it to rescue me and I never acknowledged that. Not even to myself. So, I wanted to say thank you."

Michael picked up the glass of water that he had brought over to have with his meal. He lifted it towards Pauline. "To Alex," he said.

Pauline retrieved her glass of water, too, and chinked it against his.

They drank to the memory of their friend.

Over the couple of hours that followed, they talked more and the friendship that they had once forgotten became real once again.

TEN

MICHAEL'S optimism lifted out of his body and drifted out of the window which had been opened a crack to allow in some fresh air. It left the House of Commons and floated over the London skyline until it was lost among the noise and pollution of Britain's capital city.

He had thought the working group on the perceiver crisis would bring some solutions to what was happening out in the world, but all it brought was empty talk. After a while, Michael stopped listening to the words the people around the table were saying and took a look into their thoughts. He found no inspiration there. No great idea that was going to solve the problem facing perceivers and the people close to them.

Around the table, squeezed into the small room next to the debating chamber of the House, were four backbench MPs of various parties and a representative from the cure programme who Michael had never seen before. They had given their names at the beginning of the meeting and he had already forgotten what they were. They were suits to him. They wore the uniform of the establishment with either shirt and tie or jacket and blouse and their minds were entrenched in establishment thought. But then he looked down at himself and the uniform of suit and tie that he had put on that morning and he wondered if he was any better.

When he had introduced himself, he had told the other people in the group that he brought an insight to their meeting because he worked closely with the perceiver community. At the request of the Prime Minister, he didn't tell them he was a perceiver.

The whole thing was a sham.

The representative from the cure programme was a woman with a silk scarf round her neck tied in an ostentatious bow. She kept looking down at her notes as she spoke to the others sat around the table. "The truth of the matter is that the cure programme works," she said. "We have cured more than five thousand teenagers to date, all of whom are leading lives as normal citizens."

One of the MPs, a stout woman who wasn't afraid to allow streaks of grey to grow through what was left of her brown hair, tapped her pen increasingly loudly on the table. "If it worked, we wouldn't all be sitting here," she said. "It's not the children you've cured that are the issue, it's the ones you haven't."

"Then the cure programme needs to be given more resources," said the ostentatious bow woman. "We can carry out fresh screenings and cure any of the stragglers."

A male MP, with a full beard and a tweed jacket, raised his eyebrows at that. "I don't think it is the stragglers who are a problem," he said. "From what I understand from the news reports, this is a deliberate attempt to use perceivers to pry into people's private thoughts. Did you see the telly last night? They're being trained by the army! I wouldn't be surprised if there is a government agency behind this."

The stout MP laughed. "It's always a conspiracy with you, isn't it?"

"Just because I'm paranoid, doesn't mean they're not out to get me," he said with a grin.

Michael perceived that the two MPs, despite being on the opposite side of the political spectrum, had a long history of being in Parliament and had a mutual respect for each other, even though they disagreed on a political level. It was a very odd thing to experience: two people who were both friends and enemies at the same time.

"The cure programme has worked to calm public disquiet in the past," the ostentatious bow woman said. "It can work again in the future. It's a question of making the commitment."

Michael's anger boiled over at that point and spilled from his mouth. "You can't cure everyone," he said. "Especially not after Pankhurst brought in Perceivers' Law. People have the right to live as they are."

The ostentatious bow woman shook her head. "We all know Pankhurst is likely to be voted out at the next election—"

The stout MP tutted loudly. "I think you underestimate John Pankhurst. People didn't think he'd be re-elected last time and they were wrong."

"I don't think people will make that mistake twice," said the ostentatious bow woman. "Especially not now that it's been revealed perceivers were working for the army. No one's going to believe Pankhurst didn't know about that. What I'm saying is, if we cure them, the problem goes away."

"The problem," said Michael, trying — and failing — to remain calm, "is not the perceivers, it's the people who don't understand them. If people realised that perceivers are ordinary people, then they wouldn't hate them."

"That's rather naive if you don't mind me saying so," said the stout MP.

Michael did mind. He wanted to tell her that he was a perceiver, that he wasn't evil. But he had promised the Prime Minister and so he kept his mouth shut.

"The fact is," the MP continued. "They could be anywhere. They could be prying into the minds of our most important business people, they could be eavesdropping on the thoughts of our police and intelligence services. There could even be a perceiver in this room right now looking into our heads and we wouldn't know about it."

Michael felt his cheeks go red as he realised that was exactly what he had been doing. He reached for the glass of water on the table in front of him in the hope that taking a sip would hide his embarrassment.

But it was the ringing of the stout MP's phone that provided the distraction.

"Sorry," she said, as she pulled her phone from her jacket pocket and answered. "Hello? I'm in a meeting … Oh. Oh, right. Yeah, thanks."

She got up from her seat and grabbed her papers.

"What's wrong?" said the bearded man.

"The Prime Minister's making a statement in the House," she said.

"Is it about the fiscal deficit again?" said the bearded man.

"It's about perceivers," said the stout MP.

PAULINE was standing by the filing cabinets at the back of her office when Michael found her. She had the top drawer open of one of them and a stack of files piled up on top of it.

Michael barely noticed the other woman working at her desk when he rushed in.

Pauline turned. "Michael!"

"You have to come," he said. "The Prime Minister's making a speech."

"Isn't that what Prime Ministers do?" she said.

"About perceivers!" said Michael. "The Prime Minister is making a speech about perceivers."

He grabbed her hand and pulled her from her filing.

He led her down the corridor, but after a few moments it was obvious that she knew the way better than him and he ended up being the one chasing her to the debating chamber.

Not being MPs, they couldn't go on the floor of the House, but they could go into the public gallery. A man looking like an extra from a period drama, in black frock coat, white bib shirt and white bow tie — as per the Houses of Parliament tradition — glanced at their passes, made sure they had turned off their mobile phones and led them to a row of seats behind security glass high up along one side of the chamber.

Down below, Members of Parliament were still streaming in. So many of them, that they had nowhere left to sit and were standing in a cluster by the door.

The Prime Minister stood at the lectern, to jeers of approval from his party. He looked, as he always did in public, smart in his suit with his hair brushed neatly from his face. He had chosen a more sober tie for the occasion, a dark purple with only bright yellow polka dots to express his individuality.

"The last few days have revealed news about perceivers that many have found shocking," said Pankhurst, looking up to glance at the MPs in front of him. "These reports have spoken of perceivers working with the police, with the justice system and in other ways in society. I have to tell the House that these news reports have been, by and large, true."

Jeers rose from many of the seated and standing MPs. This time they were jeers of disapproval and came from members of parties other than his own.

"Many people found the development of perceivers in this country something to be feared," he continued. "I say they are something to be celebrated. For centuries, people have tried to discover who is guilty of a crime and who is innocent. A guilty man may say with a straight face that he did not commit the crime and, until now, we had to rely on painstakingly gathered pieces of evidence to ascertain whether he was telling the truth or not. With perceivers, we can know for certain. No more do we have to worry that an innocent man has been sent to jail or a guilty man has been allowed to walk free."

The murmurs of approval from Pankhurst's party were subdued and Michael perceived that even they were uncertain about whether they could support his view.

"There has been a lot of talk in the media about breaching human rights," Pankhurst continued. "I remember a time when such voices of dissent were raised on the subject of CCTV cameras. People felt those, too, were invading their privacy. Now we take CCTV for granted and, every day, criminals are caught on video and brought to justice. It is my belief that, in time, people will appreciate the use of perceivers in the same way."

Pankhurst turned the page of his prepared statement. The MPs remained unusually quiet. "Which is why the use of perceivers so far has been on a small scale. It has been a pilot project which I have now asked to be suspended while an assessment is made on how effective it has been and how we can use perceivers going forward. So it is my directive that all work with perceivers in public life be stopped as of this moment."

Pauline turned to Michael. "Does this mean I'm out of a job?"

He shrugged.

Below them, the opposition MPs were getting restless. One shouted, "Disgraceful!" Another responded, "Resign!"

The Prime Minister ignored them and continued with his prepared statement. "But I have to tell the House that Britain is not alone in developing perceivers. I know the world believes that perceivers were only born here, but I have to tell you that other countries have secretly been plotting to use perceivers for their own ends. I am unable to go into details for security reasons, but let me say that if we abandon the perceiver programme, we allow other countries to exploit perceivers, possibly to our detriment. Which is why I authorised the army to train some of our strongest and most capable perceivers to work in the national interest. I make no apology for that, as safeguarding the country's security is one of the priorities of this government."

Pauline transmitted her thoughts to Michael, *So that's it, everyone knows about us.*

Looks that way, Michael replied.

What now?

He shrugged again.

They continued to listen to the Prime Minister speak until the leader of the opposition stood up to ask questions and it was clear nothing more of substance was going to be said.

Michael and Pauline made their way out of the public gallery and turned their phones back on.

Pauline's was the first to bleep. Her already deflated mood deflated another notch. She sighed.

"What?" said Michael.

"It's from the woman in my office." She turned the screen of the phone for Michael to see the text message. 'Come and speak to me ASAP,' it read.

"Looks like I'm out of a job," Pauline explained.

Michael's phone bleeped. He had two missed calls and a text.

"Are you out of a job too?" said Pauline.

"If I gave up university just to get sacked, I'm going to be …"

He read the text. It wasn't about work. It wasn't from anyone in Parliament.

'Can you call me as soon as you get this?' it read, and was signed off, 'Tony Patterson.'

Pauline looked over his shoulder. "Who's Tony Patterson?"

"Inspector Patterson," Michael clarified.

"The policeman you used to work with? What does he want?"

"I suppose I better ring him and find out."

ELEVEN

THE police station at Paddington was a sprawling block of a building which had all the architectural flare of someone who valued the concept of cheap above the concept of impressive.

Inside was not much better, although its tired decor and cheap plastic seats screwed to the wall were disguised by a number of waiting members of the public. Either waiting around for a relative to be released on bail or to see a police officer about their nuisance neighbour. At least, that's what Michael gleaned from them in the moments before he closed his perception down.

He told the sergeant behind the high barrier of the front desk that he was there to see Inspector Patterson. As soon as he had finished filling out his security pass, Patterson appeared to take him out of the public area and into the main part of the police station.

In the quiet of the corridor, Patterson appeared less stressed than when Michael had last seen him. He still wore a suit that looked like it had been stored in a bundle in the corner of a room rather than hung up in a wardrobe, and his wiry hair still defied any attempt to lay neatly on the top of his head, but there was an assuredness and a confidence about him that Michael hadn't perceived before. It suited him. In fact, despite the two years that had passed since they had last seen each other, Patterson looked no older.

"Thanks for coming," said Patterson, as he led Michael down the corridor of featureless white.

"No problem," said Michael.

"The woman said she needed to see someone in charge of perceivers. I didn't know who else to call."

"Who is she?"

"She's Russian, but her English is pretty good. Her name is Katya, or so she says," said Patterson. "She arrived on a tourist visa and went straight to a police station asking for asylum, but she refused to say more until she talked to someone in charge of perceivers. That's when I got the call."

"Isn't your new job supposed to be solving murder and serious crime?" said Michael.

"That 'new' job that I've been doing for two years? Yeah, it is, but some people in the Met still know me as the perceiver cop. I thought the time that we worked together was secret, but it's not easy to keep a secret in an organisation full of detectives."

At the end of the corridor, they entered into a stairwell. A sign on the wall helpfully revealed that the stairs led down to the cells.

"You locked her up?" said Michael.

"We didn't have anywhere else to put her," said Patterson. "If she went off to an asylum detention centre, I wouldn't have any jurisdiction. Not as if I can hang on to her for much longer here, we're a bit short of space for actual criminals."

Another desk sergeant waited for them at the bottom of the stairs. This one had no public riffraff to deal with and the desk he stood behind was actual desk height. Both Michael and Patterson signed in and were led to a door constructed of iron bars which allowed them to see down to the row of cell doors. Lifting a set of keys from a ring attached to his belt, the sergeant unlocked the gate then escorted them past two cell doors before stopping at a third. After peering through the spy hole and seeing nothing untoward, he unlocked the door.

It released the stale body odour smell of someone who had not been able to wash for several days. Michael tried not to let the unpleasantness of it show as the young woman inside stirred from where she had been lying on the narrow cell bed. She was white to the point of being pale while the colours of the clothes that she wore in layers of dress, jumper and cardigan had begun to merge into the same grubby brown.

As she sat up and pulled the police-issue blanket over her knees, Michael saw the one salient detail which Patterson had neglected to mention: she was pregnant.

Very pregnant. She hitched up the blanket even further to cover the bump, but it still showed.

"Katya," said Patterson. "This is the person I told you about."

She stared with wide eyes at Michael. For a moment, he thought he felt her touch his mind. But that suspicion was only fleeting and, as he perceived her, he detected only a norm. A very frightened, uncertain and troubled norm.

"Hello, I'm Michael," he said.

"You're a perceiver," she said with a heavy Russian accent. "Aren't you?"

Michael shot a glance back to Patterson, but the policeman shook his head and Michael perceived that it was not a piece of information he had told her. "Why do you say that?" he asked her.

"I've waited so long," she said.

She burst into tears. Literally. Her fear, uncertainty and troubles spilled from her eyes. Sobs took over her whole body until she shook.

Michael felt uncomfortable. He wasn't sure what to do. He turned to Patterson, but he perceived the man was just as clueless.

He turned back to Katya. Her face was already wet with tears. They dripped from her chin and rained onto her jumper. He thought about putting a comforting arm around her shoulders, but then he thought it might be inappropriate and he continued to stand helpless in front of her.

"Do you have a hanky?" Michael asked Patterson.

Patterson fumbled in his jacket pockets. He checked his inside pocket. He delved both hands into his trouser pockets and retrieved nothing.

The woman — who was almost still a girl, really — kept crying.

Michael pulled the sleeve of his shirt down over his hand and stepped forward. "Don't cry, please," he said. It wasn't very comforting, but he wasn't sure what else to say. "Sorry I haven't got a hanky."

When Michael got close enough and Katya didn't pull away from him, he reached over and dabbed the cuff of his shirt onto her damp face. The softness of his touch calmed her sobs until only tears fell. It was awkward to reach standing in front of her, so he sat beside her on the bed to wipe the remainder of her tears. By the time she had stopped crying, the end of his shirt sleeve was damp.

"Waited so long for what?"

Katya looked up at Patterson as if reluctant to speak in front of him.

"I'll wait in the corridor," said Patterson. "If you need me, I'll be right outside the door." He stepped out of the cell and closed the door behind him. It bounced off the doorframe and remained open a crack without the lock sealing it in place.

Katya looked up at Michael, her eyes red with crying. "Can you help me?"

"Help you with what?"

"Can't you perceive it from me?" she said.

"If I went deep into your mind I could," said Michael. "But it's easier if you tell me."

She sniffed and wiped her nose on her own sleeve. "They made me pregnant," she said.

"Who's they?"

"The people who want to make perceivers in Russia. I thought it was to make babies for women who couldn't have babies. There are many people like that, it's very sad for them. I needed the money and having a baby is a better job than cleaning toilets, so I agreed to do it. But that was before…"

"Before what?" said Michael.

"Before I overheard them talking. The doctor, his Russian was not that good, so he talked in English. They thought I didn't understand them, but my father was a diplomat and he wanted me to learn English so I could work abroad some day, like him. That's when I heard them say they were breeding perceivers."

Michael looked down at her swollen belly where she carried her baby.

"I thought I was having a baby for a childless couple who wanted desperately to have a family. I imagined how they would love him and bring him up to have a happy life," she continued. "But all they wanted was for me to breed a mind-reading soldier. They lied to me."

Michael sat back and felt the cold of the cell wall behind him. He thought back to his last mission to Russia, the one that had got Alex killed. They had gone to steal the perceiver research of Doctor Lucas, a British man who had defected to Russia. He had almost forgotten the pregnant women they had encountered when they broke into his research building.

"Can you help me?" said Katya.

Michael wasn't sure. "I'm going to try," he said.

MICHAEL stood at the point where his lounge met the kitchenette and looked, undecided, at the online pizza menu on his phone. Behind him rumbled the washing machine working on de-grubbying Katya's clothes while Katya herself sat on his sofa in front of him. His man-sized bathrobe would be too big for most women and leave them looking swamped in fluffy white material. But Katya's pregnancy meant it was a better fit for her than a robe designed for an ordinary-sized woman.

She had thanked Michael for allowing her to use his shower, but he was just grateful she had washed away the unwashed smell she had carried with her in the taxi from the police station.

"How about one meat and one vegetarian?" asked Michael.

"Yes," said Katya.

As he keyed in the options, the lock turned in his front door. He could perceive it was Pauline, to whom he had given a spare set of front door keys.

She sighed as soon as she entered and dropped her handbag on the floor like it contained a burdensome brick. She closed the door behind her with finality. "Unbelievable!" she said to no one in particular. "I don't know why I ever—"

As she turned, she saw Katya sitting on Michael's sofa and her words stopped. She stared for a few moments. She must have perceived Katya, but it still didn't answer the question in her head. She turned to Michael: *Who's she?*

"Hello, my name is Katya," said Katya, almost as if she had heard the question.

"I had nowhere else to take her," said Michael. "I hope that's okay."

Pauline raised her eyebrows. "It's your flat." She walked straight past him and headed for the only other door in the room.

Michael hit the key to complete his pizza order and followed her into the one and only hallway in his flat, which was barely big enough to accommodate two more doors to the bathroom and bedroom.

Both were closed. He heard Pauline slide the bolt on the inside of the bathroom door.

Can you perceive me? Michael asked with his thoughts.

"I'm on the loo!" She called back. He perceived a hint of her irritation before she closed off her mind to him.

Michael waited in the hall. He heard the sound of her pee, the toilet flush and the tap run as she washed her hands. He realised he was an arse to be listening in to her private bodily functions, but he didn't want to go back into the living room and speak to her in front of Katya.

Pauline must have perceived he was there because she opened the bathroom door without immediately stepping out. Instead, she leant against the frame to face him and folded her arms. "Is that woman a perceiver?" asked Pauline.

"She's a norm," said Michael.

"Then why are we having a conversation about her out here instead of perceiving each other's thoughts in there?" She nodded back towards the living area.

"It seemed impolite," said Michael.

"It's still talking behind her back, however you do it," said Pauline. "It's just that I thought she heard my thoughts when I came in."

"Coincidence," said Michael.

"So if she's not a perceiver, who is she?"

"I think she's one of Doctor Lucas's experiments."

Pauline shivered at the name. Doctor Lucas who had once held a gun to her head. Doctor Lucas who had got her locked up in a Russian military facility. Doctor Lucas who would have almost certainly carried out all manner of experiments on her if Michael and Alex hadn't got her out.

"Then that accent she speaks with is Russian," said Pauline.

"Yes. From what I understand, she ran away. I haven't got the full story out of her yet."

"Then the baby is not...?"

After a slight pause, Michael realised her meaning. "Mine? No! Pauline, how could you?"

"I come back and you've got a pregnant woman on your sofa who's naked apart from *your* bathrobe, what do you think it looks like?"

She grinned and he realised she was teasing him a little bit.

"It's not funny to block my perception of you entirely, you know," he said.

"I thought it was."

She relaxed her blocks and Michael perceived that, even though she was making fun of him, part of her was disconcerted at seeing Katya on the sofa.

"Perhaps she needs a woman to talk to," said Pauline. "If we go back in, maybe I can get the full story out of her."

THE pizzas came and Katya ate more than her share with the enthusiasm of someone eating for two who had run away from Russia. Pauline sat next to Katya on the sofa, leaving Michael to sit cross-legged among the pizza boxes on the floor. He felt bloated and too full of bread and fat, but he couldn't deny that it had tasted good.

"Tell me how you got out of Russia," said Pauline as she dropped the last piece of crust back in its box where a lone slice of vegetarian pizza lay uneaten.

"I took a plane," said Katya.

"Just like that?" said Pauline.

"I had to get a visa, but I say I am a tourist who wishes to visit London and it was no problem."

"They let you fly in your condition?" Pauline looked down at Katya's bump.

Katya smoothed her hand over her pregnancy. "When they saw I had medical insurance, it was not a problem."

I can't believe they would let her go like that, Pauline thought across to Michael. *Not if she's really carrying a perceiver baby.*

She's not lying about that, thought Michael. *Either she's telling the truth or she thinks she is.*

Michael perceived the silence between them caused Katya to be unnerved. She looked from Pauline to Michael. "What's wrong?"

"We think it's strange you left the country so easily," said Michael. "If you really are part of a Russian military experiment, you wouldn't have been granted a visa, let alone be allowed on a plane."

"I thought so too," said Katya. "I was allowed to go home between examinations, but I had a feeling people were watching me. The feeling got stronger the more the baby grew and by the time I realised I was part of a perceiver experiment, I knew I couldn't run without someone finding out. Not as if I had anywhere to run to.

"Then Lucas stopped coming to my appointments," Katya continued. "The nurses said he was busy, but they were lying. They didn't actually know what happened to him. Then one day, no one came to collect me for my examination. I took my chance and left."

"Do you think the Russians did something to him?" said Michael.

"I don't know. I left when I had the chance."

"That doesn't make sense," said Pauline. "Why give Lucas all the resources to carry out his research and then stop before getting the results?"

"It would have been a long wait," said Michael. "Perceivers don't develop powers until they hit puberty."

"I think they still wanted my baby," said Katya. "But when Lucas disappeared, it became less interesting for them. There is a saying my father brought back from one of his diplomatic assignments — taking your eye off the ball — it is like they did that, it is like they took their eye off the ball."

Michael let out a deep breath, partly because he was still taking in her story and partly because he was still digesting the pizza. "I'm glad you made it out safely," he said.

"Me too," said Katya. "Thank you for the pizza."

"You're welcome," said Michael. He picked up the box with the remaining vegetarian slice. "Anyone want any more?"

The women declined. "I'll put it in the fridge and have it for breakfast," said Michael.

"Euw! Cold pizza?" said Pauline.

"I'll zap it in the microwave to heat it up, obviously."

Michael went over to the kitchenette and found a plate to put his leftovers on.

"I'll help you clear up," said Pauline. She gathered up the other cardboard pizza box and a couple of empty glasses which had held water.

"I need to use your toilet again, sorry," said Katya. "The baby is resting on my bladder."

Pauline made play of throwing the empty pizza box in the bin until Katya was safely on the other side of the internal door.

"What do you think?" she said, keeping her voice low so Katya wouldn't hear.

"Her story's plausible," said Michael. "She certainly believes it's the truth."

"They took their eye off the ball and let her flee the country with their experiment inside of her? Seriously?"

"What other explanation is there?"

"That she's a spy sent here by the Russians," said Pauline.

"But she's pregnant!"

"Which makes for a brilliant cover. She goes straight to the police and uses them to find you, gives you some sob story — quite literally — and suddenly she's in your flat and wearing your bathrobe."

"Great theory apart from the fact that I would have perceived if she was a spy."

"Like you did with Sarah?"

Michael blushed. They had all been fooled by Sarah. "Sarah used strong perceiver blocks to stop us finding out about her. Katya is a norm. You've perceived her too. Don't you believe her?"

"So maybe they let her go and they're planning to turn her into a spy when she's settled in this country. They just haven't told her that."

Michael turned from Pauline and put the pizza slice in the fridge. "It's a possibility, I suppose," he said. "What do we do?"

The interior door opened again and they both turned to see Katya coming back into the living area, leaning back in that way that pregnant women do in order to maintain their balance. "I think I'm going to need more toilet paper by the morning," said Katya. "Sorry."

"I'll get some," said Michael. He took one step towards the end cupboard in the kitchenette where he kept all his spare packets of household items before Pauline grabbed his arm and stopped him.

We have to tell Agent Cooper, said her thoughts.

Michael glared back into her serious eyes. *No.*

He's the only one who's got experience at this sort of thing.

I'm not sure I trust him.

You worked for Cooper once, Pauline pointed out. *I still work for him, technically. He'll know what to do with her.*

That's what worries me, thought Michael.

What else are you going to do? Let her stay here? In your one-bedroomed flat? What happens when she has her baby?

I can't speak to Cooper, he doesn't know I got my perception back. He only let me go because he thought I'd lost my powers. If he finds out—

"Who's Cooper?" said Katya all of sudden from where she had resumed her position on the sofa.

"What?" said Michael.

"You were talking about someone called Cooper," she said.

"No we weren't," said Pauline. "We weren't talking about anything."

Pauline gave Michael a wary glance and he felt her blocks solidify around her mind.

Michael took a few steps back towards the lounge. "So where did you hear the name Cooper?" he asked.

"Sometimes I think I hear things and I don't," said Katya. "All sorts of strange things happen to women when they're pregnant, don't they?"

"I thought that was more to do with getting emotional and craving chocolate," he said.

"With me, I hear things," she said, stroking her bump again. "I thought it might be that the baby was passing on some of its perception to me so I could perceive thoughts. But that's impossible, isn't it?"

"Yes," said Michael, glancing across at Pauline and seeing that she didn't think it was impossible at all. "Yes, it is."

TWELVE

MICHAEL slept on the floor that night. It seemed only right to give the bed to the pregnant woman, which left Pauline with the sofa and Michael with no other choice.

He started to think, if he had to offer any more women the chance to stay at his place, he would end up sleeping in the kitchen sink.

Pauline had been ordered not to go into work until "the current controversy blows over" which, judging by the people yelling at each other on the TV news that morning, was going to be a long time. At least it meant she could spend the whole day baby-sitting Katya.

Michael got a message that the Prime Minister wanted to see him and, therefore, was the only person running around his flat trying to get ready.

With Katya in the bathroom hogging the only mirror in the place, Michael did up his tie the best he could by staring at his reflection on the glass door of the microwave.

He turned round to face Pauline who was sitting up on the sofa with her hair still a tangle from where she had been sleeping. "How do I look?" he said.

"Like someone who's dressing up to get sacked," she said.

"You don't know the Prime Minister," said Michael. "He's paranoid people are looking into his mind and he wants me there to protect him."

"You wanna bet?"

"Sure. I'll bet dinner on it. If I still have a job by the end of the day, you can cook."

"It's a deal," said Pauline. "I'll start making a list of what you'll be getting for us from the Indian takeaway, shall I?"

"Very funny," said Michael.

He checked he had everything — wallet, security pass, keys — and headed for the door.

He paused before he went out. "See what else you can get out of Katya while I'm gone," he said. "And try to find out when her due date is. I don't want to be woken up in the middle of the night to find she's having a baby in my bed."

Pauline said that she would.

Michael gave her one last glance before he left. It was so nice to have her in his life again. Then he realised she could probably perceive that from him and he dashed out to hide his embarrassment.

MICHAEL felt a presence he had not perceived in a long time, as he stood outside the Disraeli Lounge and prepared to knock.

There were two minds inside. One was clearly Pankhurst. The other was a man he had hoped never to see again in his life. Instinct told him to turn around and walk away, but the Prime Minister knew he was coming and to leave would be to turn his back on his duty and his promise to Pankhurst.

Michael knocked.

"Come in!" called Pankhurst from the other side of the door.

Michael did as he was asked.

Sitting on the second brown leather sofa, in the same position that Michael usually sat, was Agent William Cooper. The passing of two years had done little to change him. He still wore the same black suit and white shirt, but had picked out a grey and blue striped tie to wear for his visit to the House of Commons. His hair had grown down below the top of his collar with the untidiness of someone who had not had time to have it cut, and his face had the puffiness of someone who had hardly slept the night before.

His emotions revealed he was not surprised to see Michael at the door. It meant that when Pankhurst had asked Michael to come to the Disraeli Lounge, he knew that Cooper would also be there.

Pankhurst was in his usual spot on the other sofa. His tie with bright orange, red and purple triangles on it revealed that it was not a day for making sober announcements. He waved Michael inside. "Put the wood in the hole, as my mother used to say."

Michael didn't actually know what he meant and had to perceive him to understand that he was asking him to close the door.

Michael did so, and stood not knowing quite what to do next. He realised he had subconsciously brought his feet together and put his arms flat against his sides as if standing to attention. Like he used to do in the Perceiver Corps when he was called to Cooper's office.

"Hello, Michael," said Cooper.

"Hello," said Michael, for want of anything else to say.

"I hear you got your perceiver powers back."

Michael glanced across to Pankhurst who was avoiding his gaze by pouring himself a glass of water from the jug that had been left on the table between the two men. Michael didn't need to see into his eyes to perceive that he was the one who had passed that information on to Cooper without his permission.

"Yeah," said Michael.

"I'm disappointed you didn't tell me," said Cooper.

"My powers came back slowly. By which time, I had long left the Corps. I didn't need to tell you anything."

Pankhurst slammed his glass of water back down the table after hardly drinking a drop. It made a sound like a gavel as it hit the table so hard some of the water spilled over the top. "Good!" he said. "Now that's settled, let's get to business. Come sit down, Michael, so we can talk properly."

Michael hesitated. There were two sofas and already two men sitting on them. Asking the Prime Minister to shift up a bit to make room was out of the question and so he ended up going to the second sofa. Cooper shuffled towards the other end, but Michael still squashed himself up against the arm as far away as he could.

"Bill came to see me because he's worried for the future of the Perceiver Corps now that it has become public knowledge," said Pankhurst.

"I spent a lot of years building up a strong, trained group of personnel at Galen House," said Cooper. "I don't want to see it destroyed in the panic of public opinion."

"I told Bill about the working group," said Pankhurst. "I thought you might be able to give him a steer on their thinking."

"I think they'd order every perceiver in the country to be cured if they could," said Michael.

"We can't let that happen," said Cooper. "We already know the Russians are developing perceiver spies, as demonstrated so dramatically at the G8 summit. If we squander our advantage now, we'll never get it back."

Michael glanced over the table at Pankhurst. "You told him about that?"

Pankhurst shrugged in reply as if to say that he may have mentioned it.

"The working group all pride themselves on coming at the problem with an open mind," said Michael. "Apart from the woman from the cure programme who thinks she'll get a promotion and a bump in salary if a new programme is set up to cure every single perceiver in the country. None of the others came to the table with any ideas on how to solve the mess."

"I think," said Pankhurst. "That the idea is they go away, investigate, and come back with some ideas that aren't informed by preconceived notions. It's how these things work."

"So I gather," said Michael, inwardly thinking that the word 'work' was ill chosen.

Pankhurst looked at his watch. "I have some reading to do ahead of this afternoon's visit to this new railway line the government's found itself spending a bloody fortune on," he said. "I'm going to need you there, Michael. The place is going to be full of people you haven't vetted and I have to go round shaking babies and kissing the hands of builders." He paused to adopt a quizzical expression. "Or is it the other way round?"

He got off the sofa, grinning at his own joke, and headed towards the door.

"What time, sir?" Michael asked after him.

"Barrington's going to give you all the details," said Pankhurst. "But it's not for a few hours yet, so it'll give you two plenty of time to talk."

As Pankhurst hurried out, he took with him the calming sense of mediation that he had somehow brought to the room. Perhaps that's why he had succeeded in politics.

The door closed and Michael was left alone with Cooper.

"You should have told me," said Cooper. "About your powers."

"Once you signed off on that paperwork, I was no longer yours to order around," said Michael. "I'm still not yours, I work for the Prime Minister."

"Do you think that's going to do you any good?" said Cooper. "This working group nonsense is just something to give Pankhurst some ammunition to fire at the press. If anyone asks what he's doing about the perceiver situation, he can point to the working group and say he's got people looking into it. But things are moving too fast to wait for reports to be written and committees to discuss them."

"I know," said Michael.

"I got a call this morning to say protestors have gathered outside the base demanding that perceiver spies come out and make themselves known. The news is full of people baying for blood."

"*I know!*"

"I'm not going to let everything I worked for be torn down."

Michael stood up and turned away from him. Cooper was so arrogant that he even admitted that all he was concerned about was himself. Not the perceivers, like Pauline, who lived in Galen House and had more to lose if they were exposed than he did. If it came to it, Cooper could probably retire on a decent pension and take up golf or gardening somewhere remote. The perceivers in his charge had nothing. Having been separated from their families to live and train at Galen House, it was their home, their work and their life.

Michael went to the window and looked out across the rooftops of the surrounding buildings, covered in droppings left by the pigeons. He took a deep breath and worked to push aside his personal dislike of Cooper. "What do you know about the Russian perceiver programme?"

He turned his back on the window to see that Cooper was reclining on the sofa like he was perfectly at home. "I know what you know, that Doctor Lucas was trying to breed perceivers while developing a serum to give norms perceiver powers."

"What would you say if I told you I have information that Lucas and the Russians appear to have lost interest in the breeding programme?" said Michael.

"I would say, that's very interesting, but it doesn't make sense."

"Why?"

"Because if they want home-grown perceivers which they can use as spies — and I'm sure they do — it's their best shot. The serum only works for a short while before it turns people suicidal: a problem which we know Lucas wasn't able to fix because of the mess at the G8. If the Russians were going to use it to turn their secret service agents into perceivers, pretty soon they wouldn't have any secret service agents left."

"So why use it at all?" said Michael.

"They were probably desperate for the information they could perceive from the heads of state at the summit. It's a spy's all-you-can-eat buffet."

"That's what I thought."

"But you don't think that now?" said Cooper.

"I don't know what to think. It's just that having one of your soldiers kill himself at one of the highest profile meetings in the world doesn't do much to keep their work secret."

"Perhaps you should tell me more about the source of this information."

Michael hesitated. "Pauline said I should."

"She's a very sensible woman."

"If I tell you who told me, can I trust you to look after her?"

"You can always trust me, Michael," said Cooper.

Michael had never trusted Agent Cooper, but he told him anyway. All things considered, he had no one else to tell.

THIRTEEN

ENGLAND was dark. The blackness of the night closed in and embraced the black of the tarmac on the motorway. Through it, in his black car and wearing his black suit, drove Cooper at a speed-limit-busting ninety miles per hour.

His headlights, and the headlights of the other drivers, could only illuminate a small patch of night in front of them. Sometimes the lights of the drivers on the opposite carriageway hurt their eyes as they sped towards them, meaning that, ironically, the bright lights caused them to see less.

Katya sat in the passenger seat up front. "It's a shame we couldn't have gone in the day," she said. "I would have liked to have seen some of the English countryside."

"You would have probably seen a traffic jam," said Cooper. "Going tonight is better, honestly."

Michael and Pauline sat in the back among the takeaway burger wrappers they had collected at the drive-through on the way out of London. The oil that the chips were cooked in and the fat of the burgers left a greasy smell in the car. At least he hadn't had to pay. He had won his bet with Pauline and dinner was on her, even if it hadn't been the most sophisticated of dining experiences.

I perceived Katya while you were out swanning around with the Prime Minister, thought Pauline.

And? thought Michael.

You're right, she's telling the truth as she sees it.

You still think she could be a plant by the Russians?

If she is, she's in the perfect place, thought Pauline. *She barely stepped off the plane forty-eight hours ago and she's in a car with a man who runs the British perceiver programme, and another man who works with the Prime Minister. On the way to a military base that houses the country's strongest and most highly trained perceivers.*

Where else would you have her taken? thought Michael. *You were the one who suggested I tell Cooper about her. He says she'll be safest at Galen House.*

Because he wants to keep an eye on that perceiver baby of hers, if indeed that's what it is. I didn't say I had any better ideas, Michael, just reservations.

"Are we going to your home, Pauline?" called Katya from the front seat.

"If you want to call it that," she said, just as Cooper went past an articulated lorry which created a surge of road noise.

"Pardon?" said Katya.

"Yes, we're going to where I live." She turned to Michael. "At least I'll be able to pick up some of my stuff. I didn't exactly pack a change of clothes before I ended up staying at your place. I feel all dirty in these ones." She pulled at her blouse where it was buttoned over her chest and let it go again like it was some disgusting rag.

"Well, you look fine from where I'm sitting," said Michael. It was nice to be sitting next to her again. He hadn't realised how much he'd missed it.

Cooper reached forward to the car radio and turned it on. The calming notes of a tenor sax playing a jazz riff swept out of the speakers hidden in the car doors. Michael closed his eyes and listened to its soothing tones mix with the whoosh of passing traffic.

Pauline was there with him in his head. He perceived that her need to get back to the only place she could call home jostled with her anxiety over what she might find there.

She thought about the last phone call she had made to Galen House and allowed Michael to share in her memory. Her fellow perceivers had been locked in for two days and the base was still plagued by journalists and protestors.

You didn't have to come, you know, said Pauline's thoughts, joining her emotions in Michael's head.

I'd promised to look out for Katya, he thought back. *I need to make sure she's safe.*

That's very chivalrous of you.

Also because I think you're right. It's all too convenient to believe that her showing up like this is just about a scared young woman who's worried about what will happen to her baby.

MICHAEL must have fallen asleep because the next thing he was aware of was the tick of the car indicators waiting to turn left off a main road. The jazz music had long finished and there was quiet in the car. He perceived, other than Cooper who was concentrating on driving, the others were drowsy too.

Cooper turned onto a minor road without street lights and the dark closed in even further. Michael recognised it as the road that led to the army base where he had once lived. It gave him an eerie feeling. He had told himself that he would never go back there, and now he was breaking that promise.

He shouldn't be able to perceive anyone from that distance. Except, perhaps, the soldiers at the gate. And yet he could sense as many as twenty minds.

"People," said Michael.

"What?" said Cooper.

"I perceive people."

"At this time of night?" He swore. "Get down on the floor of the car and cover yourself in coats or something."

"What are we afraid of?" said Pauline.

"Being seen," said Cooper. Taking one hand off the wheel, he turned up the collar of his jacket and tried to hunch down into it. It wasn't much of a disguise.

Something hard struck the windscreen. Katya yelped. A sticky gloop, with broken bits of shell in it, oozed down the glass. Someone had thrown an egg.

Pauline was already in the footwell at the back of the car and pulling at Michael's sleeve for him to join her. Michael folded up his legs to crouch among the grit that had fallen off his shoes onto the interior carpet.

"I can't get on the floor!" said Katya. "I'm too pregnant." There was fear in her voice and a rising panic in her mind.

"Then cover your face," said Cooper.

As they got closer to the base, Michael perceived the mass of minds separate into those who were angry and those who were curious. The curious ones he suspected were journalists who sent bright flashes of light through the windows of the car to try to take pictures of those inside. The angry ones were protestors who slapped on the sides and the roof of the car with their palms, their fists and their feet. They shouted unpleasant things that Michael was able to only half hear through the banging.

Katya was understandably shaken by the time they got past the guards on the gate into the relative tranquillity of the base itself.

When Cooper drew up outside of Galen House and helped her out of the car, she leant on him like an elderly woman with arthritis.

"I'm sorry about the people outside," Cooper told her as he led her into the main door of Galen House. "I thought they would be gone by now, but if the TV news is doing a live report, they hang around to make a nuisance of themselves."

A porch light led their way and Michael and Pauline followed Cooper and Katya into the building.

Michael hadn't realised Galen House felt different to the outside world, but as soon as he walked through the entrance into the common area where he had once shared meals and social time with his fellow perceivers, he sensed it. He remembered sitting around one of the dining tables laughing with Alex as they struggled to eat army catering. There were other fun times, too: shouting at the television with the others in the communal area as they watched England lose a rugby match; drinking alcohol that someone had smuggled in and hiding it from Norm the Norm; playing football — badly — with Alex on the grass outside.

But the good memories were still outweighed by the bad: the roll calls, the army drills, the toilet-cleaning punishment duties. They seemed to seep out from everywhere, from the rows of dining tables laid out at the back, from the walls and even the floor. He realised he was standing not two metres away from where Kev had collapsed on the floor and told them how Peter had been killed in a stupid stunt designed to heighten his powers. Bad memories indeed.

No one was there now. It was after lights out and the perceivers would be in their beds. It made the empty room feel unexpectedly spacious.

"I need to go park the car," said Cooper. "The sergeant will come down on me like a ton of bricks if I leave my car outside the front."

As he turned to walk out, the click of an opening door above them made everyone look up to the balcony corridor that ran outside a row of offices on the floor above.

Michael perceived who it was before he saw him. He had probably perceived Sergeant Norman Macaulay's mind more in his life than anyone else he could remember. It was strangely nostalgic to perceive him again.

Norm the Norm was dressed, as always, in immaculate uniform. But, as he descended the stairs to join them, it was obvious the body inside of his neat and carefully ironed clothes was starting to feel its age. He came down slowly and somewhat stiffly while he clutched the handrail as if he needed it.

"You must be Katya," he said as he reached them.

Katya nodded, shyly.

"Welcome to Galen House," said Norm the Norm. "Normally, I would show you round, but it's late and I'm sure you would like to rest. We've prepared a room for you. Tomorrow we can get you checked over by the doctor and talk about things." He turned to Pauline. "Would you mind showing her to room A7?"

"Yes, sir," said Pauline. She took Katya by the hand and led her towards the accommodation wing.

Michael became the only one left standing with Norm.

"I didn't think we'd see you here again, Michael," said Norm.

"Me neither."

"We gave your room away to another perceiver. A nice lad, much less trouble than you." He grinned. "Room B10 is free at the moment and you're welcome to use that."

"Thank you, sir," said Michael. The 'sir' came out automatically like he had never left.

Cooper returned from parking his car and nodded an acknowledgement to Norm. "Evening, Sergeant, sorry it's so late."

Norm turned to Michael. "Agent Cooper and I have some midnight oil to burn," he said. "I'm sure you can find your own way to B10."

"Yes, sir," said Michael.

Michael heard their receding voices as Norm led Cooper back up the stairs.

"How was your meeting with the Prime Minister?" asked Norm.

"He apologised for not warning us about his announcement," said Cooper. "He said it had been urgent and he couldn't wait for me to get to London. Sanctimonious git …"

Michael headed off to the accommodation wing and realised he didn't even have to think about how to get there. The route had been programmed into his mind.

The room was spotless, as was to be expected from an army which was very particular about keeping things clean. Other than that, there was not much to it. Just a bed with sheets pulled taut over the mattress and a wooden chair tucked under an empty desk. It felt like a place to be imprisoned rather than a place to be comfortable.

Michael turned his back on it and returned to the corridor. He followed the trail to where he knew Pauline's room was and paused outside the door. He opened his perception enough to check she was there and knocked.

Pauline must have been halfway through getting undressed because, as she opened the door, she was clasping her unbuttoned blouse closed over her chest. But she hadn't pulled it up over her shoulder properly and the black strap of her bra was showing.

"Sorry," said Michael, slightly embarrassed. "I came to ask how Katya was doing?"

"No you didn't," said Pauline. "You better come in."

Pauline's room was the same as the one Michael had left, except it was entirely different.

It had the bed made to army regulations, it had the desk and chair, but it also had things that belonged to Pauline. There was a wardrobe so stuffed with clothes that the doors didn't shut properly. The desk had been turned from a formal workspace into more of a dressing table with hairbrush, lots of little pots of make-up and an ornament of a woman with the chains of several necklaces hanging from her arms. The objects in themselves didn't mean anything. It was the way that, somehow, they seemed to make the room hold Pauline's essence.

"I get into trouble if I have boys in my room after lights out, you know that," she said, doing up the buttons of her blouse.

"I'm twenty years old, Pauline. I'm hardly a boy anymore."

"You know what I mean."

"I think Norm's got too much on his mind to worry about two adults being in the same room together," said Michael. "I really am here to ask about Katya. At least, that's one of the reasons. Is she all right?"

"She's scared — who wouldn't be after that drive in? — but she's also very tired, so I think she will sleep. Being eight months pregnant takes it out of you, apparently."

"Eight months?" said Michael. She was further along than he thought.

"Didn't I tell you?" said Pauline.

"No."

Michael didn't know what else to say. He didn't know how to explain himself. Standing in the starkness of B10 had taken him back to his early days at Galen House when he was lonely and frightened. Growing up had taken away some of the fear, but the loneliness had somehow got stronger. It embarrassed him to feel that way, but he decided not to block it from Pauline.

"Fine!" she said, eventually. "You can stay in here tonight, but you're having the floor."

"The floor is fine."

"Go back to B10 and strip the bedding, I'm not having you drool on my carpet. And for goodness' sake, don't let anyone see you. Some of the perceivers here are new and eager to please. They'll report me in a heartbeat."

THE sound of smashing glass startled Michael awake.

He opened his eyes into the dark of Pauline's room and perceived the shock from nearby drowsy minds as they were all rudely pulled from sleep. The minds were unclear, indistinct, like the sound of distant traffic.

Apart from Pauline's. Her mind was waking, too, and her confusion was loud.

Michael sat up on the floor and stretched his stiff and cold legs.

"What's going on?" said Pauline, stirring in the bed above.

The room's only window shattered. Pauline yelled as broken glass cascaded onto her face and a projectile the size of a grenade pushed through the curtains and landed on the floor next to Michael.

White smoke rose from the grenade like vapour from a frozen packet of food thrust into the warm. Some of it reached Michael's nose. He choked.

Gas.

He picked it up and scrambled to his feet.

The gas stung his eyes and made them water so he could hardly see. He found his way to the window more by memory than by sight and threw the projectile back to where it came from. As the grenade bounced across the earth outside, it left a trail of white smoke behind it.

The air outside had the sting of frost about it, but it was cleaner than the tainted air in the room and Michael stayed at the window to breathe in deep. As his eyes cleared, he saw the shadowy figures of people running away. By the time he had reached out his perception, they had gone.

Behind him, Pauline launched into a coughing fit that retched deep inside her lungs like someone with a disease. "What the hell's going on?"

"Tear gas," said Michael.

"Are you sure?"

"I was at the perceiver riots, I'm sure."

The hubbub of other minds was louder now. More people were awake and more of them were confused and scared. Normally, Michael wouldn't reach out to perceive them, but it gave him an indication of the extent of the attack. He didn't know exactly, but it was clear there was more than one broken window.

Pauline was up and out of bed. Both of them had left some clothes on for modesty, but she still reached for her bathrobe that was hanging up on the back of the door. Michael found his shoes and slipped them on his feet.

"We need to find out what's going on," he said.

Pauline gave him no argument. They went out in the corridor, lit by the dim lights on night-time setting and breathed in the unexpectedly toxic air. Coughing, Michael strained to look down the corridor to where another grenade-like canister was smoking away among a scattering of splintered glass. The chill of the night breezed in from the broken window next to it.

Pauline put the sleeve of her bathrobe over her mouth and nose as she tried to control her coughing.

Michael's eyes burned like they'd been sprinkled with acid.

"One breath and run past it," said Pauline.

"No, wait," said Michael. He wrapped his mind around the canister. Its gas could hurt his body, but it couldn't hurt his thoughts. They cradled the smoke bomb as easily as if he had wrapped his hand around it. With one effort, he willed it into the air and out of the window, leaving a trail of smoke behind it.

"Come on!"

Michael grabbed Pauline's hand as they ran down the corridor towards the communal area.

The glass of another window shattered ahead of them and another gas bomb landed. It spewed out its toxicity. Michael urged Pauline to keep running ahead of him as he gripped it with his mind and threw it back outside.

Michael felt the minds of around two dozen perceivers before he saw them all gathered in the communal area, milling in clusters near the entrance with its illuminating porch light. Michael had to pull up his filters to block out their confusion and fear. Some of the other perceivers were young, maybe only fourteen, and they seemed to find comfort in sharing their distress.

What's going on? their thoughts whispered. *Are we under attack?*

Michael looked around at the members of the Perceiver Corps in their regulation grey T-shirts and sweat pants — recognising a few of them from when he used to live there — until he caught up with Pauline.

"Any idea what this is?" he asked her.

"Some of the others think it was soldiers."

"We're under attack from our own people?"

"But they're not our own people, are they?" said Pauline. "They're norms."

Norm the Norm came out of his office and ran down the stairs in a surprisingly agile manner. Cooper followed him down in a more measured walk.

"What's all this?" demanded Norm.

A dozen voices tried explaining all at once.

"One at a time," he said.

Norm shuddered as the glass window shattered behind him. A stream of tear gas arched into the room.

Michael's mind gripped it almost immediately and threw it back out again. He didn't think anyone saw. They were too busy being traumatised.

A woman's voice screamed through the broken window. "Perceivers out!"

Other voices joined her in the chant: "Perceivers out! Perceivers out!"

They dissipated soon enough as the gas overwhelmed them, but as their voices dimmed, the sounds of them banging against the sides of the building took over.

"Everyone into the dining area!" Norm ordered and herded his charges into the back like a farmer herding sheep.

It was then that Michael saw Katya emerging from the accommodation wing. Somehow, presumably in her haste and confusion, she had put her maternity dress on backwards. She clasped at her pregnant belly as she walked uncertainly towards them.

Michael elbowed Pauline and pointed. Pauline went over to help her.

"What's happening?" Katya's Russian accented voice cried above the voices of the perceivers. "You said I would be safe here. I would have been safer in Russia!"

Cooper walked up to Norm, looking as flustered as the rest of them. "What the hell's going on here, Macaulay?"

"It looks like the protestors have got in," said Norm.

"Into a secure army base?" said Cooper.

Michael stepped in. "The other perceivers think it's the soldiers," he said. Then remembered to add, "Sir."

"I thought I saw civilians," said Norm.

"The others think the attack was started by soldiers, maybe they let the protestors in."

"Do you know what you're saying, Sanderson?" said Norm, using Michael's surname like he used to when he had been stationed there.

Another gas canister sailed through the already-broken window and bounced towards them.

Outside, the crowd — because it *was* a crowd, judging by the large number of minds at the edge of his perception — broke into a chant again.

"We can't stay here," said Michael. "We're sitting ducks."

Cooper pulled his mobile phone from his pocket. "Let me make a call."

Cooper took a couple of steps away from them and dialled. After a moment, he could be heard screaming down the phone, "Then wake her!"

Michael turned and looked at the other perceivers huddled around the dining tables. Sitting on one of the tables away from them was Katya, with Pauline standing beside her holding her hand. He turned away from them and walked back towards the entrance.

"Sanderson, where are you going?" yelled Norm.

Michael ignored him. He got close enough to the window to perceive their individual minds. What he sensed was not a collection of individuals, it was a joining together of hatred and excitement fuelled by adrenaline. Like the emotions that had spurred on norms to beat up and, in some cases kill, during the perceiver riots.

The people outside were not a crowd, they were a mob.

Michael went back to Norm the Norm. "Have we got any weapons here?" he asked.

"Locked up safe in the armoury," said Norm.

Michael sighed. The armoury on the other side of the base, on the other side of the mob. "That's what I thought."

"Not that we can use them on civilians."

Michael was more thinking of firing in the air to scare them off, but the idea was a non-starter if they couldn't get to the weapons easily.

"We'll just have to wait it out," said Norm. "I'm sure they will get bored eventually and go away."

"I don't think so, Sergeant," said Michael. "You didn't perceive them."

"If you have any ideas, Sanderson, don't keep them to yourself."

He had an idea, but it wasn't something he could pull off by himself. "Can you drive one of those big army trucks?" he asked.

"It's been a while, but yes," said Norm.

"Good, I think I'm going to need you."

FOURTEEN

F**EELINGS** of shock and alarm rose from the other perceivers.

Oh, my God!

What happened?

Pauline, are you all right?

Their thoughts whispered around Michael's perception.

He followed their gaze to the back of the room where Pauline was staggering in with blood running down the side of her face.

Katya, of all people, ran to her aid. She took her arm and helped Pauline to sit on one of the dining chairs.

Michael dodged his way through the other perceivers to get to her. He perceived she was dazed, there was pain in her head from the wound, but she wasn't badly hurt.

"What happened?" he asked.

Pauline clasped her hand to the source of the blood at her temple. "I tried to go out the fire door at the back," she said. "But they were waiting. One of them threw a stone."

Katya took Pauline's hand, pulled it away from the wound and looked at it closely. "It is shallow cut, just in bad place," she said in faltering English. "Will be okay."

Michael frowned. "Why didn't you perceive them before you went out there?"

"I did!" said Pauline. "But you know how difficult it is through a wall. I perceived one or two, I thought it would be fine, but there were others out of my range…"

Michael sighed. "At least we know getting out through the fire exit is not an option."

Pauline grabbed his arm and pulled him close. She whispered, as using her thoughts to tell him something privately in a room full of perceivers was not going to work. "I perceived them when I was out there. When they realised that gassing us out wasn't going to work, they decided to regroup and try something else. I was on the verge of perceiving deep enough to find out what they were planning when the stone hit me."

Norm came striding down the middle of the hall. Some of the perceivers who had clustered around Pauline parted to let him through. "What's going on?"

"Pauline found out we can't go out the back way," said Michael, hoping that was explanation enough.

That message had obviously got through to the rest of them as the chatter in the room was getting louder, while Michael tried not to listen to the increasing number of anxious thoughts being exchanged.

The sergeant, despite being a norm, must have sensed it too. He turned to face them.

"CORPS, ATTEN-TION!"

His booming, authoritative voice cut a silence through their chatter. The perceivers who were standing, snapped their heels together and pulled their arms straight to their sides. The ones who were sitting on tables jumped off and did the same a second behind them. All expect for Pauline who stayed sat on her chair cradling her injured head, and Katya who took no notice of the shouting man.

Even Michael, despite having left the Corps, felt himself straightening up a little.

"Foster!" said Norm, looking straight at a boy of about fourteen years old.

"Yes, sir?" said the boy.

"Get the first aid kit."

"Yes, sir!"

The boy ran off.

Norm turned to the others. "The situation in here is stable for the moment, as long as we don't do anything stupid like trying to run out of fire doors unprotected. But things outside have the potential to become volatile, which is why I am ordering a withdrawal."

During his speech, Cooper approached by weaving himself in and out of the perceivers standing to attention. He was still holding his mobile phone.

"I've just spoken to the base commander," said Cooper. "She's going to order some of the soldiers to clear the protestors."

A voice rose from the perceivers standing to attention. "Is that the same soldiers who started the attack and let in the protestors in the first place?"

Unspoken thoughts exchanged between the perceivers:

They did?

Didn't you perceive them?

Every time one of them looks at me, I perceive they hate us.

Michael recognised the one who had spoken out as Kev. A boy who had become a man since they had last seen each other. Kev had grown at least a foot, there was a layer of stubble on his chin and his body had filled out with enough muscle to suggest he hit the gym on a regular basis.

Cooper looked aghast at Kev, but the teenager did not wilt under his gaze. Because, Michael perceived, Kev knew he was right.

Michael took a step closer to Norm. "I need their help, if you'll let me."

Norm nodded. "Meanwhile," the sergeant informed his charges, "Sanderson will lead the withdrawal strategy. Sanderson?"

Michael looked at the perceivers around him. The older ones knew him — and, perhaps they trusted him — the younger ones didn't know him at all. "Shall I tell you the plan or would you rather perceive it?"

The ones who weren't Kev didn't have the audacity to break the silence of standing to attention, but their thoughts were not so shy:

Perceive it!

Perceive it!

Perceive it!

"Okay," said Michael. "But be gentle."

He slowly pulled down all his blocks. He felt his fellow perceivers, eager to know what was going on, rush in on his mind. He had to use filters to push them back a little, but once they had all settled, they explored the thoughts in his head without hurting him.

He imagined the whole intricate plan. In his head, it executed itself smoothly. He tried not to think about the possibility that real life might not be so accommodating.

When he had finished, he pulled up his blocks again tight, but he still felt their curiosity, and their uncertainty, bumping up against them.

"You just have to trust me," said Michael.

Pauline, now with dried blood down her cheek, spoke out to help him. "What do you need everyone to do?"

At that point, the Foster boy came running back with the first aid kit.

"You sit there and get that cut seen to," said Michael. "The rest of you, go to your rooms, strip the bed and bring back the bedsheets."

They hesitated.

"You heard him!" Norm shouted.

Some of the younger, inexperienced ones shuddered at his voice and scampered off, followed by the more cynical older ones.

Kev paused next to Michael before he left for the accommodation wing. "Peter was right about your telekinesis, then?"

"Yeah," said Michael. "Sorry about what happened to Peter."

Kev shrugged and his mind sent out a vibe that he didn't care about it anymore. At least, not on the surface. "Peter did what he did to himself."

Pauline winced as the Foster boy dabbed at her temple with something white, which was probably a gauze pad soaked in antiseptic, by the way she recoiled from it. Katya snatched it from the boy's hand and began cleaning the wound in a more gentle manner.

"Foster!" said Michael.

The boy turned to him; startled.

"Can you go and get me a bucket of water?"

"Yes, sir!" said the boy without question and scampered off again.

Michael glanced across to Kev. "How do you fancy ripping the first sheet that arrives into strips?"

"For makeshift gas masks?" said Kev. "No problem."

After less than five minutes, Michael was standing by one pile of white bedsheets, a smaller pile of cotton strips and a bucket of water. The perceivers queued up to take a strip, dunk it in water and have it ready to put over their nose and mouth to prevent them breathing in too much tear gas.

"What the hell are you planning, Sanderson?" said Norm, suddenly at his side.

He had forgotten that the sergeant wouldn't have perceived the plan. "I need you to be ready to run," said Michael. "Can you do that?"

"I'm not dead yet," said Norm.

It made Michael chuckle. It released the tension. A little. "I also need someone to open the entrance door for me. I can't do this alone."

"I can do that," said Kev.

Michael felt guilty about putting him in harm's way, but it would be the same for anyone he asked. "Thanks."

Outside, the protestors still chanted and banged on the windows and walls.

Michael turned to the perceivers. "Here we go."

Some of them put their makeshift gas masks to their faces.

Michael kicked the pile of bedsheets closer to the entrance. He wrapped his mind around them until he held them completely in his thoughts. "Kev, now!"

Kev ran at the door and pushed it open.

Cries of, "They're coming out! They're coming!" rose up from the crowd and, in the light from the porch, Michael saw them surge forward.

Michael willed the bedsheets into the air and pushed them through the open door.

The crowd didn't know what to make of the ghost-like ball floating towards them and they backed off.

A missile — probably another stone — narrowly missed Kev's head as it whizzed through the door, hit the floor and bounced harmlessly away.

Michael willed the sheets to separate and fly out into the crowd. The people shouted and screamed as the white apparitions danced among them like ghosts released from hell.

The sheets succeeded in edging the protestors out of the way to clear a path from the door.

Michael walked out first as a protestor grabbed hold of Kev's shirt. Another pulled at his arm. Someone else grabbed his head.

Michael was helpless as he was dragged from the door and disappeared into the throng of people. All he could hear was the sound of Kev's cries.

But he had done enough and the perceivers were getting out of the building — one at a time, as that was all the single doorway would allow.

Out of the corner of his eye, Michael saw a flash of flame sail past him and heard the crash of glass and the *whoompf* of erupting flames.

Petrol bomb! screamed the thoughts of many perceivers; so loud that Michael lost concentration for a moment and lost control of the sheets. They floated, unbidden, in the night air. One descended on a protestor and they grappled with it as it covered their head and wrapped around their arms.

Michael's thoughts reached out to re-take as many of the sheets as he could and brought them deliberately down on the protestors, as perceivers ran past.

The lights of burning torches were lit one by one around him.

Not torches.

More petrol bombs.

This had to be the 'something' Pauline had perceived they had been regrouping for.

He heard a glass bottle break behind him. Followed by another. The light from the instant fire caused his body to cast a shadow along his escape path.

Michael ran.

His mind relinquished control of the sheets and they floated in the wind. One caught the flame of a newly lit petrol bomb as it descended. A woman was suddenly engulfed in flames.

Michael heard her desperate screams as he fled. But there was nothing he could do and he kept running.

MICHAEL got to the truck park to find the other perceivers waiting. Their presence had triggered the security light and the array of green-painted jeeps, troop transporters and equipment trucks could be seen in regimental rows behind them.

Pauline was suddenly at his side. "What happened?" she said.

Michael turned round. The orange light of the fire that consumed Galen House flickered on the horizon.

He just shook his head. He had no words.

"Where's Kev?" said Pauline.

"He got dragged away by the protestors," said Michael. "I couldn't reach him."

Norm, red-faced and breathing heavily, jogged up from behind them. In his hand, he held a set of jangling keys. "I don't think anyone was planning for someone to try to break into the key store in the middle of the night," he said.

Despite the danger, Michael perceived Norm was excited. Even elated. It was a long time since the soldier had seen action that didn't involve shouting at teenagers.

Michael hadn't even thought about the keys to the truck being locked up somewhere. He was glad Norm had.

"Everyone here?" said Norm, looking around at the rag-tag collection of perceivers huddled under the security light, some in their regulation grey T-shirts and trousers, others still in their nightclothes. Even Agent Cooper was there, partly camouflaged against the night in his black suit.

"Kev's not out yet," said Pauline.

Michael felt a pang of guilt that stuck in his throat as he said the words. "We can't wait for him."

"Yes, we can," said Pauline.

She pointed. Back on the road that led from Galen House, a stocky figure silhouetted against the fiery glow was half running, half limping towards them.

Behind him swarmed a mass of protestors. Protestors who were not injured and able to run faster.

"He's not going to make it," said Michael.

"Yes, he is," said Norm.

The sergeant reached under his jacket to reveal a gun holster strapped to his belt. He pulled out his pistol and, with one swift action slid back the barrel to load the first bullet. He pointed the gun to the sky.

The sky cracked with a single gunshot.

Kev, the protestors and the perceivers shuddered at the sudden noise.

Kev kept running, but the mob slowed.

"Come on, Kev!" screamed Pauline.

As he struggled to get closer, clutching his leg as he limped, his face became visible in the security light. The dark patches on his cheeks were not shadows, but bruises.

Norm the Norm took two steps towards the crowd. "Stay back!" he ordered. He fired another bullet over their heads. They ducked and stopped. One or two of them even stepped back.

"Agent Cooper!" Norm yelled. He held out the keys to his side. "Get the engine started. It's the transporter with the number plate ending FBG."

Cooper approached and put his hand around the keys Norm was holding.

But Norm didn't immediately let go. "Get the base commander back on the phone," he said, quietly. "Make sure she tells the guards on the gate that there'll be consequences if they don't let us through."

Norm allowed Cooper to take the keys and he ran over to the parked vehicles.

Kev stumbled past Norm and almost collapsed as, in his relief, he put too much weight on his injured leg. Pauline half caught him, half slowed his fall as he stopped running.

"Michael," said Norm. "Get the perceivers onto the transporter."

"Yes, sir!" said Michael, and this time he was pleased to say it.

A diesel engine rumbled to life not far behind him. He followed the sound to the transporter with the number plate ending FBG. "Come on, everyone on board. Quickly."

The perceivers didn't have to be told twice. Some of the bigger ones hauled themselves up into the back of what was effectively a small truck with benches down each side. Once in, they reached down and helped some of the smaller ones to get in.

All the while, Norm faced the protestors alone, with his gun pointing out towards them. As Michael approached, he saw some of their faces and perceived some of their minds. They were uncertain. Their chanting had stopped and the reality of the gunshots had done much to temper their resolve. Even so, among them, were people with their faces covered by scarves and hats pulled down low towards their eyes. Some of them, he was sure, were soldiers stationed at the base and he could tell by the way their jackets looked bulky, that underneath they wore bullet-proof vests.

"We're ready," Michael told Norm.

Norm, without taking his eyes off the protestors, passed over the gun. "Take this," he said. "Bill Cooper won't know how to drive a truck, not judging by the way he drives that swanky car he goes about in."

Michael took the handle of the gun. It was warm from Norm's grip and slightly damp from his sweat. "I thought you didn't have access to any weapons," he said.

"It's my personal sidearm," said Norm. "Don't fire it if you don't have to. But if you have to, don't hesitate."

"It's my personal sidearm," said Norm. "Don't fire it if you don't have to. But if you have to, don't hesitate."

Norm ran towards the truck, leaving Michael to face the mob alone.

There were more than twenty of them. Some held unlit torches, others gripped things in their fists which could be stones and one held a cricket bat. But what had once been an angry mob had turned into a reticent gathering. Michael could feel their uncertainty as they looked at the lone perceiver facing them. Several took a tentative step forward.

Michael raised Norm's gun and wrapped his index finger around the trigger.

The crowd stopped. Their uncertainty grew. At the back, a few people peeled off and disappeared into the night.

But the man at the front, with a scarf tied around his face and a woollen hat pulled down over his forehead, stood his ground. The only part of him visible under his black clothing were a pair of light brown eyes. They stared at Michael with unwavering determination as he held an unlit torch up at his shoulder like a club ready to strike.

He was a soldier, Michael could perceive it.

The soldier reached into his pocket and pulled out a cigarette lighter. He flicked a tiny flame into life and brought it close to the head of the torch. *I'm not going to let the army I love be destroyed by perceivers*, he thought, as fire engulfed the torch.

Michael aimed Norm's gun between the soldier's eyes. "Don't," he said.

"Why? Are you going to shoot me, perceiver?" said the soldier.

Michael remembered Norm's words: *Don't fire it if you don't have to. But if you have to, don't hesitate.* "Are you willing to bet your life that I'm not?"

The soldier stood ready with the burning torch, the light of its orange flames catching the flecks of hazel in the brown of his eyes. Michael stared deep into them and saw a memory of one of the soldier's friends laying in a pool of blood with his face blown off by a bullet to the head. The soldier — even though he stood his ground — knew what damage a bullet could do and had no intension of provoking Michael into shooting him.

The roar of a diesel engine broke their stand off as the truck pulled up alongside Michael. He perceived Norm and Agent Cooper were inside.

"Get in the back with the others," said Norm through the open driver's window.

Michael backed away, keeping his gun facing forwards at the soldier, until he was at rear of the truck. Stepping sideways, so the vehicle was between him and the soldier, he tucked Norm's gun into his belt.

The canvas flaps that served as doors to the soft-top were open and the faces of the other perceivers looked out at him. Two strong hands pulled him up and he collapsed onto his knees on the hard, metal floor of the vehicle. Someone banged on the inside partition that separated the driver's section from the back and the truck drove off.

As it passed by the remaining protestors, a flaming projectile was thrown into the back. Perceivers' screams erupted as the burning torch clanged onto the metal floor. Michael wrapped his mind around it and willed it out the back where the ball of flame fell, harmlessly, onto the road.

Michael stamped on the few bits of dry grass and debris which were burning on the floor and snuffed them out. Looking out of the back of the truck, he saw a human figure clothed in black run across the road and knew that the soldier had committed his one last act of defiance.

Michael pulled Norm's gun from out of his belt, but they were already leaving the group of protestors behind. The dwindling crowd shouted abuse, but it was half hearted. They had already achieved their victory: as could be seen behind them in the fire that raged through Galen House.

Michael looked around the packed benches for somewhere to sit.

"There's room here," said Kev, tapping the seat next to him.

Kev was sitting right at the end of the bench near the back with a little bit of space reserved next to him. Michael squeezed himself onto it.

He looked around to check everyone was okay. Pauline was on the same bench as him, sitting awkwardly at the other end with her body wedged up against the back partition. Katya sat on the opposite bench with her head leant back against the side and her eyes closed. The way she sat made her bump stick out even further than usual. At least they were both safe.

The truck went through the barrier at the main gate without incident and entered the dark and bumpy minor road outside. Michael perceived how the agitation of his fellow perceivers had calmed a little, despite a lingering unease.

How did he make the bedsheets fly? said their thoughts.

He did it with his mind.

Perceivers can't do that.

I heard there's some that can.

Michael shut out their thoughts and turned away. He glanced across at Kev.

Kev looked bloody awful. The bruises on his face had started to turn purple and one of his eyes was bloodshot.

"How are you doing?" Michael asked him.

"I'll live," said Kev.

"I saw what happened. I'm sorry I couldn't get to you."

Kev shook his head as if to say he shouldn't be sorry. "They stopped kicking me when you started attacking them with bedsheets. I doubt they saw that coming."

Michael grinned. "It's my sleeper weapon."

Kev laughed. Then he winced and wrapped his arms round his ribs.

"We need to get you to a doctor when we get to where we're going," said Michael.

"Wherever the hell that is," said Kev.

Michael supposed it was up to Norm.

He glanced out of the open back of the truck. The burning glow of Galen House was no longer visible. He could only see the little bit of the road behind them, as it was lit by the red of the truck's rear lights, and the ghostly outline of trees against the night sky. The wind that flapped at the sides had made his left arm and leg go numb with the cold. At first, the breeze had been nice after the heat of their escape, but now he was starting to shiver.

Kev nudged him. "What's the story with the pregnant woman?"

Michael looked over to where Katya was sitting. Her eyes were open now and she was talking to the girl sitting next to her. He watched as Katya allowed the girl to put her hands on her belly and then her eyes went wide with amazement as she must have felt the baby kick inside.

"It's complicated," said Michael.

"She's Russian, isn't she?" said Kev. "She thinks she's carrying a perceiver baby."

"How did you …?"

"Anyone brought into Galen House is going to be perceived, you know that. Especially a norm."

"Then you know everything," said Michael.

"I know you're the one who had her brought here. So, I'm wondering, is it your baby?"

"No!" said Michael. "Of course not. Why do people keep asking me that?"

"I heard that when the Russians caught you a few years back, it was because they wanted to find out how to make perceivers of their own. I bet the Russians know all about the natural borns and how the perception gene can be passed from a parent to a child."

The half of Michael's body not already chilled by the outside air turned cold. He remembered his conversation with Agent Cooper where he had discussed what happened to him when Doctor Lucas drugged him in Russia. Michael had been unconscious throughout, but the speculation was that Lucas had taken genetic samples from him. "Have you been perceiving Agent Cooper too?"

"I may have," said Kev. "I saw a lot of him after Peter died. He was even nice to me, if you can believe it."

"But that was three years ago," said Michael. "They can't still be using … whatever it was they got from me."

"Sperm can be frozen for years, Michael. If I were you, I would think about taking a paternity test."

Michael glanced back across at Katya. She now had another couple of girls clustered round her who were taking it in turns to feel her baby kick. A baby who had to have been conceived with a mother and a father, even if that conception had taken place in a test tube.

FIFTEEN

MICHAEL sat on a bench at Tidworth barracks and listened to the distant sounds of a sergeant barking at recruits as their boots hit the hard ground in unison. It was a crisp, clear day and even the sun poked out from between the clouds every so often. Despite being low in the sky because of the season, it was enough to warm his face.

Norm the Norm had driven to the military installation because it had barracks usually reserved for first year army recruits which he knew were not currently in use. He also knew someone there, who knew someone else, who was prepared to let in a truckload of refugee perceivers.

By the time the truck got there, it was the early hours of the morning and all anyone wanted to do was sleep. That, of course, was the last thing they were able to do after the night they had had. Even with shutting the perceptions of everyone else completely out of his head, Michael found that he still had his own thoughts to contend with. If sleep came at all, it was in small dozy patches.

They got up in the morning to the sound of Norm the Norm bringing spare items of uniform for the people who had escaped in only their pyjamas and bathrobes. It was khaki army uniform, not the greys like the Perceiver Corps wore, but it covered them up and kept them warm which was all that mattered. He also managed to requisition toothbrushes, toothpaste, flannels, soap and some towels for them all to have a good wash. Michael took the opportunity to have a shower, but he could still smell the soot of burning Galen House in his hair. Afterwards, he pulled a large military coat out of the pile of uniform bits and pieces and went outside to get some air.

The layout of the grass area with its perimeter fence, the collection of buildings and the roads that snaked around the complex was in a different configuration to the base they had left, but the elements were the same. Like waking up in a hotel room in a different town, it was familiar even though he had never been there before.

The loneliness of the outside, where the only minds were distant and fluttered like butterflies at the edge of his perception, was disturbed by the distinctive approach of Agent Cooper's worried thoughts.

Michael turned to see Cooper looking somewhat dishevelled. His suit looked like he had slept in it — which, given the circumstances, was highly likely — and there was a day's worth of stubble on his chin. He waved when he saw Michael watching him and joined him on the bench.

"I was told I would find you here," said Cooper.

"You were told right," said Michael.

"I thought you might want to know about Kev. He's got two broken ribs and a fractured leg. A tibia or fibula, I can't remember which."

"They broke his leg? But I saw him running."

"It's possible to run on a broken leg," said Cooper. "My brother broke his leg halfway through playing a game of football when he was fourteen and kept playing until the end. They only found out after the final whistle."

 Michael smiled at the concept.

"What's so funny?" said Cooper.

"I don't think of you as having a brother."

"I have a mother and a father too. Contrary to rumour, I didn't appear on this earth as a fully formed adult."

"I'll take your word for it," said Michael. He looked out onto the pleasant green of the grass, which was about the only vegetation which hadn't turned brown with the cold weather. He wished he could be left to sit and stare out at it alone.

"Sergeant Macaulay's ringing round, securing accommodation for the others," said Cooper. "He thinks it best, and I agree, that they're housed in small groups in several places until this whole thing blows over. So the Perceiver Corps isn't concentrated in one place."

"You think this is going to blow over?" said Michael. "Have you seen what's left of Galen House?" He yanked his phone from his pocket and pulled up the news report he'd been watching earlier. The one that had made him feel too angry to be around other people.

He passed it to Cooper, knowing that it showed the blackened empty shell of what had once been his home. The television news crews still had no clear view of it from outside of the base and so had sent their helicopter up to film from above where they could see right into the charred remains. Michael had little sentimentality left for the place, but he had perceived the horror of the others as they had looked at the footage. Not only had they lost their home, they had lost all of their possessions too.

The voice of Sian Jones spoke with that irritating hint of a Welsh accent out of the phone's speaker. She talked about a woman who was in hospital with second degree burns after "perceivers and protestors clashed". She didn't mention anything about the woman accidentally setting herself on fire while she was trying to firebomb a bunch of people.

Cooper handed back Michael's phone and he shut down the news report before he had to listen to any more.

"I'm still trying to find out exactly what happened," said Cooper.

"People are frightened of perceivers," said Michael. "I don't expect that's ever going to change."

Cooper paused. Perhaps he was thinking about what Michael said, perhaps he wasn't. Michael couldn't be bothered to perceive him to find out.

"I actually came out here to ask you if you need a lift back to London," said Cooper. "I presume the Prime Minister still wants you to work for him and I presume he's still going to go bananas if I don't get you back."

"I presume so."

"I've managed to secure an army driver to take me back to the base where I left my car. I can drive myself to London from there. I can give you a lift if you want."

Michael thought about it for a second. He really had no other way of getting back. "Yeah, that would be helpful. Thanks."

THE road back to Galen House looked less sinister in the day. The bare branches of the trees were majestic against the white winter clouds, as opposed to the skeletal outlines of the night before. The rolling hills of the English countryside stretched out to the horizon in different shades of green, some of them with the white blobs of sheep moving on them.

But, as they got closer, Michael got an uncomfortable feeling about going back in the base and asked the driver to pull over.

"Don't be silly," said Cooper. "It's safe."

"For you, maybe," said Michael. "But the soldiers inside might recognise me as a perceiver. I'd rather stay out here. You can pick me up on the way out."

Cooper reluctantly agreed and Michael got out into the cold. The sun that had pleasantly warmed his face earlier in the day was sinking below the tree line and the chill was returning to the air. He buttoned up the military coat that he still wore and stood back from the road.

Michael pulled out his phone and texted Pauline: 'How are you doing?'

She texted back almost immediately: 'Took Katya for check-up. Army doc says all fine. She thinks baby is a boy!'

'How are *you* doing?'

'Stuck here for another night, but ok. Phone needs charging. Gotta go.'

Michael sent another message asking her to let him know when Norm had found her somewhere else to stay, but he didn't get an immediate reply. Either she was busy or her phone had run out of power.

Michael looked up the road towards the army base that had once been his home. From where he was standing, he should have a view of the guarded gate at the entrance with the buildings behind. But what he could actually see was a group of civilians and three vans with news logos on the side and satellite dishes on top. They were probably all journalists. The fire had put Galen House firmly back in the news.

With the dimming of the light, the news crews had started to turn on their own light sources and areas of bright white beamed out from where they gathered. Michael, curious and cold from standing still, decided to walk up to investigate. As he got closer, he heard the irritating voice of Sian Jones carried on the wind.

She stood between one of the news vans and the fence, and was looking into a camera mounted on a tripod and pointing in the direction of the entrance. One of the bright lights Michael had seen from further down the road shone down on her from the top of a pole, giving her blonde hair an almost saintly halo.

Behind the camera stood a giant of a man, well over six feet tall, who had to bend forward to look into the viewfinder.

Michael stopped when he got close enough to hear what Sian Jones was saying:

"…has confirmed that the army base behind me was the home of an elite unit of perceivers being trained for unspecified missions. In the statement, the government condemns the attack on the building in which they say many of the perceivers were sleeping and which could have resulted in loss of life. What the statement fails to address is who carried out the attack. It was assumed earlier in the day that it was the anti-perceiver protestors who we spoke to yesterday outside of the army base, but some people I've been speaking to here have told me that it was some of the soldiers stationed on the base who staged the midnight attack. Official sources won't comment on that suggestion, but it would answer the question being asked by many: how did protestors armed with petrol bombs get into a secure and guarded military installation? And if perceivers are no threat, then why did the very soldiers who work alongside them turn against them?"

Her diatribe stopped and she kept staring into the camera for a moment. Then she relaxed and turned away as she apparently came off the air. The cameraman stood up from his stooped position, put his hands in the small of his back and leant back against them. After stretching out, he reached across to a cord dangling from the light on the pole and turned it off. The halo around Sian Jones gave way to the grey of the day's fading light. She pressed her finger to her earpiece and lowered her mouth towards the microphone on her lapel. "Yeah, that's fine," she said to whoever was listening on the other end. "Ask them how long they want, will you?"

The cameraman approached her with a large puffer jacket which she took, gratefully. Putting her arms into the sleeves and doing the zip up over her thin body made her look like she was a puffer jacket with a head sticking out of the top.

"Cheers, Andy," she said. "They need us to stay to do a piece for the six o'clock."

"It's all overtime to me," said the cameraman, who was evidently called Andy.

"Have you got any more tea in that flask?" she said.

"You drank the last," he said. "I'll see if I can score some more. ITN have some work experience kid hanging around, I'll see if they'll let me borrow him."

The tall cameraman, who seemed oblivious to the cold in his big jumper and jeans, walked off towards one of the other news crews.

Sian Jones plunged her hands into the pockets of her puffer jacket and walked away from the van. She was ambling, more than heading anywhere in particular, but still her path generally headed in Michael's direction. She didn't see him at first, as her eyes were pointed towards the ground as she assessed the best place to plant her feet on the uneven grass. When she looked up again, she gave him a cursory smile. "Afternoon," she said.

"Afternoon," Michael replied.

As she passed, he perceived her. She was thinking about what she was going to say in her six o'clock news report. It was not much different to what he had already overheard. But, as he lingered in her head, he noticed something else emerging in her thoughts: a growing sense of recognition.

Sian turned back round. "Do I know you?" she asked.

Michael faced her. "We met once," he said. "About five years ago."

"Was it on a story?"

"Sort of," said Michael.

He didn't know what he should do with himself. Make his excuses and run back down to where Cooper was expecting to pick him up, probably. But he was interested in what Sian Jones knew, and worried about what else she might reveal about perceivers.

He perceived her as her mind ran through snatches of half-remembered stories she had worked on. It was like watching a slide show of photographs on fast forward: a cute dog, a crying widow, an injured man, an embarrassed politician. Then Michael saw an image of himself as a boy reflected back at him. That was back before he became a perceiver for a second time, when he thought he was a norm.

She clicked her fingers. "You were with that girl who was asking about Brian Ransom, the perceiver guy."

It was Michael who now remembered a face from his past: Jennifer. She was the perceiver who had taken him in when he had nowhere else to turn and helped him to discover who his father was. "Yes," he said.

She was excited now, as her brain rushed to reconstruct little bits and pieces of memory from five years ago. "She was the one who led the march on Parliament that sparked off the riots. Whatever happened to her?"

"She couldn't take it anymore," said Michael. "She opted for the cure."

"That's right." Sian nodded. "I'd almost forgotten. That was back when I worked at the paper. I loved working for the paper, you didn't have to stand out in the cold for hours talking to a camera. But they had to cut the investigative reporter budget in the end, so I figured I could reach more people on the TV."

"Why are you doing it?" said Michael.

"It pays the bills," said Sian.

"No, I mean, why are you digging up all the secrets about perceivers?"

"People have the right to know."

"Do they have the right to attack perceivers in the middle of the night with tear gas and petrol bombs?"

She was getting angry now. He could perceive it. "I didn't tell people to do that, they did it on their own."

"But you told everyone where the perceivers were!" said Michael. He was aware his voice was raised, he saw a couple of people from the other news teams turn to look. But he didn't care.

"I didn't know it was going to turn violent, how could I?" said Sian.

"Because you were the one stirring up anger," said Michael. "Perceivers were fine living their own lives not bothering anyone, then you go ahead and broadcast information about them with no thought for the consequences. You need to stop before someone gets killed."

"All I'm doing is putting the truth out there," Sian insisted. "People on trial and arrested police suspects were having their minds read without their knowledge. Who knows what they were doing with that information? And who's to say that the perceivers could be trusted? They could perceive the mind of an innocent man and say he's guilty and no one would know."

"And that gives you the right to victimise them, does it?"

Andy the cameraman must have heard them arguing because, in a few strides, he came over carrying a mug of tea in each hand. "What's going on?" he asked, looking at Michael, then at Sian.

She held up her palm towards him like a traffic warden holding up the traffic. "It's fine, Andy, thanks."

Michael took a breath and tried to subdue his own anger. It was stopping him thinking clearly and getting in the way of perceiving other people's thoughts. "Everyone knows the truth now, so you need to stop saying it on the news."

"If I stop, then other journalists will take over." She threw out her arm to indicate the other news crews hanging around the base and narrowly missed whacking her cameraman in the face. He took a step back and tried not to spill the tea.

Michael looked back towards the entrance. There were more white lights shining out now, and each one probably represented a different organisation all doing a different report using the same facts and putting their own spin on it. It was the proverbial genie let out of the bottle.

"And if you think this is all there is to the story, then you're so sorely mistaken," said Sian, her pride now taking over. "There's so much more that they're hiding. A few young people shut away behind a military fence is nothing to what's coming."

"More?" said Michael. He concentrated his perception on her. He pushed away her pride and anger to look into the thoughts beneath. She was thinking about politicians. He saw images in her mind of men in suits and the tower of Big Ben rising above the Houses of Parliament.

A sudden fear blanketed her thoughts. "Are you a perceiver?" she said. "Is that why you are hanging around here?"

"You say it like being a perceiver is a bad thing," said Michael.

But what he perceived from her was not a hatred of people like him, but a fear that he would see her secrets. Not an unfounded one, either, as Michael probed further to find out what she knew.

Sian suddenly broke into song: "*Land of hope and glory! Mother of the free!*"

Her mind was full of song lyrics and images of crowds singing at the tops of their voices while waving Union Jacks at the Last Night of the Proms. "*How shall we extol thee, who are born of thee?!*"

Andy the cameraman put the cups of tea down on a patch of uneven ground so they tipped and some liquid spilled over the top. But he was more concerned with Sian. "Come on, let's go back to the van." He took her arm.

On the road nearby, a car stopped and there was the sound of a door opening and closing. Michael perceived it was Cooper, while his perceptions of Sian were coming up against only patriotic singing.

Some of the people from the other news crews had split off from the rest and were coming over to see what the fuss was about.

The cameraman pulled Sian back the other way. "*God, who made thee mighty, make thee mightier yet!*" she kept singing.

Michael shuddered as he felt Cooper touch the sleeve of his coat. "What's going on?"

"She's trying to stop me perceiving her."

"I thought the technique was to sing songs in your head."

"She's gone one step further," said Michael.

Somehow the whisper went around the approaching journalists that Michael was a perceiver and they quickened their pace towards him.

"We need to go," said Cooper.

"Yeah," said Michael.

He jogged down to Cooper's car and got in the back.

As Cooper drove away, Michael stared out of the rear window at the journalists as, for a moment, he perceived their disappointment that they had missed their chance to interview a perceiver. But it wasn't them he was worried about, he was thinking about the real story that Sian Jones claimed the politicians were hiding.

SIXTEEN

MICHAEL got back to the flat to find the sheets that Pauline had been sleeping on, folded up on the arm of the sofa. As he wandered through to the bathroom to do the necessary after his long journey in the car, he looked through to his bedroom to see the unmade bed where Katya had slept.

After he washed his hands, Michael stripped the bed and put the sheets in the washing machine. He was overtired from getting virtually no sleep the previous night and he wanted to look forward to getting into his own bed with his own clean sheets and not ones that someone else had used.

He collected the folded up sheets from the sofa and was about to put them in the machine as well when the smell of Pauline stopped him. It was wrapped up with the residue of fragrance from the washing powder, but there was enough of it to make him think of her. The sheets were soft in his hands and he held them like he was holding her.

Shaking the silliness from his head, he bent forward to put the washing in with the rest and stopped. The machine was quite full already with sheet, two pillowcases and a duvet cover. There was also the issue of getting everything dry before he could put it back on the bed again. It didn't make sense to wash both sets of bedding and leave him with nothing. So he shut the door of the machine, added the powder and set it off on its washing cycle.

Michael took the other set of sheets back to the sofa, put them back where he had found them and sat down. The cushions hugged his body with a comfort of home which was more relaxing than any other. He retrieved his phone from his pocket and read the warning message to say it was low on power. Reluctantly, he left the sofa, scrabbled around for the charger, then sat back down again and dialled Pauline's number.

The wire attached to the phone was too short for him to sit back so he leant forward with the phone at his ear. It rang for a long time and he thought it was going to go to voicemail. But, at the last moment, Pauline answered.

"Hello?"

She sounded a little out of breath, but it was good to hear her voice. "Hi, it's Michael."

"Yeah, I know. The display tells me who's ringing. Where are you?"

"Home."

"You got there okay, then?"

"Sort of." He paused. "Look, Pauline, there's something I found out."

"What?"

"I'm not really sure."

"You're not really sure what you found out?" she repeated.

"Are you coming back to London at all?"

"I haven't got a job anymore, have I?"

That's what Michael thought. It was a silly question. It was just that he had no one else to talk to. He had friends back at university, but they were norms, they wouldn't understand. The only person he actually knew in London was the Prime Minister and he wasn't the sort of person you invited over for a coffee and a chat.

"I could come up and see you, I suppose," she said. "Norm's got me somewhere to stay in Kent. I should be able to get to London from there."

"You could stay here," said Michael. He hadn't been able to perceive her to sense how she would react to the offer. It was quite possible she would end the phone call and never speak to him again, but it seemed an obvious solution. To him, anyway.

"In your one-bedroom flat?" she said, as if the idea was preposterous.

It probably was preposterous. He was being an idiot. "You don't have to," he said, backtracking to save further embarrassment. "It was just idea."

"It's a good idea," said Pauline. "It's just that I promised Katya I would stay with her."

"Then bring Katya," said Michael.

"In your one-bedroom flat?" she said again.

"It's all I have, Pauline. I miss you."

Michael felt himself go red and was pleased she wasn't there to see it.

"Well, in that case, then yeah. I'll check with Norm the Norm, but he's been run so ragged trying to find places willing to take perceivers that I'm sure he'll just be glad he's got two less people to find a home for."

"Okay, then. I'll see you ... tomorrow?"

"Probably," said Pauline. "I'll text you."

"Okay."

"Bye, then."

"Bye."

They hung up together. Michael let the phone slip from his fingers as he sat back on the sofa.

PANKHURST'S car stopped in the middle of the long driveway that led to the car factory in Dagenham. Ahead lay the glass-fronted reception area that disguised the automotive plant behind. Despite the rather grey day, it seemed to gleam as if a team of window cleaners had been crawling across its surface to spruce it up for the Prime Minister's visit. But, then, they probably had.

Michael was travelling in the car behind, which also slowed down to a stop on the driveway. Michael got out and stood waiting as still and patient as a statue. To an outsider, he must have looked like any other member of the Prime Minister's entourage standing there in a suit.

A little way ahead, a temporary barrier of steel railings had been erected and, behind that, stood a throng of journalists. Their microphones and camera lenses swung round towards the Prime Minister's car as Pankhurst emerged from the back. He had chosen, Michael noticed, a jazzy tie with bright red, purple and green circles to mark his individuality against the more conformist grey suit and pastel blue shirt that he wore.

Pankhurst headed straight for the journalists. Michael followed at a discreet distance and threw a perception barrier around Pankhurst's mind.

One of the journalists shouted out: "What's your reaction to the death of the woman who got burned at the anti-perceivers protest?"

Michael's perception barrier faltered for a moment as the news hit him. The memory of the bedsheet falling on the woman and catching fire from the petrol bomb was suddenly clear. It brought with it renewed horror as he remembered her arms fighting to get free from under the burning shroud.

Dead?

Earlier reports said she had been badly injured, but they hadn't suggested her condition was critical. The news was going to bounce back to harm the perceivers' cause, he knew it. No one would remember that the woman who burned to death had been the one throwing the petrol bomb.

Pankhurst's reaction to the question was numb and rehearsed. With all his advisors around him, someone must have passed the information to him in the car and he was ready with his answer. "First let me say that my thoughts are with Hilary Bestwood's friends and family at this tragic time…"

Michael actually saw some of the journalists roll their eyes as Pankhurst trotted out the same insincere mantra politicians always trotted out after tragic events.

"…But it will not deter me in my efforts to find a solution to this very concerning tension that has risen up between perceivers and other members of the public."

"What are you actually doing about it, Prime Minister?" asked another journalist.

"We have a number of options on the table," said Pankhurst. "We know that the choices before us are hard, but I can assure you that we shall make the right choices for the good of the country."

"What options, Prime Minister?"

He smiled, blatantly ignoring the question. "Thank you for coming. I do hope you'll be covering my visit to the highly successful Fusheema car factory."

He turned, abruptly ending the impromptu press conference and went into the building.

The rest of the visit was highly organised — and strictly timed. Shake a few people's hands here, look at some machinery there, go to another room and talk to some workers in especially cleaned overalls near where he had started.

Throughout it all, Michael protected the Prime Minister's mind. But it turned out to be unnecessary. There was no crazed Russian on perceiver serum to disrupt proceedings.

There was only a management trainee on an apprenticeship who, as soon as Michael walked into the same room as him, he realised was obviously a perceiver. The trainee looked about eighteen years old in a new suit which he wore like a shop mannequin as he desperately tried not to get it creased or dirty. The trainee immediately perceived what Michael was, and his eyes went wide and his face went pale.

He instinctively raised his barriers when he felt Michael touch his mind and Michael had to push through to ensure the trainee heard his thoughts.

Don't worry, thought Michael. *Shake the Prime Minister's hand, don't try to perceive him, and I will say nothing.*

The trainee shook Pankhurst's hand with a weak and trembling grip. The teenager didn't even try to sense the Prime Minister's emotions. He was clearly no spy, just a young man who had got his first job in a car factory and also happened to be able to read minds.

After that, dignitaries, invited guests and the press gathered in the factory assembly hall among the half-finished vehicles, engine parts and robotic machinery. A lectern had been set up for the Prime Minister and he addressed his audience who remained much quieter and more respectful than the rabble he addressed every week in the House of Commons.

Pankhurst said how proud he was to see the tradition of manufacturing return to Britain. He praised the wonderful job that the managers were doing in their commitment to an apprentice scheme which encouraged young people to … blah, blah, blah.

Michael found himself standing next to Barrington as he kept a careful eye on the crowd.

"I need to speak to the Prime Minister," Michael whispered.

"Not available," said Barrington out of the corner of his mouth.

"What's he doing after this?"

"Back to Downing Street. Cabinet meeting. You're not needed."

"Can I ride with him in the car?"

"No," said Barrington. "You work for the Prime Minister. Not the other way round."

Michael could perceive there was no use arguing with the man. So he continued to stand and perceive the crowd. The journalists among them, who were used to listening to political rhetoric, appeared to be as bored by it as he was.

Afterwards, Michael hoped to catch Pankhurst's eye, but he had more hand shaking to do and Michael continued to blend into the background.

The Prime Minister, however, had one human weakness that Michael was able to exploit. Like every other human being on the planet, he needed to go to the toilet at some point during the day. Because of Michael's ability to perceive him, he knew when that point was and made an effort to get there first.

The gentlemen's toilet, like the front of the building, looked like it had been given extra special attention by a team of cleaners. The white tiled floor and the painted white walls almost sparkled in the bright lights overhead. There were three cubicles, three sinks and three urinals, one of which was occupied by a man whose whole hair quota seemed to have been used up on his beard rather than on his head. Michael approached the urinal next to him and unzipped his fly.

Pankhurst entered the toilets, went straight into one of the cubicles and closed the door.

Barrington followed at a more leisurely pace. He checked the other two cubicles were empty and stood on guard next to the one Pankhurst had locked himself into.

The bearded man, looking somewhat intimidated, shook himself dry and tucked himself away in his trousers. He glanced once behind at Barrington, then left without washing his hands. Which Michael thought was rather disgusting.

Michael tried to pee, but his body didn't want to.

"Come on, Michael," said Barrington. "Finish up and leave."

"I just need to …"

At that moment he heard the sound of falling urine landing into the water of a toilet bowl. The sound was enough to break his psychological barrier and he squeezed a little bit from his bladder.

The Prime Minister, it seemed, was too shy to reveal an intimate part of his body at a public urinal.

Pankhurst emerged soon after and Michael was relieved to see he believed in personal hygiene as he went to the sink to wash his hands. Michael finished what he was doing and joined him.

"What options?" said Michael.

Barrington stepped forward and touched Michael on the shoulder. "Come on, now. You've finished."

"The Prime Minister told the journalists he was considering options to deal with the perceiver crisis," said Michael. "I want to know what they are."

Barrington pulled at Michael's shoulder. Not politely this time, but forcefully enough to pull him back from the sink and for his wet hands to drip onto his shoes.

"No, it's all right," said Pankhurst, waving Barrington away. "We have a few minutes before we have to leave, don't we?"

Barrington glanced at his watch, but Michael perceived he didn't actually read what it said. "Not really, sir."

Pankhurst shook the water from his hands and went over to one of the hand driers next to the sinks. It was one of those powerful ones mounted at waist height. He plunged his hands in and the resulting blast of air meant he had to raise his voice to be heard. "There are always options."

"I'm part of the working group on perceivers," said Michael. "If there are options, then we should be considering them at our next meeting."

"Ah," said Pankhurst, with regret. He pulled his hands from the drier and the roar of the air abruptly ceased. "Things are moving so fast, I fear I will need to act before the working group finalises its report."

"Then you *are* looking at options?" said Michael. He perceived Pankhurst was hiding something from him, so he looked further into his thoughts. What he saw shocked him: Pankhurst was thinking of the ostentatious bow woman who had represented the cure programme at the first meeting of the working group.

"I won't lie to you, Michael," said Pankhurst. "It would be foolish to lie to someone of your ability anyway. The truth is that I'm under pressure to extend the cure programme to all perceivers."

"You can't!" said Michael. "That would undermine perceivers' rights — the rights that you personally enshrined in law. Anyway, it would be impossible."

"A report's landed on my desk which lays out how it might be done." He thought of the ostentatious bow woman again.

"You're not seriously considering it?" said Michael.

 But he perceived that Pankhurst was.

"Nothing has been decided yet, Michael. Now, if you'll excuse me, I have a Cabinet meeting to attend."

Barrington stepped aside as Pankhurst headed for the door and formed a deliberate barrier to stop Michael from following.

"Is there something you're not telling me?" Michael called after Pankhurst. "Sian Jones thinks there's a wider conspiracy going on. Is that true?"

But Pankhurst had gone and if he knew anything about what the journalist had hinted back outside the army base, then the glimpse of his thoughts as he walked out revealed nothing of it.

Michael tried to walk around Barrington, but Barrington side-stepped and continued to block him. "You do not speak to the Prime Minister without permission again, do you understand?"

"I was just asking—"

"I tolerate your presence because the Prime Minister requested it and because your actions at the G8 summit were commendable. But you're not his friend and you certainly do not ambush him in the toilets. One more stunt like that and I will not tolerate your presence any further, is that clear?"

Michael didn't say anything.

"Is that clear?" Barrington repeated.

"It's clear," said Michael.

"Good," said Barrington. "You ride in the car behind, as you did on the way in. Once we arrive back at Downing Street, you make yourself scarce. Everyone who will be there you have vetted before, so your presence is not required."

Barrington turned on his heel and walked out.

SEVENTEEN

MICHAEL didn't know why he watched the television, it only made him angry.

Claudia Angelheart had come out of the woodwork and proudly announced that she had resurrected Action Against Mind Invasion. The same organisation who had mounted a counter-demonstration to perceivers on that day when they clashed and five people died.

Her stupid face with too much make-up was all over the news, demanding action. "We let them live among us once before and look at what happened," she told whatever journalist would listen. "It's time to revoke Perceivers' Law and take back control of our own minds. The only way to do that is to cure them all."

The news programmes also ran that clip of Pankhurst repeatedly. The one where he proclaimed: "We have a number of options on the table. We know that the choices before us are hard, but I can assure you that we shall make the right choices for the good of the country."

Michael nearly took his shoe off and threw it at the television screen. If the TV hadn't come with the furnished apartment, then he might have done. Instead, he lifted the remote control with his thoughts, brought it over to his hand and changed the channel to watch a comedy panel show.

At least someone had something to laugh about.

Pauline let herself in with the key that Michael had given her. She looked cold in the khaki trousers, shirt and jumper that she was wearing. When she had taken some clothes from the pile of uniforms that was offered to the perceivers at Tidworth barracks, she must have neglected to find a coat.

It was gone ten o'clock and he was surprised to see her. He had texted her through the day and, apart from a few messages earlier on saying she was still planning to come, she had said nothing.

He perceived a tiredness about her that was more than lack of sleep. "Hello," he said. "I'd almost given up on seeing you today."

"I was waiting for Katya," said Pauline.

Michael opened his perception a little further and confirmed that he and Pauline were the only ones there. "Where is she?"

"Cooper wouldn't let her come. He issued orders that she be questioned. I thought they would question her and let her go, but it got late and they hadn't even turned up yet."

"Do you think they have suspicions about Katya?"

"No more than we do," said Pauline. "They just want to be sure, I guess. I told Katya I would stay with her, but she said it was fine and I should come to see you in London. I think she knew I didn't really want to stay there. Perhaps that baby inside of her was allowing her to perceive me a little."

Michael got up off the sofa. He took the kitbag from her shoulder and felt how light it was. "Is there anything in here?" he said.

"Just the nightclothes I was wearing when the attack happened."

He put it down by the door. He perceived her more deeply now that they were close. There was a melancholy wrapped up in her tiredness. "Why don't you take a seat. Do you want something to eat or drink? There's pesto and pasta. Or I can make coffee?"

"Coffee sounds great," said Pauline. "I shouldn't because I should sleep, but … coffee sounds great."

She availed herself of the bathroom while Michael made coffee in the kitchenette.

When he came back into the living area with two mugs, Pauline had changed into her nightclothes and was sitting on the sofa.

She saw him looking at her. "It feels so good to take the uniform off," she said. "I've *got* to get some more clothes to wear."

"You can go shopping tomorrow," said Michael.

"I left all my money and cards and stuff at Galen House."

"I can lend you some money."

"Really?"

"Sure."

She took one of the mugs of coffee from him and sniffed at the deep bitterness rising in the steam. "Thanks," she said. "For the coffee and the other thing."

Michael sat beside her. "We can't have you walking around London naked, can we? Even if would be fun."

She kicked him playfully in the shin.

He laughed.

She laughed too, but the breaking of her stoic emotions allowed her darker feelings to surface. Like a bird flying up in the sky only to be shot down with a bullet and come plunging back to earth.

Her face contorted as she lost control and tears came.

She turned away from Michael. But even if he hadn't seen that she was upset, he could feel it.

Her body trembled. She put her mug of coffee on the floor. "Sorry," she said. "I'm so sorry."

"Don't be," said Michael. He put his coffee next to hers and moved up closer on the sofa. He perceived her first to make sure she wouldn't shrink from him, then he put a comforting arm around her shoulder.

"Everything I had was in Galen House. *Everything*. And they just burned it down like it was a meaningless pile of wood on bonfire night."

"I know," said Michael.

She sniffed and found her self-control from deep inside. She wiped her eyes with the sleeve of her bathrobe and calmed herself even though the feelings of loss and betrayal still raged under the surface.

"I'm such a fool," she said. "It's only stuff, isn't it? I can get more stuff."

She said the words, but she didn't believe them. What had burned down was more than stuff, it had been her home for four years and she was, effectively, homeless.

On the television, the smarmy show host from Wales was laughing about whatever the cocky comedian from London had said.

"What's this?" said Pauline.

"Oh," said Michael, looking at the television screen. "Three people on one team each tell a story and the three people on the other team have to work out which one is telling the truth."

"Sounds dull," she said, and picked up the remote control which was next to her.

Michael was about to say he thought the programme was actually quite funny, but she flicked a button and the screen abruptly changed to the news. The bulletin that Michael had been watching earlier had changed to a discussion programme. Three guests sat in a semicircle amid moody lighting and a screen behind them which showed a photograph of burning Galen House. Questioning the guests was an old male journalist Michael didn't recognise. He recognised one of guests, however. It was Claudia Angelheart.

"Turn it off," said Michael. "It will just make you angry."

He reached for the remote control, but Pauline pulled it away from him. He wished his telekinesis was strong enough to rip it from her hand. "Someone needs to tell that woman she's talking nonsense," she said. You can't cure everyone. I mean, even from a practical point of view."

"The Prime Minister has a report from someone at the cure programme who says that you can."

Pauline shifted in her position on the sofa to face him. "He's considering it?"

"Apparently," said Michael.

On the TV, one of the other guests had managed to get a word in edgeways. He was a young muscular man in his early twenties whose blonde hair was receding from his temples. "Curing people is not the answer," he said. "Perceivers are here. You can't disinvent us. Even if you were able to track down every perceiver in the country and make them take the cure, you've got to understand that the thing which turns people into perceivers occurs at the genetic level. It's something that can be inherited. The young people who were the first to develop perception after the vitamin pill scandal are old enough to have children now. The chances are, their children will be perceivers too. What are you going to do, sterilise us all? Like the Nazis tried to do in the Second World War?"

Recognition crept up on Michael as he watched. "Oh my God," he said to himself.

"I don't believe he's saying it, either," said Pauline.

On the TV, the journalist was getting excited. "Are you saying the cure doesn't reverse perception?"

"It stops people being able to perceive," said the young man. "It doesn't stop them from being perceivers inside and it doesn't stop their children from growing up to be perceivers."

Pauline was getting angry. "That's only going to antagonise norms even more." She stopped; she perceived Michael. "That's not what you're 'oh my God'ing about, is it?"

The young man's hair wasn't as bright blonde as it used to be and his muscular frame was disguised by the cut of his suit, but it was definitely the person Michael remembered. "That's Otis."

A name came up on the screen as the camera closed in on him: *Oliver Smith, Perceiver.* "It says he's called Oliver Smith," said Pauline.

"When I knew him, he called himself after his initials that spelled Otis. His name is Oliver Something Something Smith. He used to be the boyfriend of Jennifer Price, the girl who led the perceiver movement before the riots. They must have found him from somewhere to talk on behalf of perceivers."

The picture had cut back to Claudia Angelheart who had become very animated at the thought of a whole new generation of perceiver children.

"Telling the world that we're all going to have perceiver babies isn't going to help," said Pauline.

"But it's true, isn't it?" said Michael.

"Speak for yourself," said Pauline.

The camera was back on Otis. The more Michael looked at him, the more the cosmetic changes to his face over the years seemed to fall away and he saw the same teenager he had known back before the Perceiver Corps. "The politicians didn't tell you perception is inherited because they wanted to lull you into a false sense of security," said Otis. "Even if you accept that the cure is a solution, it's only a temporary one. The politicians knew that right from the start, but they didn't say anything because it suited them to make people believe that everything was fine."

Pauline hit the 'off' button on the television remote and Otis's face disappeared into the blackness of the screen. "You're right," she said.

"What?" said Michael.

"Watching that stuff makes you angry."

She moved closer to him and leant her head on his chest. "If we stay here and close the curtains, turn off the TV, the radio and don't look at the internet, we can pretend none of this is happening. We can exist in our own little world."

"The world will still be there in the morning," said Michael.

"But not tonight," said Pauline. "Tonight I want to feel like every-thing is okay. Just for a little while."

Michael allowed her to relax back into him. The warmth of her face on his chest and the strong beat of her heart lulled him into a soothing rhythm. He could perceive her thoughts were still troubled, but as she lay there, he sensed them lose their turbulence as sleep claimed her.

Michael lifted her head from his chest and lowered it down onto the sofa. She stirred, but didn't wake. He found the spare set of bed-clothes he had just cleaned from the day before and lay them on top of her. She looked serene in the semi-light of his darkened flat.

Removing her un-drunk mug of coffee from where she might kick it over in the middle of the night, he took one last look at her asleep on his sofa. He had been going to offer her the bed again, but he didn't want to disturb her. It was better for her to lie there and dream about a world where perceivers were not hated and their future wasn't under threat.

The real world could wait until the morning.

EIGHTEEN

Michael indulged Pauline with a shopping trip in Oxford Street in the morning. It was a shopper's paradise where all the most well-known clothing chains in the country had their largest stores, in what was one of the busiest areas of London.

Pauline was like a child in a sweetshop. For a woman with no clothes of her own, she was literally spoiled for choice. She took so many items to the fitting rooms that the shop assistants wouldn't let her take them all in. Michael allowed her to have her fun. She smiled, she laughed and she didn't think of the perceiver crisis once. Even though it meant Michael standing for lengthy periods outside of changing rooms waiting for her, he didn't mind. Seeing her happy was reward enough.

Most of the clothes she was trying on were a fantasy, as Michael could only afford to buy her one outfit. In the end, she chose a pair of black jeans, a black T-shirt with a picture of a white cat on it and a black jumper. She decided she could make do with the set of army boots she had been given, but refused to make do with the scratchy wool socks that went with them, and so added a set of underwear to the bill.

Afterwards, they retreated to a burger place where Michael stood in the queue for drinks and Pauline went off to the toilets to change.

Being Oxford Street, it was packed with people speaking all sorts of languages, mostly tourists or foreign students, although he noticed some English voices among them. As Michael turned from the counter with Pauline's chocolate milkshake and his own coffee, two people had just vacated a table by the window. He claimed it quickly before anyone else came and sat on the bright plastic chair next to the bright plastic table and looked out through the window at the dull winter's day and the stream of dull people walking by.

Pauline emerged all in black, as Michael had always known her when she wasn't in her Perceiver Corps regulation greys. She still wore the smile she had worn in the shops. She also still wore the tag from the jumper which was sticking out of the back of her neck.

"What do you think?" she said, opening her arms so he had a full view of her outfit.

"They suit you," said Michael. "Apart from one thing. Sit down."

Puzzled, she sat down. But then she perceived him and realised what he was doing.

Michael got up and went round the back of her chair. The tag was attached with a thin bit of plastic which he couldn't break. So he brushed her hair out of the way and leant forward to bite it in two.

Pauline giggled and squirmed a little in her seat. "Your breath tickles."

The plastic was no match for Michael's teeth and he was able to thread it out from the jumper and place the two halves on the table along with the offending tag.

"Thanks," said Pauline when he sat down. "Not going to work today?"

"I'm not wanted," said Michael. "I'm not sure they want me at all anymore."

"Why do you say that?"

"The working group on perceivers that I left my new life for is being overtaken by events. Anyway, I'd rather spend the day with you."

Pauline sipped at the straw which was sticking out of her drink and noisily drew chocolate milkshake up into her mouth.

Michael looked around at the other people sitting at the plastic tables near them. He could hear all their conversations about what they should buy and how much things cost. It was too crowded a place for him to talk properly to Pauline.

I spoke to Sian Jones a couple of days ago, Michael thought.

Pauline looked up from drinking her milkshake.

She said what she has been reporting on isn't the real story, Michael's thoughts continued. *She said the politicians are hiding something.*

Pankhurst? thought Pauline.

If he knows anything, he's keeping it deep within his mind where I can't easily perceive it. I don't think he's clever enough to do that.

If not Pankhurst, then who?

I don't know, but I want to find out, thought Michael. *Want to come?*

Pauline smiled. *Yeah. After I've finished my milkshake.*

SIAN Jones worked out of Broadcasting House, not too far to walk from the burger place in Oxford Street. It was tucked behind the frontage of old buildings which faced the road as if embarrassed to show its modern glass-fronted exterior to the world.

As soon as Michael and Pauline turned off the street to walk down the paved entrance to the front door, it was obvious that finding Sian Jones in that haystack was not going to be easy. At least twenty people were in the process of leaving the building and walking in their direction to the street, while at least another twenty were approaching it alongside them.

"What's your plan?" asked Pauline.

"Go up to the reception desk and ask for her," said Michael.

"What if she doesn't want to see you?"

"I'll think of another plan."

The reception area on the other side of the glass was bigger than any other Michael had been in. Once he stepped inside, he realised why. It had to accommodate a lot of people. As well as a few visitors in business suits who were probably there for a meeting of some sort, there were others who were waiting to be guests on a television or radio show. There was even a trio in straw hats with a guitar, a cello and a violin.

Past a couple of bored-looking security guards in uniforms of white shirt and tie was a long desk with three receptionists. Michael chose the one who looked the most friendly; a woman with dyed auburn hair pulled back in a ponytail and a telephone headset over the top, who looked hot in the formal jacket she had to wear.

"Hello," said Michael with a smile. "We're here to see Sian Jones."

"Sian Jones," the receptionist repeated. The name clearly meant nothing to her.

"She works in television news," Pauline added. "She's a journalist."

"Let me ring the newsroom," said the receptionist. She tapped out a few numbers on a panel in front of her. After a moment, her expression changed and she began a conversation with someone who had apparently answered the phone on the other end. The call didn't last long before the receptionist hung up. "Someone's just gone to find her," said the receptionist. "She's in today, but doesn't seem to be at her desk. Why don't you take a seat?"

Michael and Pauline found a seat among the eclectic crowd and waited.

Someone came and got the trio in straw hats and they went through the security doors into the main part of the building. Other people sitting on the seats near them were also collected and taken through. Michael and Pauline remained.

"Let me go and ask again," said Pauline. She went back to the reception desk, leaving Michael sitting alone. He watched the comings and goings in the reception area for a little longer and was beginning to suspect that 'think of another plan' was what he was going to have to do, when a tall man he recognised came through the security barriers. It was Andy the cameraman and he looked in a hurry.

This could be his Plan B. As one of Sian's colleagues, he was more likely than most to know where she was. All he had to do was follow him out and ask him. Even if he didn't answer, Michael could perceive him and find out — assuming he didn't burst into a rendition of *Land of Hope and Glory* in the middle of the street.

But Andy didn't head for the door, instead he approached one of the security guards who looked rather shocked to have a tall man loom over him. A tall, angry man at that, as Andy soon lost his temper. "Well, can't you check?" the cameraman yelled at him.

The people assembled in reception turned to look. The security guard gave an apologetic shrug.

"You know what?" yelled Andy. "Just forget it!" He stormed out of the front doors.

Michael perceived him as he passed and realised that his anger was born of concern. He was worried about Sian Jones.

Michael got up from where he was sitting and followed Andy out. The cameraman had legs long enough to complete two strides where it took Michael three to cover the same ground and he had to hurry to keep up. At the same time, Michael reached into his pocket and pulled out his phone. He called Pauline.

"Hello?" she said.

"I've thought of another plan," he replied. "Catch me up. Go out of the main doors and turn left."

"Wh—?"

But he had no time to explain. He hung up and put his phone back in his pocket.

Out on the street, Andy had taken a left turn onto the main road and was heading for the tube station. As he disappeared down the steps into the London Underground complex, Michael realised he had only a few minutes to either lose him or lose Pauline. He glanced behind and saw Pauline hurrying in his direction.

Michael stopped at the top of the steps to the tube station and waved for Pauline to hurry up. She broke into a run.

Someone coming up the steps swore at him to "get out of the bloody way".

Seeing that Pauline was almost there, he did as he was told and descended underground.

He'd waited too long. The station was full of people all going different ways, like a nest of worker ants all following their own path and all looking the same. Their thoughts chattered at the edge of his perception, but none of them felt like the worried and angry mind of the cameraman.

Pauline bumped up behind him. "What the hell's going on?"

Michael grabbed her hand and pulled her towards the ticket barriers. Andy had to be on the other side of them somewhere. Michael tapped his Oyster card to the reader and the barrier let him through. He waited precious moments on the other side as Pauline found her ticket in one of the pockets of her new jeans and came through.

Michael turned. There were two down escalators and two options.

Out of all the dawdling tourists and hurrying Londoners around him, he picked out the head of the cameraman disappearing down the one that led to the Central Line. If Andy hadn't been taller than most of the other people around him, Michael might have lost him.

He followed, with Pauline behind.

On the London Underground, the rule is that people standing on the escalators stand on the right, allowing people in a rush to walk down the left. It only works if people don't block the left hand side.

Thankfully, that morning, some thoughtless person had dumped their suitcase in the way and had stopped Andy striding out of view.

At the bottom, Andy headed for the westbound platform, with Michael and Pauline not far behind him.

What's going on? Pauline asked with her thoughts.

He's worried about Sian Jones and he's going to find her, Michael replied.

It took only a minute for the tube train to arrive and for Andy to get on. Even though it was packed, Michael and Pauline squeezed themselves onto the same carriage. Crowded was good because it meant Andy didn't realise he was being followed. Even when the train emptied out a little bit on the subsequent stops, he was too wrapped up in his thoughts to notice Michael and Pauline.

Thoughts that Michael was able to perceive. Sian had not turned up to work that morning, which wasn't like her, especially as she was excited about the story she was working on. She wasn't answering her phone, either. Several other calls to several other people revealed no one had heard from her. Some of her colleagues in the newsroom thought it best to check to see if she had swiped in with her security pass and if she was, therefore, in the building somewhere with a flat mobile phone battery. Andy had volunteered to ask one of the security guards, even though he believed — he *knew* — that if she hadn't turned up in the newsroom, she hadn't turned up for work at all.

Andy was heading for her flat. She lived, Andy's thoughts revealed, alone with her cat, which meant if something had happened to her, there was no one to raise the alarm.

Michael perceived Sian's address from Andy's mind and he could have stopped following him to make his own way there. But the best way to get to Sian's flat was by the tube train that they were already on and so he sat with Pauline with his back to Andy in case he recognised him from their fractious meeting outside of the army base.

It was not an inconsiderable walk from the tube station to Sian's flat. Michael and Pauline hung back a little and crossed the road so as not to be so obvious about it, but Andy must have sensed he was being followed. Michael perceived that either he didn't care or he deliberately decided not to notice because the only thought in his head was getting to Sian's flat.

What are we going to do when we get there? thought Pauline.

Either she'll be there and we can ask her what she meant about the story being bigger than the Perceiver Corps, or she won't be there and we can come back to ask her later, Michael replied.

What if something really has happened to her? She might have fallen down the stairs and hit her head or something.

Michael didn't have an answer for that and he let his indecision speak for him.

The parked cars along the road that Sian lived in gave Michael and Pauline a little bit of cover as they tried to both keep up with Andy and not get too close so that he would turn round and challenge them.

The cameraman's pace slowed down as he approached what his mind said was where Sian lived. Like all the other houses in the street, it was a Victorian terrace with a postage stamp of an overgrown garden between its front wall and the street. And, like half of the other properties in the road, it looked like it had been converted into maisonettes.

Michael tucked himself in behind one of the parked cars as Andy walked up the short garden path to Sian's home. Pauline crouched behind him.

Andy put his hand out to the front door, but rather than knocking, he gently pushed and the door swung open.

He went in and Michael caught a moment of his concerned thoughts before he disappeared into the building.

Michael and Pauline crossed the road.

"Sian?" Andy called from inside.

Michael and Pauline waited on the street, next to the patch of overgrown garden.

"Sian!" Not a call for her to respond, but a scream of panic. "Sian! Sian! Jesus! *Sian!*"

Andy appeared in the doorway and Michael perceived a rush of horror as the tall man leant on the frame of the open front door, his eyes damp with the sheen of tears and his face pale. His trembling hand pulled the mobile phone from his pocket.

There was a singular image in his head: a blood-splattered bedroom and, at the centre of it, the wide staring eyes of Sian Jones's corpse.

NINETEEN

SIAN Jones's death was on the news by the time Michael and Pauline got back to his flat. The journalists on the television did their best to report it like any other murder, but it was clear in their faces — even without being able to perceive them through the screen — that this was not like any other murder to them.

Their colleague had died in the most brutal way and they were still trying to process it.

Michael and Pauline were still trying to process it.

On the television, a reporter stood on Sian Jones's street in front of a strip of police tape and told the camera what she knew, which wasn't very much. The reporter said it was a suspected shooting. The reporter said early indications were she had been dead for some hours and might have disturbed a burglar when she got home from a late shift.

The reporter didn't say what everyone had to be thinking: that Sian Jones was probably killed because of the story she was working on.

Michael got fed up of watching the TV, got off the sofa and went into the kitchenette. "Do you want some coffee?" he asked.

"Not really," said Pauline.

"Me neither." He took a glass from the cupboard and filled it with water from the tap.

Pauline turned off the news, which had started to repeat the same information they'd heard ten minutes ago anyway, and came over. She put her arms around Michael's waist and rested her head on his back. The warmth of her touch was nice, but the perception of her thoughts was troubled.

Michael drank from the glass. The water was cool and it soothed him a little. "We've got to find out what story she was working on," he said.

"We could ask her colleagues," said Pauline.

"I got the feeling this was her scoop. If she did tell anyone about it, they're not going to tell us. I was thinking more of getting hold of her research."

"I don't see how. If she kept it at work, it's in a newsroom manned twenty-four hours a day in that building with security guards and security doors. If she kept it at home, then it's at the site of a major crime scene crawling with police officers."

"I know," said Michael. "Know any good computer hackers?"

"I don't even know any bad ones," said Pauline.

A knock on the door made Michael turn. "Who's that?" he said.

"Could be Katya?" suggested Pauline.

Michael put his glass down by the sink and headed out of the kitchenette. Pauline's arms slipped from his waist and her residual warmth dissipated into the room.

As he approached the door, he perceived through it. "It's not Katya."

He opened the door to reveal Inspector Patterson wearing a coat over his usual crumpled suit. His stern expression didn't change. "Can I come in?"

Michael stepped aside and allowed the policeman to enter. He paused just inside the door and looked around. "Nice place."

"The government's paying for it," said Michael. "I don't suppose I'll be here much longer."

Patterson's gaze settled on Pauline. "You two back together again?"

Michael tried to perceive the answer from her, but she blocked him. The only answer he got was the one she was prepared to give to Patterson. "I needed somewhere to stay," she said. "My home burnt down. You probably saw it on the news."

"Ah, yes."

"Do you want some coffee, Inspector?" said Michael.

"This isn't a social call, Michael."

"I know. You've come about Sian Jones."

Patterson's stern expression became suspicious. "Are you perceiving me?"

He was, but not on a deep level. Not that he needed to. It was obvious. "You're the perceiver cop. The journalist who was working on the perceiver story has been murdered and suddenly you're here. Am I putting two and two together correctly?"

Patterson didn't reply, but he didn't have to. Michael perceived he was right.

"Maybe I'll have that cup of coffee," said Patterson.

Michael returned to the kitchenette and made three mugs of coffee for three people who didn't really want it. With two mugs balancing precariously in one hand and one held easily in the other, he brought the drinks over.

Patterson had taken off his coat and was sat on the sofa next to Pauline. It was a sofa which was big enough for three people, but only if Michael squeezed himself in between them. Given the circumstances, it seemed inappropriate and so Michael sat on the floor.

Patterson took out his phone and the stylus he used to write notes on it. Michael saw that he was also starting the recording app, like he used to do when he interviewed suspects and witnesses back in the time when Michael worked with him.

Michael tried to work out which one Patterson thought he was — suspect or witness, but it seemed even Patterson wasn't sure.

"Do you want to tell me what you were doing at Sian Jones's house?" said Patterson.

"Nothing," said Michael.

"You were seen," said Patterson. "The witness gave a description good enough for me to recognise it as you."

"What Michael means," said Pauline, "is that we didn't do anything. When we got there, she was already dead."

"The witness said you had a loud argument with her a couple of days before."

"You really think I could have killed her?" said Michael.

"I think you had motive," said Patterson. "She's the one who broke the perceiver story, she revealed where your training base was and indirectly got your girlfriend's home burnt down …"

Pauline flinched at being called Michael's 'girlfriend'. Patterson didn't seem to notice.

"… You have military training, you can fire a gun. I'm told the army keeps tight control of its weapons and you can't just walk out with one, but amid all the fire and the confusion the other night, it might have been possible."

"No!" said Michael. He scrambled to get himself off the floor. He felt vulnerable with Patterson looking down on him from the sofa. Standing, he felt he could regain authority in his own flat. "I didn't kill her. I didn't want to kill her. I went to her house to talk to her, but she was dead by the time we got there."

"Do you think a perceiver did it?" asked Pauline.

"Officially, we are keeping an open mind and pursuing several lines of inquiry," said Patterson.

"Unofficially?" said Michael.

"A perceiver with a grudge makes sense."

"Does it?" said Michael.

"On the surface," said Patterson. "But I've been at crime scenes where someone has been killed because of a vendetta and they're messy. People get angry, there's usually some sort of fight, the victim has defensive wounds and there's stuff all over the house where people have thrown things. This crime scene was clean. The gunshot wound made a mess, there was a lot of blood as you'd expect, but there was no evidence of a confrontation. It looks like someone was waiting for her to come home and shot through a pillow so the neighbours wouldn't hear. There was some effort to make it look like a burglary gone wrong, but it was a half-hearted one."

"Are you saying it was a professional hit?" said Pauline.

"I'm saying a perceiver with a grudge makes more sense," said Patterson.

Michael walked over to the window and came back again. Pacing did nothing to subdue his nervous energy. "She told me before she died that she was working on something else. She suggested that all the perceiver stuff she had reported on so far was just the tip of the iceberg and something bigger was coming."

"What?" said Patterson.

"I don't know," said Michael. "We wanted to ask her, but it seems someone else got there first."

Patterson's stylus hovered over the screen of his phone. He hadn't written a word of it down. "Someone with the power and resources to hire a hitman?"

"It makes more sense than a perceiver with a grudge," said Michael. "Don't you think?"

"I think you might be putting two and two together and making five," said Patterson.

"Then help us get to the truth," said Pauline. "If she was working on a big story that got her killed, the details could be on her computer. If you could get us access—"

"I can't."

"Or a copy of the files," said Michael.

"You two seem to forget that you don't work for the police anymore," said Patterson. "Even if I could give you access, I wouldn't. Until we establish what happened, you two remain suspects. I can't let suspects in a murder inquiry tamper with computer evidence, they'd bring back hanging just for me."

"You really think we're suspects?" said Pauline.

"We're keeping an open mind and are pursuing several lines of inquiry," said Patterson.

"For the record," said Michael, "we didn't do it. We need to find out who did before the perceiver crisis explodes into something worse. Sian Jones knew something and she was killed for it. No disrespect to you or your police colleagues, but I'm not prepared to sit back while you gather evidence strong enough to stand up in court. We need to act now."

"I can't help you," said Patterson. "I came here on my own as a favour to you because of our time working together and because I respect you. If you want to speak to the journalist's colleagues and see what they know, then that's entirely up to you as long as you don't impede my criminal investigation."

Patterson drank back his coffee. He stood up and handed the empty mug to Michael. "Is that your bathroom through there?" he asked, pointing to the only internal door in the room. "I just need to pay a visit."

He turned off the recording app on his phone and laid it down on the sofa along with the stylus. As he headed for the door, he thought to himself: *I'll just leave my phone there. I'm sure it'll be safe for five minutes.*

Once he had gone, Michael turned to Pauline. *Did he leave that there on purpose?* he thought.

Pauline picked up the phone and start scrolling through. *It's got the statement made by the man who found the body.*

What does it say?

She looked up from the screen and smiled. *It starts off with his name and address.*

ANDY Mostello, which turned out to be Andy the cameraman's other name, opened the door to his flat with a cat tucked underneath his arm that didn't want to be there. It was a relatively mature cat which was completely black, apart from a white patch down its front, and it was wriggling like crazy against Andy's strong grip.

The man himself was in a bit of a daze. By the scratchy beard on his chin and the unhealthy colour of his face, it looked like he had not slept at all. By the smell coming from the inside of his flat, alcohol was probably involved.

Andy's home was a step down the property ladder from Sian's converted house. It was one of up to fifty flats in a purpose-built concrete block with cold and uninviting stairwells that led to up to five separate floors where blank corridors allowed access to a row of identical front doors. The only thing that distinguished Andy's flat from that of his neighbours was his door was painted yellow, while both the ones on either side were painted blue.

Michael perceived that Andy was expecting to see someone like the postman or a delivery guy standing on his doorstep, so when he saw it was Michael and Pauline, his brain took a moment to realise who they were. As soon as it did, he broke into a sudden panic and hurled the cat at Michael.

The cat screeched a *meow* and Michael jumped backwards as the furry projectile landed on his neck. Alarmed and probably trying only to save itself, the cat extended its claws and reached out to find something to hold onto. The first thing it found was Michael's face and it tore at the skin on his cheek.

Michael yelled, grabbed at the furry ball and pulled it off him. The cat's pawing claws dug into his coat, but Michael yanked it free and dropped it to the floor. It dashed away across the corridor and down the steps.

As Michael wiped the blood from his cheek he saw that the door was still open because Pauline was standing in the doorway. Just beyond her, was Andy. For a tall man who was physically a match for both of them — even at the same time — he was gripped with irrational fear.

"We only want to talk," said Pauline.

Michael stepped forward and looked over Pauline's shoulder to see Andy with a mobile phone in his hand.

"You killed Sian!" he said.

"We didn't," said Michael. "We came to talk to her. The person who killed her was there long before we were."

In the pause that accompanied Andy thinking about what Michael had said, a voice spoke through the speaker of his phone. "Emergency. Which service do you require?"

"Please, let us talk to you," said Pauline. "We want to find out who killed Sian as much as you do."

Staring at them, his mind conflicted, Andy lifted the phone to his ear. "I'm sorry," he said into it. "Wrong number." He hung up.

"Thank you," said Michael. "Perhaps we can come in and talk properly."

A sudden panic came over Andy. But it wasn't a panic brought on by fear, it was brought on by worry. He stared at the open doorway. "Where's Trixie?!"

"Who's Trixie?" said Pauline.

"Sian's cat," said Andy. "I took her in when the police sealed off the house. Sian would have wanted someone to look after her."

Michael felt a dread in his stomach. "Would that be a black cat with a white patch down its front?"

"Yes," said Andy.

"It ran out and down the steps."

Andy pushed his way past them and out in the corridor, shouting the name of the cat as he went. "The bloody thing's been trying to get itself run over ever since I brought her here. I've been trying to hold on to her every time I open the door, but she's a slippery cat."

He seemed to have forgotten he was the one who had literally thrown the cat out of his flat.

Michael and Pauline ended up spending the next twenty minutes walking up and down the road shouting the cat's name until it was obvious that either the cat didn't know what its name was or it didn't want to be found.

Pauline was the one who suggested going back to the flat to get some cat food to tempt it out of hiding, and that's when they found Trixie: sitting outside of Andy's door all innocent as if nothing had happened.

Michael felt the most enormous relief from Andy as he bent down and picked the animal up. He squeezed and cuddled the cat, even though Trixie clearly didn't like being held, and wiggled to get free. The stupid cat was the only thing he had left of his murdered colleague and he treasured it.

Once inside, Andy got some cat food for Trixie and moved a couple of old pizza boxes and a collection of junk mail out of the way so Michael and Pauline had somewhere to sit in his tiny living room. It was barely the size of Michael's kitchenette and, with his furniture in there as well, there was hardly any room for people.

"Sian was working on something when she died," said Michael. "Did she tell you what it was?"

"How do I know I can trust you?" said Andy.

Michael thought about it. "Who else can you trust?"

"I could trust the police," he said. "Or people at work. Sian isn't the only journalist I work with, you know."

"But we're the ones who are here," said Pauline. "We're the ones you decided to invite into your home."

Andy looked directly at Michael. "You're a perceiver, aren't you? Sian knew you were, that's why she did that stupid singing and caused a scene outside of the army base." He smiled at the memory, then turned to Pauline. "I suppose you're a perceiver too."

"Yes," said Pauline.

"Then you can perceive that I don't trust you."

"But I perceive you want to," she said.

Andy paused. He looked to the ceiling. He looked to his hands clutching each other as he rested them in his lap. He looked at his shoes. Anywhere but directly at them. "Sian gave me something before she died. Just for safe keeping, I don't think she thought she was in danger. I want you to know, that if I give it to you, it's not the only copy."

"We understand," said Michael.

Andy reached into the front pocket of his jeans and pulled out a flash drive.

"What's on it?" asked Pauline.

"Journalist stuff," said Andy. "Research and notes and things. Whatever she was working on. I don't know what it was, but she was excited about it. Like journalists get when it's a big story."

Pauline reached over to take the flash drive, but he kept his hand held tight around it.

"I don't care about the story," said Andy. "I care about my friend and she cared about the story. If I give you this, promise me you'll honour her memory and find out who killed her."

"We promise," said Pauline.

Michael perceived Andy was still reluctant. Half an hour earlier he thought they'd come to kill him, after all. "I want to be honest with you," he said. "Sian Jones has stirred up a lot of anger against perceivers and that's been difficult for us. But it was coming sooner or later. The more perceivers were sent out to read people's minds, the more people knew about it and the more likely it was that someone was going to blow the whistle. If there's worse to come, if there's something we don't know about — something that made it worth killing to keep quiet — then we can't sit around and wait for it to happen. We need to find out about it now so we can stop it."

Michael held open his hand. Andy unfurled his fist to reveal the flash drive. He tipped his palm and the drive rolled off and dropped into Michael's possession.

TWENTY

THE onions and red peppers released their sweetness in the heat of the frying pan and filled the kitchen with the smell of their caramelised flesh. Michael gave them one last stir and pushed them with his spatula onto the warm and waiting plate next to the hob.

He tipped a glug of olive oil into the hot pan and it instantly sizzled. Into that he tipped the raw strips of chicken from the packet and the oil spat some more as it sealed the meat.

Pauline was at the other end of the worktop, well away from the danger of hot oil, scrolling through documents on Michael's laptop computer. "Smells amazing," she said. "Is it nearly ready? The only thing I had all day was that stupid milkshake."

"It'll be a couple of minutes," said Michael. He picked up the packet of spices which had been with the packet of chicken and ripped the top open with his teeth. He added the contents to the pan and the aroma of chilli and garlic overwhelmed all the other cooking smells. He realised how hungry he was.

"How are you getting on?" he asked Pauline.

"This isn't just her journalist research," she said. "It's like Sian Jones dumped everything she had on her computer onto the flash drive. There's everything on here, from a list of people's birthdays she's not supposed to forget, to how she's saving up for a trip to Australia next year."

Michael laughed. "You'll figure it out."

The microwave bleeped. It kept bleeping until Michael took out the plate of tortillas he'd put in there to warm up.

"Give me a hand with all this stuff, will you?" he said.

Pauline left the laptop and helped Michael take all the bits and pieces of the meal over to the sofa. There wasn't actually room for everything and so they ended up putting the plates of chicken, vegetables and tortillas, and the bowls of guacamole and sour cream on the floor, and sitting down beside it as if they were Japanese.

"Looks amazing," said Pauline.

"I only did what it said on the packet," said Michael. He picked up a tortilla, spooned on some onions, peppers and chicken, dolloped a spoonful each of sour cream and guacamole and rolled it all up together. As he put one end in his mouth, a blob of sour cream fell out of the other end and dropped on the carpet.

"Arse!" he said.

Pauline giggled. She had also made a fajita from the assembled ingredients, but she held her hand out at the other end of the wrap to catch the drips as she took a bite.

"You really need to get a table for this place," she said.

Michael finished his fajita and went back to the kitchenette to fetch a cloth. He also got a couple of extra plates for them both, even though it was shutting the fajita door after the sour cream horse had bolted.

"Have you found anything in Sian's computer files which aren't when her mother's birthday is and how much it costs to go to Australia?" asked Michael.

Pauline finished her mouthful before speaking. "There's a lot of stuff in there about perceivers, but it's all mixed up. Some of it she's reported on, some of it she hasn't but a lot of that stuff isn't what you'd call a big story. It's more like other examples of perceivers being deployed in areas of public life. There also seems to be some research from other stories she's been working on, up to around two years ago. I mean, there's a load of background on an MP called Peter Wauluds, if you can believe a name like that."

"Wauluds?" said Michael.

"Yeah — heard of him?"

"I've met him. He's a perceiver."

Pauline's mouth hung open as she was about to take a bite of her fajita. "Are you sure?"

"Bald guy? Tries to disguise it with what little wispy hair he has left?"

"That's him."

"When I told Pankhurst, he made him resign as a minister," said Michael. "What sort of research has she got on him?"

"Nothing that stood out," said Pauline. "He grew up in one place, went to school in another place, first elected somewhere else ... it all looked routine to me."

Nevertheless, when she had finished, she brought the laptop over for Michael to go through while she volunteered to clear up.

Pauline was right. Sian's research was not stored in any kind of logical fashion. The stuff on Wauluds, however, was in one folder which made it easier to go through. It didn't make it any more interesting. A lot of it was just public information available with any internet search. There was even a copy of his Wikipedia entry.

"This is interesting," said Michael, eventually.

"What?" said Pauline from where she was loading the dishwasher.

"Peter Wauluds used to work for Ransom Incorporated."

"Your father's old company? The one that produced the vitamin pills that made babies grow up to be perceivers?"

"Yeah."

"Bit of a coincidence, isn't it?"

"Not really. My father gathered together a lot of natural born perceivers to work for him back then."

Pauline came back to the living area, drying her hands on a tea towel. She put the towel down on the sofa and sat next to it. "Give me that."

Michael handed her the laptop and got off the floor. His buttocks had gone numb and he decided that sitting next to her on the sofa was much more comfortable. As well as easier to look over her shoulder. She had opened the folder about Wauluds so that it filled the screen with little icons representing documents and images. One of them was a text file labelled 'contacts'. She clicked on it.

It was a list of recent times and dates going back a week and annotated with a kind of typed shorthand. The first three had the letters, 'msg lft'. The fourth had, 'not there (lied)' next to it. The fifth was a time on the day after she died with no annotation.

"Looks like she made several attempts to speak to him," said Pauline.

"Hmm," said Michael. He went back to the folder and opened an image file which was titled 'MP interests'. It was a screenshot from a webpage.

"I looked at that," said Pauline. "I thought it was going to say he was interested in golf and action movies, like the personal interests from a dating site, but it's a list of companies."

The screenshot was from the parliamentary website under Peter Wauluds's name. "MPs have to declare their financial interests to Parliament," Michael told her. "It's so they don't make policy about transport when their wife runs a train company, that sort of thing."

One of the company names, to whom Wauluds was said to be an 'advisor', seemed familiar.

"Look up Agroph Chemicals," he said.

"What is it?" said Pauline.

"Just look it up."

She gave him a sideways glance, but did as she asked.

The internet revealed the answer almost immediately. Agroph Chemicals had bought up a lot of the assets of Ransom Incorporated when the company was broken up after the vitamin scandal.

"That means nothing," said Pauline. "Your father destroyed all the equipment and the research that created the vitamin pills before he went to jail, didn't he?"

"As far as we know."

"Then the fact that a man who used to work in the pharmacy industry is still acting as an advisor doesn't mean anything."

"Not until it's found on a flash drive that used to belong to a journalist investigating perceivers. And especially not if she was killed because she was getting too close to something."

"What do we do now?" said Pauline.

"Find out more about Peter Wauluds."

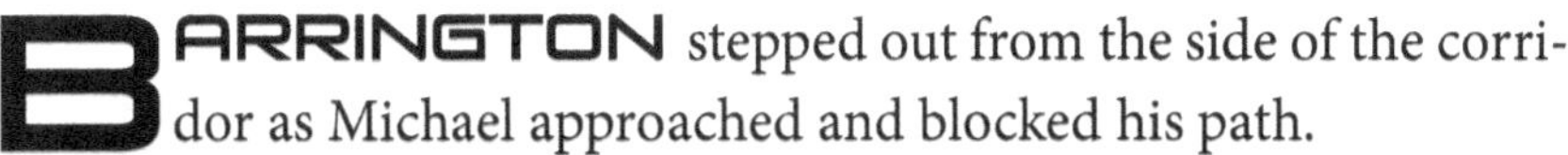**B**ARRINGTON stepped out from the side of the corridor as Michael approached and blocked his path.

"What's going on?" said Michael.

"This way," said Barrington.

He led Michael through a door into the nearest office. Michael hadn't been in there before. It was one of the nicer offices in the House, with a window that looked out onto Parliament Square, similar to the office that Pauline had worked in, but with only one desk in it. Behind the desk sat a woman with short grey hair and glasses who looked up from the phone call she was embroiled in and gave Barrington a smile as she kept talking.

"… I'll be sure to pass that on," she was saying. "Well, of course the Minister will be delighted, but I'm afraid his diary is rather full at the moment …"

Barrington stood inside the door and stared at the woman. Michael waited beside him, perceiving that he wanted to talk to him alone.

"Hold on a second," said the woman, putting her hand over the mouthpiece of the phone. "I'm sorry, Mr Barrington, do you want something?"

"Can I borrow your office, Maureen?"

She continued her puzzled stare while she spoke again into the phone. "Why don't I check with the Minister and give you a call back? … Yes, yes, I have your number … by the end of the day, absolutely. Yes, thank you. Bye."

She hung up the receiver.

"Thank you, Maureen," said Barrington.

She headed for the door. "I'm going to get myself a cup of tea," she told Barrington as she passed him. "Don't touch anything on my desk while I'm gone. I'll know if you do."

She left Barrington and Michael alone in the room. Barrington closed the door after her.

Michael perceived the words Barrington was practising in his head and realised he was about to be fired.

Barrington walked further into the room, but he did not sit. He took a moment to look out of the window at the view before turning and addressing Michael. "I'm going to have to ask you to hand in your security pass and leave," he said.

Michael was expecting it, but it still came as a blow. "Why?"

"Certain members of the press have seen you with the Prime Minister and questions have started to be asked. The cover story that you are some kind of intern isn't going to stand up to much scrutiny and, with the perceiver crisis how it is, I have concluded it best for you to leave."

"Does Pankhurst know about this?"

"I've discussed it with him."

"But, with the perceiver crisis getting worse, that's exactly the time I should be here. I'm supposed to be on the working group finding a solution."

"There is no working group anymore," said Barrington. "I believe the Prime Minister is looking at a solution of his own."

Michael said nothing. He concentrated on Barrington's mind to find out what he knew and found the answer. "Pankhurst is seriously considering a programme to cure everyone?"

"All I know is that, with the murder of that journalist, the perceiver issue has risen to the top of Mr Pankhurst's agenda. Having someone like you around will attract the wrong kind of attention. Especially, as I learn from my colleagues in the police force, that you are a suspect in the journalist case."

"I'm a witness!" insisted Michael.

"Do you think the press on a witch-hunt is going to make that distinction?" Barrington held out his hand. "Your security pass, please."

Michael pulled the pass off from around his neck and slammed it into Barrington's palm. "I actually came in today hoping to speak to you because I have information about a security threat," he said.

Barrington wrapped the cord of Michael's security pass around his picture ID and secreted it in his pocket. "What information?"

"If I tell you, will you promise to look into it and tell me what you find out?"

"No," said Barrington.

"Fine," said Michael. "You've asked me to leave, I'll leave." He reached out for the door handle and had opened it a crack before Barrington managed to sprint across the room and close it again.

"I don't make promises," said Barrington.

Michael figured he had nothing to lose, and if he did Barrington a favour, maybe the man would be willing to offer him the same courtesy later down the line. "You need to look more closely at Peter Wauluds," he said. "Sian Jones was about to break a big story about perceivers. He was avoiding her calls and she was going to make one last attempt to speak to him, until someone had her killed."

Michael reached for the door again and Barrington let him go. But all the way to the exit, as Barrington escorted him to make sure he actually left the building, Michael was perceiving the security chief and knew that he was going to do what he asked and use his resources to investigate Peter Wauluds.

TWENTY-ONE

MICHAEL had made a promise to Patterson that he would go down to the police station and make a formal statement about Sian Jones. Pauline had already done her duty, but it was something Michael had been putting off until Patterson left a message on his phone to say that if he didn't get his arse down to the police station before the day was out, he would send someone round to arrest him.

So Michael made a statement. It wasn't to Patterson himself, but to some of his colleagues who plied him with predictable questions and wrote down the occasional note on their pads of paper. He suspected he learnt more from the police officers than they learnt from him, as he was perceiving them all the while.

They didn't think he did it, which was the main thing. His fingerprints weren't anywhere at the crime scene and the witness who had seen him there, Andy Mostello, confirmed that he had only seen him outside of Sian's flat. All this was confirmed by another witness and CCTV which showed Michael and Pauline following Andy from the tube station.

The officers talked to him for less than half an hour, gave him a cup of disgusting police tea, and thanked him for his time.

Michael had intended to go straight back to his flat, but as he walked out into the reception area of the police station, he sensed another perceiver.

Looking up, he saw a face he had seen only a few days before on the television. The face that had caused him to utter, "oh my God". Flanked by two plain clothes police officers was Otis, with his dull blonde hair ruffled from the wind outside and his muscular frame more obvious in the casual jacket and jeans that he wore.

Otis? asked Michael's mind.

Otis looked at Michael with blue, confused eyes. He perceived him and Michael let him. *Michael?*

The two police officers led Otis through the security door that led into the main part of the building.

What are you doing here? asked Michael.

Same as you, probably.

The door was closed behind Otis and halted their conversation.

Suddenly, Michael didn't want to go home. He wanted to talk to his friend.

Texting Pauline to say that he wasn't going to be back at the flat anytime soon, he ventured outside to find a cup of tea that hadn't been processed by some disgusting police tea machine. After passing by two coffee shops which were closed because it was after office hours, he ended up with a packet of crisps and a screw top bottle of Coke from a convenience store.

The police station was quiet when he returned. Apart from the desk sergeant and a nervous woman sitting in the corner playing with the tassels on the end of her scarf, he was the only other person in there.

"Excuse me," said Michael to the woman in uniform behind the desk. "My friend came in about ten minutes ago. Youngish, blonde, muscular guy. I'm just checking he hasn't left yet."

"Not out this way," she said.

"Good," said Michael. "I'll wait."

"He could be in there for hours," she said.

"I'll wait."

Michael sat on one of the hard plastic seats in the public area and leant back against the wall behind. Above the main desk, a television screen played a series of silent adverts on a loop that warned people to beware of pickpockets and not to leave valuables out on display in their cars. He pulled out his phone and opened up a game he hadn't played for ages.

After a while, the nervous woman got out of her seat. Michael felt an unstoppable wave of relief from her as a young man emerged from the other side of the security door. He was tall and lanky and barely old enough to be an adult, legally speaking. He muttered something about being released on police bail and she hugged him, much to his discomfort. Then they left, taking their confused emotions of relief, anxiety and love with them.

Fifteen minutes later, the battery on Michael's phone died and he went back to staring at the screen with its helpful hints on how to avoid getting his pocket picked.

He was beginning to wonder if the desk sergeant had been right about Otis being in the police station for several hours. Michael had assumed Otis was there, like he had been, to give a statement in less than half an hour. But if Otis had been arrested, then the police had twenty-four hours to question him before he had to be charged or released. Michael was happy to wait, but not that long.

At last, about an hour and a half after Otis had passed Michael in the reception area, he emerged again. One of the plain clothes policemen said goodbye to him at the security door and left him to it.

Michael stood up. "Hello, Otis."

Otis looked his way. Instinctively, he increased his filters in the presence of another perceiver, but not enough to block out that he was unfazed by his encounter with the police, if a little tired. "No one's called me Otis for a long time," he said.

"What do I call you?" said Michael. "Oliver?"

"Sounds odd when you say it. I like Otis fine."

"Why are you here?"

"The Sian Jones case. You?"

"Same."

"They think a perceiver did it," said Otis. "They thought I might know who. I told them perceivers don't go around shooting people. They didn't believe me, but they know I wasn't the one who did it, so they couldn't keep me."

"I saw you on the TV the other day, Otis."

"With that bloody Angelheart woman!" *If I was going to commit murder, she'd be the first in line.*

Michael laughed.

The desk sergeant looked up at them. It was like she was mentally projecting her disapproval in their direction.

"Come on, let's go," said Otis. "I need to get home and my wife'll kill me if I miss the night bus."

They stepped out into the cold. The temperature had dropped several degrees since Michael had gone into the police station and he wasn't dressed for it. Above him, despite the light pollution of the London sky, a few stars could be seen twinkling in clear patches between the clouds and it felt like it wouldn't be long before frost started to form.

"You're married?" said Michael as Otis walked to the bus stop.

"Not really," said Otis. "Strictly speaking she's my partner, but I call her my wife because we had a baby together. It was a bit of a surprise, to be honest, but now Matilda's here, I wouldn't have it any other way. So we're saving up to get married. Trying to. Nappies are expensive."

As he thought of his family, Michael perceived he was happy. It wasn't something he had ever expected from Otis, but then a person could change a lot in five years. When Michael thought back to everything that had happened to him since he and Otis had last seen each other, he realised how much.

"Your baby will grow up to be perceiver, then," said Michael.

"I expect she will."

"Congratulations."

"Thanks. Talking of which, I better let my wife know I'm on my way." Otis pulled his mobile phone from his pocket and turned it on.

The tiny machine responded with a series of pings and alerts that came so rapidly one after another it was like it was playing a little tune. An ominous tune.

Otis touched the screen on his phone and Michael perceived his dread. "This has to be some kind of hoax," said Otis. "We've been down this path. We fixed this five years ago."

"Fixed what?"

Otis touched the screen again and the familiar sound of Pankhurst's voice emerged. He held it out so Michael could see the video playing on it.

"… The experiment has failed," Pankhurst said from a podium placed outside of Ten Downing Street. "We were willing to allow perceivers to live among us. We even experimented with allowing perceivers to act as useful members of society by looking into the minds of criminals. But, still, they did not respect the privacy of honest, hard-working people. It has been made clear to me, in recent days, that we cannot allow this perversion to continue to exist on our streets. Therefore, regrettably, I shall be ordering the full-scale curing of all perceivers from midnight tonight."

Michael felt sick. He felt betrayed. The man who had made him give up the chance of a normal life at university to bring him to London had turned his back on him. He had turned his back on all people like him.

Otis was right, it was déjà vu.

Pankhurst had thought curing perceivers was the answer before. Michael had persuaded him otherwise. It had taken a riot, five dead people and a deftly worded argument to bring about the introduction of a law to allow norms and perceivers to live alongside each other.

Suddenly, in one speech, Pankhurst had thrown it all away.

Otis was just as horrified. He barely had the strength to hold the phone up. He stopped the video and the Prime Minister's words were cut dead. He ran out in the road, waving his arms like a madman.

"Taxi!" shouted Otis.

A black cab screeched to a halt and barely managed to avoid running Otis over.

Michael perceived his panic, but he didn't understand it. "What are you doing?"

"I can't afford to wait for a bus," said Otis. He rushed up to the driver's open window. "Can you take me to Stepney, mate?"

The taxi driver indicated that was okay and Otis went to get in. Michael was already standing by the back door. "Was is it, Otis? Can I help?"

"The police know I have a list of perceivers," said Otis. "After Jennifer was cured, teenagers kept contacting her wanting to know if they should take the cure too or live under Perceivers' Law. She didn't want anything to do with all that stuff anymore and I sort of took over running the network. All the data is secure, but… I've got to get home and warn everyone and then … I don't know … destroy all the data? Start a new protest movement? I should have seen this coming. When the journalist died and people blamed perceivers … I should have seen this coming."

Michael stepped out of the way and allowed Otis to climb into the back of the taxi. "Bye, Michael. It was good to bump into you again. A shame it wasn't under better circumstances."

Otis closed the door and the taxi drove off, leaving Michael standing on the pavement and wondering what the hell he was going to do.

TWENTY-TWO

PAULINE opened the cupboard nearest the fridge in Michael's flat to find two shelves containing only a half-used packet of pasta and an unopened packet of rice. She slammed the door shut again and opened the cupboard next to it.

Michael watched from just outside the kitchenette. He had intended to go in and unload the dishwasher, but Pauline had been rushing from one end to the other for the past five minutes and he decided he was better off keeping out of the way.

The second cupboard contained coffee mugs and china bowls.

"What are we going to do?" she said.

"I don't know, Pauline." He was tired. It was late when he got back, then he spent another night hardly sleeping.

"Doesn't he know that you can't just go around curing perceivers with an injection? That injection thing is a myth, a lie to keep parents happy. They'll need other perceivers to go into our heads and cut off our power. How the hell does he think he's going to get enough perceivers to do that to all of us in the country?" She opened a third cupboard and found where he kept the teabags and the coffee. "Christ, do you not have any breakfast stuff in this flat?!"

Michael stepped forward and went to the cupboard under the counter where he kept an emergency box of cornflakes. He'd had to put it there because the box was too tall for the other cupboards. He handed it to Pauline. "Pankhurst knows all that. I can only assume the report drawn up by the woman from the cure programme addressed all those things."

"I suppose they've got all the records from the schools where they screened everyone. Even the ones they cured will be on record and the register of births will say if they've had children or not."

"It doesn't matter how they're going to do it, Pauline, the fact is they've announced that they are. We're officially public enemy number one."

Pauline went back to the cupboard with the china bowls and pulled one off the top of the stack. "You need to speak to Pankhurst," she said, shaking the box of cornflakes harshly like it was the box's fault. The bowl was more than half full by the time she stopped.

"That's going to be difficult since he sacked me and had my security pass taken away."

She went to the fridge, opened the door and stared at the inside. "Michael, have you got no milk?"

He sighed. It was one of the things he had meant to do on the way back from the police station. "Sorry, I forgot to get some."

"For Christ's sake!" She slammed the fridge door shut so hard that the whole thing rocked on its base. "Can you not manage to do the simplest thing?"

Pauline spun round with her arms out in front of her. They collided with the bowl and it leapt into the air, sending cornflakes flying everywhere. The bowl hit the hard kitchen floor with the sound of smashing china. Shards shot out in all directions as cornflakes rained down on them like confetti.

She cried out with rage.

Michael felt it too. The helplessness, the anger, and the fear over what was going to happen next. When he perceived the same things from her, it only made his emotions more intense. He took a step towards her, to comfort her. "Pauline, I…"

She walked straight past him, pushing him out of the way as she did so.

He watched as she sat on the sofa and reached for the TV remote.

"Don't watch that, it'll only make you angry," said Michael.

"If they're going to come for me in the middle of the night, I want to know about it," she said.

With the mood she was in, there would be no consoling her. Not that he had anything to say. He could tell her that everything was going to be all right, but that would be a fairy story.

Michael found his wallet from the trousers he was wearing the day before and headed for the door. "I'm going out," he told her.

She didn't reply. She just continued to sit in front of the television, watching the news and torturing herself.

Out on the street, the cold of the day soothed Michael's hot cheeks. Drizzle fell on his head and on his arms and cooled him still further.

He went to the shop at the end of the road and picked up a bottle of milk. He got bread and butter in case Pauline fancied toast, some cheese which would work for a sandwich later in the day and a packet of chocolate biscuits because he fancied them.

When he got back to the flat, the television was playing to itself and there was no sign of Pauline. He was about to open his perception to find her when he heard the shower running. He turned off the TV and crunched over the fallen cornflakes to put the provisions away.

After picking up the pieces of broken china, while Pauline was still in the bathroom, he got out the vacuum cleaner.

Only half the floor was cornflake free by the time Pauline came out of the bathroom. She had her body wrapped in a towel with her wet hair dripping down her back. "Didn't you hear the door?" she yelled over the sound of the vacuum.

"The what?" Michael stamped on the 'off' button on the base of the machine and the motor wound down to reveal the sound of insistent knocking.

"It really is Katya this time," said Pauline.

She opened the door to see that her perception had been right. Standing in the corridor, with a belly so large it looked like she might topple over, was Katya.

Katya's face broke into a smile and she came in to give Pauline a big hug. "Pauline, I'm so sorry I was so long."

But Pauline's need for it to be Katya at the door had fooled her perception and, as the pair stepped back from their embrace, she became aware that Agent Cooper had followed Katya through the door.

Michael watched it all from the centre of the living area where he had stopped vacuuming. It wasn't the fact that Agent Cooper was at his flat that interested him, it was the feelings he perceived coming off him. He was defeated, frustrated and even a little scared.

"Agent Cooper!" said Pauline. She pulled the towel tighter across her breasts.

He nodded. "You're both here. That's good."

"I'm going to go put some clothes on," said Pauline and scampered off towards the bedroom.

"I need to go too," said Katya in her heavily accented English. "Baby make me go pee all the time."

It left Michael and Agent Cooper facing each other.

It reminded Michael of how they had faced each other on the stairs of the fire escape at his father's office some five years before. Michael was a scared kid then, with no memories of who he was or what he was doing there. But he still had had an instinct not to trust

Cooper. It was an instinct that had never gone away, even when he had worked for him. Back then, Michael had been armed with a knife. Five years later, he stood holding the handle of a vacuum cleaner. On the face of it, Michael had lost ground. But, in the intervening years, what Michael had learnt had given him more ammunition than a weapon ever could. He could perceive that Cooper thought he was there to help Michael, Pauline and Katya. But the truth was, he was there to help himself. He was always acting to help himself.

"I had some intelligence operatives interview Katya," said Cooper.

"And?" said Michael.

"She's a scared young woman who thought she was having a baby for a childless couple, but found out she was really part of a military experiment."

"So not a spy, then."

"She was able to give us some more information which ties in with what we've been able to glean from our operatives in Russia. It seems, to all intents and purposes, that the Russian perceiver programme has collapsed. All that is left is some perceiver serum that someone in the Russian military got their hands on and has been using in a reckless attempt to gather information to impress their superiors. There have been a few incidents, nothing quite as newsworthy as a soldier blowing his brains out all over the President of the United States, but incidents nevertheless."

"That's good," said Michael. "It means the Russian perceiver programme is no longer a threat."

"It means Pankhurst can go ahead and destroy all the perceivers in Britain in the false belief that they are not needed to protect the country against the Russians — or any other foreign power — using perceiver spies. Just because the bear has gone back to his cave to sleep, it doesn't mean that he won't wake up again in the morning, even more hungry than before."

Pauline emerged from the bedroom in the jeans and T-shirt that Michael had bought her. Her hair was still damp, but no longer dripping.

"Agent Cooper, we weren't expecting you," she said.

"I had an urgent meeting with the Prime Minister," said Cooper. "He called me in after last night's announcement."

The frustration that he had brought into the room with him became louder in his mind.

"What did he say?" said Pauline.

"He's ordered the break up of the Perceiver Corps," said Cooper. "He said that all members are to be cured in order to prove to the public that he's serious about tackling the problem."

"Cured?" said Pauline. Of all three people in that room, she was the one who was the most shocked. Cooper had clearly been processing the information on the way over and Michael had half expected it.

The sound of the toilet flushing broke through their conversation and Katya emerged from the bathroom. She leant back against the doorframe. "What's going on? You all look like someone's died."

"It's nothing for you to be worried about, Katya," said Pauline.

"I think you lie." Katya rested her hand on her pregnancy like she was protecting the baby inside. "My son helps me know things. He helps me know that you are all worried, which makes me worried."

Cooper bowed his head, not making eye contact with any of them. Michael could perceive his regret as he spoke. "I'll try to protect as many of you as I can, but that's going to be a handful at best.

"But that's…" stuttered Pauline. "That's… ridiculous! We work for the government. We've done everything you've asked. We've done more than you asked."

She was thinking about Alex again and of the moment that he drew his last breath. Michael struggled to push the image out of his mind.

"I told Pankhurst I have spent my life building up the Perceivers Corps. I told him the Ministry of Defence has spent millions training an elite force. I reminded him that there were natural borns before the vitamin scandal, I told him that if natural borns exist in Britain then chances are they exist in other countries. He heard none of it. All he's thinking about now is the next election and his political legacy. He doesn't want to go down as the prime minister who allowed perceivers to walk free to read the minds of innocent members of the public. He wants to be remembered as the prime minister who saw the error of his ways and worked to eradicate perceivers once and for all."

"What do we do?" said Pauline.

"Run," said Cooper.

"That's it?" said Michael. "That's your plan?"

Cooper turned to him. "I'm sorry, Michael, but Pankhurst wants you to be the first. I think Barrington told you that the press were asking questions about you, it was only a matter of time before they found out what you are. It also seems they have found out *who* you are. By which I mean, who your father is. If the story hasn't broken already, then it will soon. Pankhurst thinks that curing Brian Ransom's son will be the best publicity stunt to launch his campaign to cure all perceivers."

Michael felt a moment of their pity before he locked out all other feelings but his own. Feelings that were making his hands shake. It wasn't so much the fear of not having his powers. He had lost his ability to perceive before and it wasn't so bad. But being rounded up like a criminal and having them stripped from him like he was the subject of a public execution … No, he couldn't bear that.

Then what would happen to him? Would they throw stones until they beat him to death?

Or would they not need to?

His father had tried to cure him before. Back when he was a teenager. Ironically, to keep him safe from Cooper. It had worked in that it had taken his powers away, but Michael was so strong that it had destroyed all his memories in the process. The cure was the reason he didn't remember anything about his childhood. Where other people had memories of a loving mother and playing football with the rest of the boys in the school playground, he had a blank space. He even envied the people who had had a horrible childhood, who were bullied at school, or made to sit in their room instead of going out to play at home. At least they understood where they came from. He didn't understand any of it. He never would. His past would always be nothing.

He couldn't let someone touch his brain again.

"I'll die first," said Michael.

"I came straight here after the meeting," said Cooper. "I don't know when or if they're going to come for you, but obviously they know where you live, so you might not have much time."

"What about me?" said Katya. "You said staying with Pauline was fine. That I would be safe. You said I could have my baby in a London hospital."

"Sorry, Katya," said Cooper. "That was before I met with Pankhurst. You should be safe, there's no paperwork linking you to the perceivers. Officially, you're here on a visitor's visa. I could take you back with me, but honestly I think you'll be better out here."

"You'll be fine with us, Katya," said Pauline.

"You hope," said Michael. He threw the handle of the vacuum cleaner aside and it struck the wall with such force that a little bit of plaster fell onto the carpet. The least of his worries.

He headed for the bedroom.

"What are you doing?" said Pauline.

"Grabbing a couple of things and heading the hell out," said Michael.

"Michael, wait!" said Cooper. "While I was at the House of Commons, Barrington gave me something for you."

Cooper held out a piece of folded notepaper. Michael took it and opened it up. It was the name and address of a company called Clairone Labs in a place called Erith.

"What's that supposed to mean?" said Michael.

"Barrington said you would know."

TWENTY-THREE

MARY Ransom walked through her new and spotless open front door onto her gravel drive and put her arms around her son. "Michael, thank God you're all right."

Michael allowed his mother to hug him. He loved the way she treasured squeezing him so tight that he could barely breathe. Even though he could not love her back in the same way, perceiving it from her was comforting. In such a hostile world, comfort was something to be savoured.

She stepped back from him and only then, it seemed, did she notice Pauline and Katya beside him.

"You must come in," she said.

Mary led them through into her home which still had the faint smell of fresh paint about it. The inside was so spotlessly clean, that it was difficult to believe it was the same house as the one which had been soiled by vandals.

In fact, to Mary, it wasn't the same house. As she walked them through the hallway and up the stairs, Michael perceived that it no longer felt like home to her. The rooms and the walls and the furniture inside of it were still the same, but the perceiver-hating vandals had taken away the sense of safety that they used to bring. Whereas millions of other people up and down the country were able to go inside their house at night, lock the door and relax, Mary Ransom would always feel a little bit on edge in her own home.

"I thought I'd show you to your rooms first, then you can come downstairs when you're ready," said Mary.

She showed Katya to a room at the top of the stairs with a single bed in it. "If there's anything you need, you let me know," Mary told her. "Even if it's a bit crazy. I remember when I was pregnant with Michael, I couldn't get enough of chocolate spread and banana sandwiches."

"Thank you," said Katya. She then asked for directions for the bathroom and rushed in there blaming the baby for sitting on top of her bladder again.

"I've put you two in the guest room," said Mary.

Michael had stayed in the guest room before, but it was only when he stepped inside it and saw the double bed laid out with two sets of guest towels on it did he realise what she was saying.

Pauline realised it too. "Oh no, Mrs Ransom, we're—"

"There's no need to explain, Pauline dear," she said. "I was young once, you know. I'm going downstairs to put the kettle on."

Michael waited until he perceived his mother was out of earshot. "I'll sleep on the floor," he said.

Pauline giggled.

"What?" said Michael. Even perceiving her, he couldn't work out what was funny.

She pushed the door closed and laughed even louder.

"What?" he said.

"Perceivers are about to be persecuted up and down the country and we're worried about our sleeping arrangements." She sat down on the bed so hard that it bounced several times before it settled.

Michael sat down more gently beside her. "It's not that I don't want to sleep with you," he said. He was close to her, he could smell the shampoo she had used to wash her hair that morning. Even though it was his shampoo from his bathroom, it smelled nicer when the fragrance came from her hair.

"Is that a double negative?" she said. "Does that mean you *do* want to sleep with me?"

"You can perceive that I do," said Michael. "Although, I'm not sure I'm comfortable doing it in my mother's house."

Pauline laughed again. "After the shit we've been through today, I think sleeping is about all I'm going to be good for."

Michael stood again. "Come on, let's go down and allow my mother to treat us to some hospitality."

"In a minute," she said. "I want to know what Cooper gave you at the flat."

"It's an address."

"An address for what?"

Michael pulled the piece of notepaper from his pocket and handed it to her.

It read:

Clairone Labs

Gatehouse Industrial Estate

Erith

It was signed, *Barrington.*

"What's Clairone Labs?" she said.

"I looked it up on the train," said Michael. "Clairone is a subsidiary of Agroph Chemicals. It researches new medical drugs, that sort of thing. I can only assume it has something to do with Peter Wauluds."

"What are we supposed to do about it?"

"I don't know yet," said Michael. "The one thing I *do* know is that I'm not going to sit around in my mother's house waiting for someone to find and cure me."

TEN minutes later, Michael was sitting in the lounge of his mother's house staring at the back wall. He remembered when it was decorated with cream wallpaper with illustrations of delicate blue flowers on it. Until it was desecrated by the vandals. Since then, all the subtlety had been stripped away to be replaced by a bold floral pattern with large and striking purple petals. It was a statement that she had reclaimed the wall for herself, but it did not eclipse the memory of what had been written there in red and green paint. The words 'Perceiver Scum' haunted the room like a ghost that wouldn't be exorcised.

Michael took his gaze off the wall and pulled his mobile phone from his pocket. He typed Clairone Labs into the search box.

Mary came in with a tray containing four mugs of tea. She offered one to Katya first, who had an armchair all to herself, before she came over to the sofa where Pauline sat next to Michael.

"Thanks, Mrs Ransom," said Pauline as she took a mug for herself and one for Michael. She passed it over.

This is so ridiculous, thought Michael as he took the mug from her. *This morning we were running out of my flat with barely enough time to pack a bag and now we're all sitting around drinking tea.*

Until we come up with a plan, we can spend five minutes drinking tea, thought Pauline. *It makes your mother happy.*

Mary took the last remaining mug to the other armchair and sat herself down. "When are you due, Katya?"

"Two weeks," said Katya. "The doctors think."

Mary smiled. She nodded. She sipped from her tea. "I bet you can't wait."

"Not really," said Katya. "Like your son, my son is a perceiver baby. I don't know what's going to happen to him after he is born."

Perhaps it was her Russian accent, or the fact that she was speaking in her second language, or perhaps it was just her plain honesty, but it brought the pleasant afternoon chit-chat to a halt.

Mary changed the subject. "How about some cake? I have some in the kitchen. Katya? Pauline? Michael?"

"What?" Michael looked up from the internet.

"Is there something important on your phone, Michael?" asked Mary.

"Not really," he said. "Unfortunately." He closed down the internet and put his phone in his pocket.

"Nothing on Clairone Labs?" asked Pauline.

"The company doesn't even have a website," said Michael. "There's an entry at Companies House, but all that gives me is a list of directors' names I've never heard of and public accounts going back ten years or more. Pages and pages of them."

"Clairone Labs?" said Mary. "The medical research business?"

Michael sat up. "You've heard of it?"

"When your father …" she trailed off, not able to bring herself to say the words *went to jail*, even though she thought them. "When your father's business had to sell up, some of it went to Clairone. I only know because he made sure I had some investments to give me an income and the Clairone shares turned out to be next to useless. As far as my accountant could see, they never made any money."

"You're a shareholder?" said Michael.

"Not anymore," said Mary. "My account suggested I sell them. He thought the company was some sort of tax write-off. They funnelled all their loss-making research through there. Why? Is it important?"

"Probably not," said Michael.

Pauline sat forward. "Do you think they could have been carrying out some sort of research linked to perceivers?" she said.

"Any lab could be, in theory," said Mary. "But if you're asking if any of the perceiver work my husband did at Ransom Incorporated was transferred to this company, then absolutely not. He destroyed it all. He was ashamed of what he had done."

"Is there any way of finding out?" said Pauline.

"In my experience, sometimes the best way of finding out something is to ask," said Mary. "If they say 'no' and they're lying, you could perceive them and know that the answer is really 'yes.'"

Michael took a mouthful of his tea. "Do you know what this tea needs?" he said. "A nice piece of cake to go with it."

Mary laughed. "Michael, I'm forty-nine, I'm not senile. You could just say, 'Mum, would you mind leaving the room so we can discuss something in private?'" She put her tea down and got up from her chair. "I'll get everyone a nice piece of cake. I hope lemon drizzle is all right for you all."

Pauline waited until Mary had closed the door to the lounge behind her. "You're not seriously thinking of going and asking them?"

"No," said Michael. "I'm already assuming that Clairone has something to do with perceiver research, otherwise why did Barrington give me the address? Getting a yes or no answer out of them won't help. We need to get in there and do some proper snooping around."

"You think it will save you from this cure you are so scared of?" said Katya.

"Who says I'm scared?" said Michael.

"My son," she said.

Michael shivered. Being perceived by other people his own age was something he was used to. Being perceived by an unborn child through his mother was something that was too weird.

"To be honest, Katya," said Michael. "Even if we find what we're looking for, I don't know if it'll save me. But it's the only information we have, so I need to follow it."

TWENTY-FOUR

MICHAEL paced up and down Mary's hallway, listening to the ringing tone on his phone. It rang longer than he hoped, longer than it should if someone was going to answer.

At the point where he was about to give up, the ringing stopped. Inspector Patterson answered in an urgent whisper. "Michael, what the hell are you doing?"

Michael stopped walking. He put his hand out for the railing of the stairs and hung on to it. "Inspector Patterson, what's the matter?"

"People are looking for you."

"That's why I left London."

"You should come back, Michael, face up to it."

"I can't," said Michael.

"You're lucky they haven't put out a warrant for your arrest."

"I haven't broken any laws."

"Which is why they haven't," said Patterson. "Yet."

Michael closed his eyes and rested his head against the railing. It was all moving too fast. "How long have I got?"

"A couple of days, maybe," said Patterson. "Everyone's running around like headless chickens here. Officially, it's not a police matter, but if there's going to be violence, the police will have to step in. There's a lot of discussion … well, I can't talk about it, especially not to you. But put it this way, I'm the one who they see as a perceiver cop, so I've been called into a lot of meetings."

"So now would be the wrong time to ask for a favour?"

"I can't help you, Michael. I'm sorry. Apart from anything else, they'll be watching me, they know I'm your friend."

"It's just a little favour. I need a phone number."

Patterson said nothing. All Michael could hear was his breathing. "Inspector Patterson?" Michael waited for an answer. "Tony?"

"What phone number?" said Patterson, eventually.

"It's for one of the people you interviewed over the Sian Jones murder. His name is Oliver Smith."

OTIS raised his perceiver blocks as he walked into Mary's lounge. Perhaps it was instinct for him when meeting another perceiver, but Michael suspected he was more trying to mask his tired and worried thoughts.

Michael and Pauline stood up from the sofa. "Thanks for coming, Otis," said Michael.

"No worries," said Otis. He forced a smile across his worried face. "You must be Pauline. Michael tells me you were with the Perceiver Corps, I didn't realise there were so many of you about."

"Michael tells me you're a natural born," she said. "I didn't realise there were so many of *you*."

This time, Otis's smile was genuine. As he relaxed, he allowed his blocks to weaken and the three of them shared their nervous, but determined emotions.

"Did you speak to your father?" said Michael, sitting back down again.

"Yeah," said Otis, sitting in the nearest armchair. "He remembered you. He said you were that 'nice boy' who came to pick up the chemical analysis report with me."

It was what had made Michael think of Otis. Otis's father worked for a company called Randall Miller and Parnell Research Labs and had analysed the contents of the injection they gave to perceivers before they cured them. It was Doctor Smith who discovered the injection was only a sedative used to make perceivers compliant to the cure procedure and not the cure itself, as the public had been led to believe.

"Does he know anything about Clairone Labs?" said Michael.

"Not much more than you already found out," said Otis. "He thinks they're involved in military research, which is why everything is so secretive."

"A biochemical company involved in military research?" said Michael. "Like chemical warfare?"

"It could be. Or they could be researching a new anti-malaria drug for troops sent to the jungle, as far as my father knows."

"But will he help us?" said Pauline.

"He made some calls and managed to get an appointment to look round. He put out a research paper last year which was well received in the scientific community. He got a lot of head-hunting calls from people inviting him to job interviews after that. I thought he was bragging, but apparently, it's not far from the truth otherwise he would have been given a flat 'no.'"

"That gets your father inside," said Pauline. "What about us?"

"We're going to have to play it by ear," said Otis. "He thinks he can sneak off at some point, on the excuse of going to the loo or something, and open a fire door. Unless they're really serious about security and escort him to the toilet. Which, he says, could happen."

"Thanks, Otis," said Michael.

"Thank my dad. I didn't think he would do it until I perceived him with my daughter. He knows perception is hereditary and he fears his grandchild has it. After what Pankhurst said, he's worried about what's going to happen to her. He's not the only one."

Because Otis had weakened his blocks and because Michael and Pauline were strong, they both perceived how scared he was for the little girl called Matilda. Before he wrapped up his emotions again and hid them behind his blocks.

"When's this appointment?" asked Pauline.

"Eleven o'clock tomorrow," said Otis. "We'll need to leave no later than nine."

"We'll be ready," said Michael.

MICHAEL slept with Pauline that night. Not in the way that people usually meant when they talked about sleeping with someone. In the way that involved two people lying in one bed together and trying to sleep.

His body wanted sex. The hormones inside of him were insistent and they made him respond when Pauline slipped in between the sheets next to him. He hid it from her, but hiding his body was easier than hiding his mind. He could put up his blocks, but every time he dozed off, they weakened and he knew she was able to perceive his feelings.

Feelings of wanting to hold her, to feel the smoothness of her skin and the beating of her heart as he pulled her close. But sex was a distraction and so he kept his distance. They had a big day ahead and they needed sleep.

Not that they got much.

ONE of the advantages of asking Otis for help was that he could drive. He didn't actually own a car, as living in London meant it was easier for him to use public transport, but it meant he could borrow Mary's Vauxhall Astra and get them to Erith without crashing — which is what would have happened if Michael had had to drive.

Erith was the other side of London to Beaconsfield, which meant a journey around the M25. If Katya had been with them, she would have seen a little bit of the English countryside which she had been asking about, and one of the notorious traffic jams which Cooper had talked about.

Despite the traffic, and one stop for a "comfort break", as Otis called it, they made good time.

Gatehouse Industrial Estate was basically one purpose-built road which curled around itself with little spurs off to offices and warehouse-type buildings, each with their own car park out the front. Clairone Labs was one such building. There was no fancy glass-fronted reception, no big and bold sign across the front advertising its business. It was just a rectangular office block with a set of double doors at the entrance. There was also no security to stop them driving into the car park, although Michael did see several CCTV cameras positioned at strategic points around the building.

Otis parked and turned off the engine. He pulled out his mobile phone and sent a text. "My dad knows we're here," he said.

Otis asked Pauline, who was sitting on the backseat, to pass over a rucksack he had left in the footwell. Out of it he pulled three folded pieces of white cotton cloth and handed one each to Michael in the front passenger seat and Pauline behind him.

Pauline unfolded hers. "Lab coats?"

"Put them on when we get inside. It'll help us blend in."

"People really wear these? Not just on TV?"

Otis laughed. "Not just on TV. If you spill chemicals on your shirt, you need a new shirt. If you spill chemicals on your lab coat, it just looks lived in."

They sat in Mary's Vauxhall Astra for five minutes before another car drove in. "That's my dad," said Otis.

He parked up close to the building where there were a couple of visitors' spots and got out. The man in his fifties, who Michael recognised as Doctor Smith, looked very little like his son from a distance. It was probably because what little hair he had left had turned to grey. Doctor Smith acted as if he didn't know they were there and went into the building with not so much as a glance behind.

"What now?" said Pauline.

"We wait," said Otis.

It was a long wait. Twenty-five minutes before Otis got a text to say his father had accomplished his mission.

"Here we go," said Otis.

They got out of the car and went round to the back of the building. They found two fire exit doors. The second one was ajar.

"Lab coats," said Otis.

As Michael and Pauline put on their lab coats, Otis pulled a packet of cigarettes from his pocket, along with a lighter. He put a cigarette in his mouth and sucked air through it as he put the tiny flame to the end. The cigarette end glowed orange for a moment as Otis's face turned red and he subdued his coughing to blow out a plume of smoke.

"Otis, what are you doing?" said Michael.

"Plausible deniability," he said.

Pauline led the way in through the fire door and into a long corridor which looked like its only purpose was to lead to the fire exit. "Someone's coming," she whispered.

Michael perceived it too. A curious mind belonging to a woman who turned into the corridor on stealthy flat shoes. She was a short woman and physically not a threat, but being discovered was still going to be a problem.

Otis took another breath of smoke and threw the cigarette out of the fire door which he closed with a bang.

"What's going on?" said the woman, striding in their direction. "I had a note come up on my screen that the fire door was open."

"Yeah, sorry," said Otis. As he spoke, smoke came out of his mouth. "I was gasping for a cig."

She regarded him with a hard stare. Michael perceived her as she evaluated what he said. Bad luck for them, she was the receptionist and knew that she hadn't signed in three visitors that morning. "Who are you?"

Mind control, Pauline suddenly thought.

Yeah, thought Michael.

Pauline walked up to the woman, stringing out her apology as she got closer. "Sorry, we're the research students working on the new project. Did nobody tell you we were starting today?"

Michael followed and, as Pauline kept the woman's attention focussed on her, Michael went hard into her mind. He pushed her doubt and her suspicion away to get to the centre of her thoughts.

She gasped.

Mind control was not pleasant if the subject resisted. It took a strong perceiver to do it and, unless there was time to be subtle, a norm would almost certainly feel it. Michael hated to manipulate people's minds like that, but he hated being caught even more and so he did what he had to. Fortunately, the woman was already running a routine in her mind where she left the reception desk to check on the fire door. She had formulated two possible outcomes: in the first one she found nothing of concern and went back to the reception desk; in the second, she found something not right and raised the alarm.

Michael held her thoughts in his mind and twisted them until the truth became a lie. She believed that she had seen no one at the fire door and her mind headed down the road of the first outcome.

Pauline took hold of the woman's arm and physically turned her around so she was facing away from them.

She staggered a little and put her hand out to the wall to steady herself. Then she walked back the way she had come. Michael perceived she was thinking that there must be some sort of the glitch on the system and would have to make a note to tell the manager.

What the hell was that? asked Otis's thoughts.

Mind control, thought Pauline.

Can you teach me to do that?

Absolutely not, she thought back.

As they walked along the corridor, Michael whispered to Otis, "Why didn't you warn us the fire door might be monitored?"

"They aren't always," said Otis. "And if they are, the smoking trick usually allows me to get away with it."

"Usually?" said Michael. "How many buildings have you broken into?"

Otis didn't say, but Michael perceived there had been a few.

They made it to the stairwell without encountering any more suspicious members of staff. In theory, the stairwell was a helpful place to be because there was a chart on the wall explaining what departments were on what floor. What was less helpful was that, other than the admin offices on the third floor and toilets and kitchen area on the ground, the departments were labelled Lab A, Lab B and Lab C.

"Any word from your dad?" asked Michael.

Otis checked his phone. "No, but then he only agreed to let us in, not to give us any information."

"We need to perceive someone," said Michael.

The sound of footsteps on the stairs above them made Michael look up. A man in scuffed shoes and wearing jeans under his lab coat was coming down.

Michael pushed Otis back into the shadows in the hope he could perceive him from there, but Pauline stepped forward.

Pauline, what are you doing?

She ignored him.

"Excuse me?" she said to the man as he reached the ground floor. "We're the research students."

To Michael's horror, she pointed behind her into the dark and blew any notion of them hiding from sight.

Michael looked into the man's mind and got ready to control him.

The person on the stairs, who turned out to be a bearded man in his thirties, nodded as if it was all perfectly normal. "We were wondering where we were supposed to be. I know that one of the labs is super secret and we're not supposed to go in there, but I don't know which one. I thought it was Lab D, but there isn't a Lab D. I must have mis-heard."

"Oh no, that's Lab B," said the man. "You really don't want to go in there. You're probably in Lab A because I'm in Lab C and we haven't got any research students."

"Thanks," said Pauline.

"You're welcome," said the man. As he walked past Michael and Otis, he gave them a smile and nod and continued on his way. To the kitchen, according to Michael's perception of him.

What was that? thought Otis.

It's called being polite and charming, Pauline thought back. *Sometimes the best way of finding out something is to ask.*

The chart on the wall said that Lab B was on the first floor, so they climbed up one set of stairs to the landing which had a choice of turning left through a set of double doors or right through a different set of double doors. Both of them led to Lab B, according to the sign.

Michael took an executive decision and turned left.

On the other side of the double doors was a corridor with windows which looked out onto the car park. It contained only one other door, presumably into the lab. It had no handle, just a square black box on the side with a little red light in the corner. It was similar to the devices on some of the doors in the House of Commons. It required an electronic key to open it, usually a security pass placed over the black box, which would respond by turning the red light green.

They didn't have a security pass.

"What now?" said Otis. "We can't ask it politely to let us in."

Michael told him to be quiet as he put his face to the door. He opened his perception wide and pushed it through the wood. For some reason, he imagined there would be lots of minds on the other side of the door. But he perceived almost nothing. Apart from the dull presence of one person. Far away so he could barely sense them.

Well? asked Pauline. *Do you want me to knock and ask to go in?*

Michael held up a finger as a gesture for her to wait. He locked onto the mind and tried to explore it. It was deep in concentration and he was able to pick up a few stray thoughts which didn't mean anything to him: *Growing medium … photosynthesis.*

The mind became clearer. At first Michael thought it was because he had a stronger grasp of it, then he realised it was because the mind was coming closer. He was going to withdraw, to warn the others that the person was coming to the door. He was going to tell them that they needed to decide whether they were going to force their way inside the lab, or force their way inside the man's mind to find out what he knew.

But the mind was familiar. Hauntingly so. A strong intellect and a methodical pattern to his thoughts that was keeping the turmoil of madness at bay.

Recognition turned Michael cold. He pulled out his perception and stepped back from the door.

"What?" said Pauline. She didn't perceive the man behind the door, she perceived Michael and then she knew what he knew. The coldness of recognition spread over her too.

An electronic bleep chirped from the black box as its red light turned green and the bolts that held the door closed clicked to the unlocked position.

The door opened.

A man in his fifties with dark-rimmed glasses and holding a security pass that was hung around his neck, stood in the doorway. His mouth fell open.

It was difficult to tell who was the most shocked: Michael and Pauline … or Doctor Lucas.

TWENTY-FIVE

"**YOU** fucking bastard!" screamed Pauline and charged at Doctor Lucas with her head down like an enraged bull.

She struck the scientist in the stomach and the pair of them went sprawling inside the lab. Lucas landed on his back with the ugly smack of his spine hitting the hard floor. His glasses went flying off his face and under one of the benches. He cried out in pain as Pauline fell on top of him and pinned him to the ground.

Michael and Otis rushed in afterwards.

Michael looked around. As his perception had forewarned him, Lucas was the only person in the lab. It was a large expanse of a room with as many windows as the corridor they had left, except that these looked out onto the other buildings on the industrial estate. The light from the winter sun shone onto what looked like window boxes on the inside of the windowsill, with strange red moss-like stuff growing in them. The rest of the lab was laid out with rows of benches, equipped with scientific instruments.

Pauline had Lucas on the floor between two of the benches and was relentlessly hitting him.

She threw a fist into his cheek. "You put a gun to my head!"

A second fist landed on his other cheekbone with a thud. "You killed Alex!"

He cried out in pain and tried to bat away her punches with flailing arms. Her fury broke through his defences and struck his chest, his nose and his ear. "You. Evil. Murderous. Bastard!"

Michael rushed over to her and tried to pull her off, but she shook him free. She landed another couple of punches before Otis was able to grab hold of her arm and, with Michael, drag her fighting body from the stunned, bruised and bleeding scientist.

He scrabbled back from her, his feet pushing against the floor as he slid backwards like an upturned crab.

Michael walked between the benches to catch up with him. Lucas staggered to his feet and backed away until he could go no further. His body hit one of the window boxes and he was stuck between Michael and the window.

Pauline pulled herself free from Otis and came running over. The pathetic, frightened figure of Doctor Lucas drew back from her, but he had nowhere left to go.

"What are you doing here?" she demanded. "You're supposed to be in Russia."

Otis came up behind them. "You know this person?" he said.

"He experimented on perceivers," said Pauline. "He captured me, and Alex died to get me out of there."

"So what's he doing in a research lab in Erith?" said Otis.

"That's an excellent question," said Michael.

The last time he had encountered Doctor Lucas, the scientist had injected himself with the perceiver serum and was able to block Michael's perception. This time, there was no barrier to Michael reading his mind. He stared at the man's bleeding face and saw beyond its physical exterior into his brain where terrified thoughts chased each other around like a mad dog chasing its tail.

"No, no, please don't perceive me!" he said. "I'll tell you. I'll tell you everything, but leave my mind alone."

Michael stopped. Lucas was telling the truth.

"What are you doing?" Pauline glared at Michael. "If you won't perceive him, I will."

She pushed Michael out of the way and Lucas's terror filled the room.

Michael put a restraining hand on Pauline's shoulder. "There's no need. Not if he's going to tell us."

"You trust him?" she screamed. "After all he's done? You're going to trust him to tell us everything?"

"We'll know if he's lying, Pauline."

"Hey," said Otis. "I don't know what this guy did to you, but you came here for information and if he's willing to give it to you, that's got to be better than pulling it from his head."

Pauline didn't move away from Doctor Lucas. She stared at him. Michael could tell that she was perceiving him. Not hard enough to extract thoughts hidden deep inside his mind, but enough to know that the fear of it would make him talk.

They allowed Lucas to sit on a stool by one of the benches. He pulled a handkerchief from his trouser pocket and Otis dampened it under one of the taps in the lab so he could dab the blood from the broken skin on his face. The others stood as he leant his elbow on the bench behind him and talked.

"I was made an offer," said Lucas. "The British government knew that I was working with the Russians and that I had produced the perceiver serum for them, imperfect though it was. I had done things in this country which, shall we say, could get me in trouble with the law, but the government officials said they were prepared to overlook that. They said they could offer a research position in England if I, in turn, was prepared to bring my research home and destroy everything that I had built in Russia."

"Who made that offer?" said Michael. "Was it an MP called Peter Wauluds?"

"It was made through an agent out in Russia," said Lucas. "She told me her name was Julie, but I doubt that was her real name. I think she chose something English to make me feel more comfortable talking to her. Whoever it was further up the chain who authorised it all, I don't know."

He was telling the truth. Michael would have perceived if it was a lie. "Did you destroy it all?" he asked. "Everything you had done in Russia?"

"As much of it as I could. There was a certain dissatisfaction among the Russians about the perceiver serum. They wanted it to be perfect, they didn't understand that biochemical science takes time, that it is about refining your results, about learning from your failures. So I played into their hands and ended that trial claiming that it was unsuccessful. No one seemed to notice that I destroyed my research, apart from a few vials of the serum which I believe got into the hands of one of the Russian generals. The rest of it, without me, was bound to collapse. The Russians liked the idea of creating a whole generation of perceiver children like Brian Ransom had done in Britain, but they had little appetite for waiting for those children to be born and grow up. It is my understanding that, after I had been smuggled out of the country, that line of research was moth-balled."

"Is this the thing that Sian Jones was going to expose?" said Pauline. "That Britain is carrying out research into perceivers? Doesn't seem something worth killing for."

"It depends what the research is," said Otis. "Why don't you ask him what the research is."

Michael looked around the lab. "Well?" he asked Lucas.

"When I told the Russians that the serum trial was unsuccessful, it was a lie," said Lucas. "When I came back to England, I was able to combine the work I was doing in Russia with the research Brian Ransom had done in the UK and tweak the formula. We were able to develop a serum which targets only the part of the genetic code which turns ordinary people into perceivers, and not the part of the brain that turns people mad. Unfortunately, it's very difficult to manufacture, as the basis of the chemical is extracted from a living perceiver. That's when we decided to synthesise it using a rapidly growing species of moss which was developed in the pharmaceutical industry to grow substances for use in medicines. It makes the moss turn red for some reason."

Michael looked around the lab again. The red moss growing in the window boxes took on a new significance. "You're growing stuff which can turn norms into perceivers?"

"It has to be extracted and concentrated to have any great effect," said Lucas. "The stuff we've spliced into the moss will only give people a tiny sense of what it is like to be a perceiver. A sort of perceiver-lite, if you will. Once extracted and concentrated, it forms a new serum which we believe is safe enough to be injected by intelligence agents out in the field and strong enough for them to easily and effectively perceive the minds of their targets."

"That's it?" said Pauline. "A new way to turn norms into perceivers? I don't believe it. That's not worth killing someone over."

She bolted forward and grabbed Lucas by the lapels of his lab coat. He was not a small man by any means, but her frustration was such that she lifted him up off the stool. "What are you not telling us?" she screamed. She widened her eyes and pushed in hard with her perception.

Lucas cried out. Half with the pain she was causing inside of his mind, half with the fear of what she was going to do.

"Pauline, stop!" Michael pulled at her arm, but she wrenched it from him.

Two years since the death of Alex and all that hurt was pouring out of her, into the probing of Lucas's mind.

Then it stopped. Pauline withdrew in shock. She stood there, her eyes still wide, but her perception closed down. "He wasn't hiding *what* he was working on," she said, almost to herself. "He was hiding *who* he was working with."

She pulled at the security pass around his neck so hard that the cord broke, and she turned and ran.

"Pauline!" Michael called after her.

She ran out of the lab and back into the corridor. Michael was steps behind as she slammed her palms on the double doors that led into the stairwell. The doors were still swinging on their hinges as Michael got there, just in time to see her slam her palms on the second set of double doors.

He entered a corridor which was the mirror image of the one they had just left. Windows looking into the car park were on his right. A single security door was on his left. Pauline touched Lucas's pass to the black box. The red light turned to green, the bolts of the door clicked to their unlocked position and she pushed it open.

Michael followed to see Pauline had stopped just inside the door of the mirror image lab. More red moss grew in window boxes along the back. More benches ran in rows down the length of the lab with more scientific equipment laid out along them.

Sitting at one of the benches was a man. There were microscopic images of the moss displayed on a computer screen in front of him. He was about the same age as Lucas, with a full head of grey hair and a neatly trimmed beard.

When he turned to look at Michael, it only served to confirm his identity. Michael had already perceived who it was.

It was Brian Ransom. His father.

TWENTY-SIX

MICHAEL looked at his father.

His father looked at him.

Pauline watched them both.

They perceived each other.

Disbelief, understanding, hatred and love mixed themselves together like brightly coloured paints stirred into a brown, muddy emotional soup.

"Michael," said Ransom, eventually. "How did you know I was here?"

"I didn't," said Michael. "You're supposed to be in jail."

"I'm on day release." Ransom lifted the leg of his trousers to reveal an electronic tag strapped to his ankle.

"Why did they let you out?"

"They needed someone to work with Doctor Lucas," said Ransom. "Someone who knew about perceivers, someone who could interpret the old research we did to create the vitamin pills."

"I thought that research was destroyed," said Pauline.

"Apparently, not all of it," said Ransom. "When parts of my company were split up and sold, some of it ended up here at Clairone Labs."

There was water in Michael's eyes. Water that felt like acid burning its way through his sight and turning his vision to mush. "Doctor Lucas?" he said. The pain of the acid was affecting his voice and causing his mouth to tremble as he spoke. "Doctor Lucas who had you kidnapped by two mind-controlled thugs in the middle of the street? Doctor Lucas who had you chained to a radiator and made you piss in a bucket? Doctor Lucas who experimented on perceivers and didn't care who he hurt in the process?"

Michael turned away from his father. He was disgusted. What made it worse was how his father sat there and talked so calmly about it as if it were nothing.

Otis came rushing through the door. "What the hell's going on?"

Behind him, walking awkwardly after his beating, was Doctor Lucas. "I'm sorry Brian, I couldn't stop them."

Ransom couldn't help but see Lucas's injuries and the bloodied handkerchief in his hand. "Saul, what happened? Are you all right?"

The scientist opened his mouth to answer, but Michael's anger wasn't going to give him the satisfaction. He swore, if he still had Norm the Norm's sidearm with him, he would have shot Lucas through the head there and then and been done with it. "Oh yes, let's all feel sorry for Doctor Lucas!" he yelled, swirling around and glaring at every single person in the room like it was all their fault. "Poor Doctor Lucas who has hurt — how many people?"

"Michael, calm down," said Ransom. "I can explain."

"Honestly, Dad, I don't think you can."

Michael walked out into the corridor. He was going to stand there where there were fewer emotions flying around to think about what he was going to do next. But when he stepped outside, he knew it wasn't far enough away. He turned to the double doors and ran.

He ran out into the stairwell and down every step, thumping his feet down on them as if to punish them. Without thinking, he went back the way they had come in and found himself in the corridor which led to the fire door. He didn't hesitate for a moment and kept running until he was nearly there, then he lifted both hands and pushed down hard so the door had no choice but to open. It swung wide — probably sending a little notice to the computer belonging to the woman with the stealthy flat shoes — and let him out into the open.

A cold wind blew in the shade of the building, but Michael didn't care. He welcomed the winter air chafing at his skin and the way it took the heat away from his cheeks.

He walked around to the front of the building. He thought about getting back in the car, but that would be swapping one claustrophobic inside space for another — and, besides, Otis still had the keys. So when he got to the front entrance he just stopped. There was a little doorstep there — more like a kerb, really — and he sat down.

Was that the big story that Sian Jones was working on? That Brian Ransom, the man who was jailed for using his research to make perceivers, was being let out of jail to do new research into how to make more perceivers? It was big enough to make the headlines. But big enough to kill for?

And what did it have to do with Peter Wauluds? Perhaps it had nothing to do with the MP. Perhaps she had found out that he was a perceiver and was going to expose him, and her research into him was no more complicated than that.

Pauline came and joined him.

She sat on the kerb and pulled his arm until his hand came out of his pocket and then she clasped her fingers around his. It did more to warm him than the faltering winter sun that was beginning to sink behind the industrial buildings on the other side of the car park.

"Are you all right?" she asked.

"No," he said.

She squeezed his hand tighter.

"I might as well give up now," said Michael. "Call Pankhurst, tell his men to come get me and submit to the cure."

"Don't say that."

"Katya was right. This whole crazy quest, ringing up Otis, getting his father to let us in the fire door and all the rest, it was never going to save me."

Pauline said nothing. Instead, he felt her perception nudge at the edge of his filters. He let her in because he had nothing to hide. They had all seen his shame on display in the lab with the father who had done everything to betray him.

Just to have her mind there felt nice. It was like the touch of her hand, but more intimate. There were no other minds around, the people who worked at Clairone were safely inside the building, so he didn't even have to block anyone else out. They just sat there, letting their thoughts intertwine and their emotions combine, until there was no difference between them.

Until another presence entered their perception and they pulled up their blocks. It was Brian Ransom. He wasn't as strong as them, but he could perceive their surface thoughts. Thoughts that they didn't want him to perceive.

"Excuse me, Pauline," he said. "I would like a word with my son."

She looked up at him as he stood beside her. Michael kept staring out ahead.

Is it okay? Pauline asked Michael with her thoughts.

Yeah, it's okay, he replied.

Pauline stood up from the kerb. "Where are the others?" she asked.

"Still in the lab," said Ransom. "A man called Doctor Smith — his real name, apparently — is in there. Lucas is showing him our moss."

"See you later, Michael," said Pauline and she left.

Ransom sat down next to Michael. He tried to perceive him, but Michael blocked him out.

The sun sank further behind the buildings.

"They came to me in prison," Ransom said. "They told me, the Russians had developed a serum that could turn normal people into perceivers. But it was only temporary and with a terrible side effect that turned the users mad if they had too many injections. They said it wasn't perfect, but it could be improved with more research and they were worried the Russians would develop a drug that would turn their secret agents into the perfect spies. If the Russians had it, then pretty soon the Chinese might have it, the Japanese would have it. It would be like the nuclear arms race all over again.

"Except that we, Britain, would not have it," Ransom continued. "Britain had effectively had two leading researchers in the field of perception and both of them had been prevented from carrying out their work in this country. One was Doctor Lucas, who defected to Russia under the lure of more money and resources. The second was me, who they put on trial and threw in a jail cell. If Britain was to maintain a presence on the world stage, they told me, then we needed to resurrect our research. That meant getting me out of jail, getting Lucas to come back home and getting us to work together."

"So you accepted?" said Michael. It was not so much a question as an accusation.

"I welcomed the opportunity to get out of prison, I don't deny it. Even though they take me back to my cell and lock me up again at night. But I also welcomed the chance to resume my research into perception. I had screwed up with the vitamin pills, I knew that I had. But I also knew if I could take Doctor Lucas's perceiver serum and perfect it, then children like you wouldn't have to be co-opted into any Perceiver Corps. People who wanted to be spies or soldiers or special agents, would be the ones turning themselves into perceivers, and they would be doing it willingly."

"Doctor Lucas offered you the chance to work with him when he had us both imprisoned in Russia and you turned him down, do you remember that?" said Michael. "You said you had a vision for peace, that if everyone could perceive each other, then hatred and misunderstanding would be things of the past. But all that happened was that normal people came to hate perceivers and no matter how much we tried to explain that we're not evil mind readers, it made no difference. That's why you told Doctor Lucas to go to hell back then, even if it meant coming back to Britain and going to jail."

"That was different," said Ransom.

"Was it? I was proud of you then. I'm not proud of you now."

"If you could only understand what we're doing here—"

Michael got up from his position on the kerb and raised his arms in frustration. "No, I don't understand, Dad! You're turning perceivers into a weapon. Once Pankhurst has got his wish and cured us all, that's what perception will be: a weapon to inject into soldiers to help them defeat the enemy in a war. Not the bringer of peace like you thought it was going to be all those years ago."

A ringing sound emerged from Michael's pocket. It was his phone.

He retrieved it and was going to turn it off, but the screen said it was Mary Ransom calling.

"It's my mother," said Michael. "Your wife. Do you want to tell her what you've been up to when she thought you were safely locked away in jail?"

Michael held out the phone to Ransom. Ransom turned his head away. "Don't tell her, please."

"So you *are* ashamed at what you're doing?" said Michael.

It was a rhetorical question which he didn't give his father time to answer as he accepted the call.

Mary sounded flustered. The police had been to the house, she said, looking for him. She had told them she didn't know where he was and managed to get rid of them. But, with all the stress in the house, Katya went into labour. Because Otis had taken the car, she had to call an ambulance.

Michael thanked her, said he would deal with it, and hung up.

"I have to go," Michael told his father. "What are you going to do?"

"I don't feel like going back into the lab. Not today," said Ransom. "I'll probably just sit here until the van comes to take me back to prison. What other choice do I have?"

"There's always a choice, Dad," said Michael. "There's always a choice."

TWENTY-SEVEN

OTIS drove them to Wycombe Hospital, which was the nearest maternity hospital to Mary's house in Beaconsfield and where the ambulance had taken Katya. They said their goodbyes and Otis left to take the car back to Mary and then to make his way home to the woman he called his wife and their child.

The last time Michael had come to a hospital, he had experienced a man's death. The memory of it existed in the smell of the chemical they used to clean the floors and wash the bedclothes. It clung to the uniforms of the nurses as they moved from patient to patient. It was in the floral pattern of the curtains used to partition each bed and in the anxious faces of the relatives who sat waiting for news.

That was what he *saw*. But what he sensed with his perception was entirely the opposite. The people who sat waiting, the staff who attended the patients and even the patients themselves were happy.

There was an optimism about them, a feeling of hope and expectation. Because the maternity ward was about life, not death.

In among all the happy, but anxious minds was one that Michael recognised. Looking beyond the movement of busy nurses around the nurses' station, was the familiar black suit of Agent Cooper. He was standing by a collection of chairs meant for relatives, and speaking into his mobile phone; too engrossed to notice Michael and Pauline approaching.

Pauline touched Michael's arm to bring him to a stop in the middle of the corridor. A doctor in a hurry had to dodge to get round them.

"What's he doing here?" she said.

"I called him," said Michael.

"You did what?"

Katya's baby was conceived as part of the Russian perceiver programme, he told her with his thoughts, not wanting any norms to overhear.

"I don't see how that matters," said Pauline out loud.

"He has a legitimate interest," said Michael. "Anyway, Katya is a single mother in a foreign country, she needs some sort of support and I don't think — given the circumstances — that we are the ones who can offer that to her."

It did little to alleviate her suspicions and Michael felt Pauline's perception reach out to his mind. He instinctively resisted. "What are you not telling me?" she said.

A nurse carrying a pile of sterile bandages had to take a wide path to get round them. Pauline gripped Michael's sleeve even tighter and dragged him to the side, out of the way.

"Michael?" she asked again. "Are you going to tell me or do I have to pull the information from you?"

It was an empty threat because she knew he was strong enough to block her.

But he decided to tell her anyway. The only reason he hadn't mentioned it before was that it never seemed to be the right time.

He took a deep breath. It was harder to say the words than he had imagined. "Do you remember when I first went to Russia? When Doctor Lucas kidnapped my dad and I went to find him?"

"Yes," said Pauline.

"Doctor Lucas had me drugged and took me away for … something. I never knew what. I was unconscious the whole time. There was speculation that he might have taken something from me. He was researching perceivers so it made sense that he would want to take genetic samples to analyse. One theory is that he didn't just take a blood sample. There's speculation he might have also taken some of my sperm."

Michael let the words hang between them.

"You think Katya is carrying your baby?" she said.

"I don't know. Possibly."

"That was three years ago, Michael."

"Sperm can be frozen — three years, thirty years, it doesn't matter. If the Russians wanted perceiver babies to be born, the easiest way would be to fertilise a human egg with sperm from a perceiver donor."

Pauline blocked off her feelings so he couldn't read them. "What's all that got to do with Cooper?"

"I want him to run a paternity test," said Michael. "I need to be sure."

He nudged Pauline as he saw that Cooper had finished his phone call and was heading their way. "You're here," he said. "Katya's been asking for you."

Cooper led them to a private room where Katya lay propped up on a hospital bed looking tired, sweaty and pleased to see them. By her side was a midwife in blue tabard uniform.

The midwife looked up as they came in. "I'm sorry, three's too many of you to be in here," she said.

"We just wanted to see that Katya was okay," said Pauline.

"I'm okay," said Katya, lifting herself up on her elbows so she could see them better. "I think my baby wants to come soon."

The midwife turned to Michael. "Are you the father?"

He choked on his own breath. "What? No."

"We're friends," said Pauline.

"Then you need to leave, this is not a party," said the midwife.

"No, let them stay," said Katya. "Except Agent Cooper. He can go."

Katya's face suddenly contorted. She gripped hold of the handles on the side of the bed and let out a scream so loud that it hurt Michael's ears.

"What's wrong?" he said.

"Nothing's wrong," said the midwife. "It's just a contraction." She went round to the bottom of the bed and looked between Katya's legs. "That's good, Katya. Not long now."

"I'll just be outside," said Cooper and left the room.

Katya's scream subsided and the midwife looked up at Michael and Pauline. "If you two want to make yourselves useful, you can hold her hand."

Michael went round one side of the bed and Pauline went round the other. Katya clasped both of their hands tightly.

Michael allowed himself a moment to perceive Katya, but then another contraction came — and, with it, the pain — and he quickly withdrew his perception.

After that, the only pain he felt was his own as Katya's nails dug into his hand tighter and tighter with each new contraction, while the midwife made encouraging sounds at the bottom of the bed.

Katya's screams turned to shouted Russian words, which Michael could only imagine were swear words, as the midwife interspersed them with English. "Baby's nearly here, Katya. You're doing well. Just one last push. Come on, that's it. Give me all you've got."

Her face red with determination, Katya squeezed Michael and Pauline's hands as she let out one last, long, primal grunt.

The baby's head appeared from between her legs and the rest of him plopped out onto the bed. A wet, wriggling, tiny human being. So alive and so real, it was difficult to believe he had been inside another person.

The baby gurgled at suddenly being thrust into the world and started to cry. Which turned into a piercing scream as the reality of leaving the safety of Katya's womb touched his skin.

The midwife scooped him up and wiped the residue of the foetal sack from his face. "Well done, Katya! It's a boy!"

She placed the baby, still attached to its umbilical cord, onto Katya's chest and the new mother cuddled him close. Her eyes brightened as she looked at him with a smile that was full of love.

Michael opened his perception and felt a rush of euphoria. It was like no experience he had ever had before. Happiness was such an inadequate word. Katya was floating on her emotions. Her excitement, contentment and strong instinct to protect her child eclipsed her exhaustion and worries like a drug.

"Would you like to cut the umbilical cord?" asked the midwife.

Michael saw that she had sectioned off a small piece of the blue-tinged cord from where it snaked out from the baby's belly button. She offered him the scissors.

Michael was about to refuse, but he realised there was no one else and so he took the scissors. The cord was surprisingly tough, but he managed to cut through it and release the physical link between the mother and child. Katya's baby was officially his own, independent person.

The midwife hustled them out after that so the little boy could be cleaned up properly and weighed and whatever else it was that needed to be done after he was born.

As they went out into the corridor, they passed Agent Cooper and Michael heard him ask the midwife for a sample of the umbilical cord to send off to the lab.

There were two chairs outside Katya's room and, as Michael sat down, he realised how exhausted he was. Not as exhausted as someone who had just given birth, but mentally drained.

"What now?" said Pauline.

"Figure out a way to get back to my mother's house, I suppose," said Michael.

"I meant, *what now*?" said Pauline. Even though the words were the same, the meaning she conveyed was more long term.

Michael thought about the question for a long time.

He didn't expect the answer to come from his perception. But, as he sat there outside of Katya's hospital room, he perceived a familiar presence.

Michael looked up the corridor and confirmed what he already knew. Inspector Patterson was there and he was coming for him.

Michael got up from his chair. Pauline got up, too, and stood behind him.

Patterson stopped. He was no more than ten paces away. It was not only his suit that looked crumpled and uncared for, it was his whole body. Michael perceived him and felt his regret.

"I'm sorry about this, Michael," said Patterson.

"Sorry for what?" he asked, even though he knew the answer.

"I've come to take you in."

"For what?" said Pauline. "He's committed no crime."

"Emergency legislation," said Patterson. "They could have sent someone else, but I thought it would be better coming from me."

"What will happen?" asked Michael.

"I don't actually know. It's not up to me."

Michael was suddenly very afraid. Once he was in police custody, that was it. Game over. He looked around the hospital corridor for something to protect himself. Some sort of weapon.

His mind gripped onto the chair that he had been sitting on. He wrapped his thoughts around it and willed it into the air. He projected it, with all his fear and anger, at Patterson. Patterson sidestepped as the chair whizzed past him and crashed to the floor behind.

Gasps rose from the nurses at the nurses' station.

"Don't make it difficult, Michael."

Patterson took a step forward. Michael's thoughts seized the second chair and hurled it at him. Patterson ducked and it sailed overhead.

Michael looked around. There was a clipboard on the nurses' station. His mind picked it up and sent it spinning at the police officer. It hit him in the back. Patterson jolted, but he kept walking.

Michael's mind lifted a pen, a box of tissues, a thank you card, another patient's chart on a clipboard, an empty sample tray all into the air. They struck Patterson's body and bounced off in quick succession like a handful of pebbles thrown at a tank.

"Don't do this, Inspector Patterson," pleaded Michael. "Tony, please."

He perceived the policeman didn't want to, but he did it anyway. Patterson knew that if he didn't take Michael in, someone else would.

Patterson stood in front of him. "Turn around."

As Michael turned, out of the corner of his eye, he saw a fire extinguisher attached to the wall in the corner where the corridor ended. He explored it with his thoughts and held it with his mind. He could pull it from the wall and send it sailing through the air to strike Patterson on the head.

He could run.

But run where?

He perceived from Patterson that there were other police officers in the hospital. Even if Michael had some place to run to, he probably wouldn't make it.

So he let Patterson secure the handcuffs around his wrists and lead him away.

There were probably only days left before he was subjected to the cure.

TWENTY-EIGHT

THE turn of a key in Michael's cell door clicked the bolt free and it opened.

Michael had perceived who it was outside, but it was still surprising to see Barrington walk into the stark, grey environment of the police cell.

The security chief looked somehow smaller in the casual jeans and polo shirt he wore, instead of the suit Michael was used to seeing him in. He brought with him the smell of freedom, with his freshly showered mix of deodorant and moisturiser. It was not enough to blot out the stale air of the cell, but it made Michael think of the outside.

He swung his legs around off the narrow bed with its squeaky plastic-covered mattress and tossed the grey police-issue blanket aside.

The custody sergeant standing next to Barrington informed him that he would be waiting in the corridor in case he was needed. He left, pulling the door closed behind him but not locking it.

"Your policeman friend is very persuasive," said Barrington.

"If he was that persuasive, he would have let me go," said Michael.

Barrington chuckled. "Quite so."

"Did he tell you his theory about the Sian Jones murder?"

"Yes."

"And?"

"Professional hit. Interesting."

Michael perceived Barrington didn't entirely believe Patterson's theory. Which was bad. Because, out of all the crazy things that Michael wanted to tell him, that bit was the most believable.

"Did he tell you what's going on at Clairone Labs?"

"He did," said Barrington.

"And?"

"Also interesting. It reminds me of how the West treated Nazi scientists after the war. The Second World War, that is, not all the other terrible things that have happened since. Many of them were taken to America, not only to deprive post-war Germany of some of its more brilliant minds, but also to advance America's technical ability. The same man who developed rockets that bombed Britain in the forties went on to be a major player in the race to put man on the moon. Which America won, of course."

"What is the connection with Peter Wauluds?" asked Michael. "When I asked if you could investigate him, you gave me the address to Clairone Labs. I know he's listed as one of their advisors, but I can't find out any more. Certainly not while I'm stuck in here."

"Okay," said Barrington. He walked the two short steps to the bed, which was little more than a padded bench attached to the wall, and sat himself down next to Michael. "This is what I've been able to find out about Wauluds. Listed as part of his parliamentary financial interests, alongside Clairone, are a couple of defence companies which have major contracts supplying other parts of the world with weapons. All above board, of course. Wauluds was smart. Accepting a job as justice minister presented no conflict of interest as far as parliamentary standards go, but it did put him on the map as far as political ambitions."

"Except Pankhurst got him to resign," said Michael.

"As a minister, yes. But not as an MP. The word around Westminster is, it's a temporary blip in his career. Wauluds is tipped for big things, maybe even the next prime minister if he plays his cards right. Everyone knows Pankhurst is on his way out. Either Pankhurst will lose the next election or his own party will vote him out and try to get someone more popular in as a last-ditch attempt to hold onto power."

"You seem very certain."

"I've been working around politicians for a long time," said Barrington. "I can see which way the wind is blowing. Why do you think Pankhurst is having this sudden panic about perceivers? The general election is just a year away, either he swings the public mood in his favour before then, or he works damned hard to repair his legacy ahead of being ousted from office."

"I don't see what that has to do with Wauluds and Clairone."

"Think of yourself as an ambitious politician," said Barrington. "You want to ingratiate yourself with the right people. The right people being the people who are on the way up, like Wauluds, not the people on the way down like Pankhurst. Maybe you got yourself noticed as an MP and got promoted to a ministerial position in the Department for Business, Innovation and Skills. The same department that grants export licences to companies who want to sell weapons to foreign powers. Wauluds has nothing to do with that committee, of course, it wouldn't be allowed because of his links with defence companies. But, what he does have, is influence. A word in the right ear, asking someone to approve an export licence on the understanding that, maybe down the line when he is prime minister, that favour could be reciprocated."

It was all coming together in Michael's mind. Like pieces of a jigsaw scattered around the room and gradually being uncovered in the dark corners where people had hidden them. "You think Wauluds wants to sell the perceiver serum to other countries?"

"Developing an injection which turns ordinary intelligence agents into perceiver spies would be useful to Britain, but imagine how valuable it would be as a commodity. Clairone Labs licences the patent to one or more of the defence companies which Wauluds has an interest in, they sell it to foreign powers and make a ton of money, allowing Wauluds to pocket the profits."

"Can you prove any of this?"

"At the moment, it's just a theory," said Barrington.

"A theory which, if it got out, would destroy Wauluds," said Michael. "A theory that he might think would be worth killing someone to keep it quiet."

"The only thing I have on record about Wauluds is that he is the one who approved Brian Ransom's day release from prison while he was still justice minister. That's a fact that he can't hide because he had to put his name to the paperwork. Wauluds, of course, used to work for Ransom back when the perceiver vitamin pills were developed. So he knows some of the science and some of its potential."

Michael stood up. His head was firing with ideas. "We've got to tell someone." But as he looked around the four grey walls of his cell, he knew that he couldn't do it while locked up in there. "You've got to get me out."

"I don't have that power," said Barrington.

"You can't let me stay in here, not with something like this. If they cure me, there's no telling for certain what's going to happen. I've been cured before and it destroyed my memories. Being cured a second time…" Michael shivered at the thought.

"I'm open to suggestions," said Barrington.

"Get me in a room with Pankhurst and Wauluds. Pankhurst is still prime minister, he still has power until his party or the electorate chuck him out. We need to put all this to Wauluds and I need to perceive him and we have to tell Pankhurst. We can't let the world turn perception into a weapon for people to use on each other."

Barrington nodded. "I'll try," he said. "I don't make promises, but I'll try."

TWENTY-NINE

MICHAEL pushed down the leg of his jeans and tried to cover up the electronic tag which was strapped to his ankle. Even with the material over the top, the bulge was still visible. It made him feel like a criminal. Perhaps, in the mind of the country, he was.

The terms of his release meant he was allowed out in the day, as long as he obeyed the overnight curfew and was tucked up safely at his mother's house by ten o'clock. Under Mary Ransom's stairs, the Ministry of Justice had installed a box which would sound an alarm if it didn't detect the presence of Michael's electronic tag during curfew hours.

It was already eight o'clock and Michael was still at Barrington's flat in Harrow in north London. Michael was supposed to wait patiently there until the security chief returned home. The waiting bit he had just about figured out, the patiently aspect was something he was getting worse at the more the minutes ticked by.

Like a lot of homes in London, 'cosy' would have been the polite term for Barrington's living room. His wife and teenage son had been shipped off to the in-laws for the night, but they had left evidence of their existence behind. It appeared that Mrs Barrington was into home toning regimes, judging by the women's gym kit folded up on a selection of hand weights in the corner. The son appeared to be studying the history of the First World War, according to the battered school text book by the side of the armchair. The rest of the stuff could belong to anyone in the household, with a PlayStation stuffed under the TV, shelves stuffed with paperback books — mostly on Indian cooking — and a few ornaments of dragons which might have been brightly coloured if it weren't for the layer of dust on them.

It had been more than half an hour since Barrington had left Michael sitting on his bijou two-seater sofa, and he had virtually memorised all the titles written down the spines of the Indian cookbooks on the opposite wall.

The front door opened.

Michael widened his perception and sensed that it was Barrington. The mind that he had brought with him was instantly recognisable as Pankhurst.

The door banged shut again and Michael felt the tremor through the house. Indecipherable male voices talked in the hallway on the other side of the wall. Then the final barrier between them, the living room door, was opened and Barrington led Pankhurst into the heart of his home.

The Prime Minister looked somehow less prime ministerial as he had taken off whatever brightly patterned tie he had been wearing that day and was just in a suit with open-necked shirt. However, it was what was in his mind that Michael was more interested in.

Michael had promised weeks ago when Pankhurst offered him a job that he would not perceive him. But sacking him, ordering that he be cured and sending his friend the policeman to lock him in a cell violated that agreement as far as Michael was concerned. He ignored Pankhurst's tired and slightly nervous emotions and looked deeper into his mind.

Michael perceived no remorse at what he had done. Pankhurst was riding high at what his announcement over perceivers had done for his public approval and he was full of confidence following a meeting with senior members of his party who had agreed to back his continued leadership into the next election.

Other questions remained unanswered. Michael wanted to ask Pankhurst outright, but he had promised Barrington that he wouldn't. So he thought them instead:

Why did you turn on perceivers when we had done nothing to you? Do you know how much pain you will cause when you force people to be cured? Do you realise you've criminalised an entire generation who has done nothing wrong? How can you live with yourself?

But Pankhurst couldn't hear Michael's questions. He was just a norm.

Barrington joined them. "Remember," he said. "No politics in my flat. I know the two of you are on opposite sides of a certain debate, but you left that debate when you left Westminster. This meeting is about Wauluds and Wauluds only."

"I heard you in the car, Barrington, there's no need to repeat yourself," said Pankhurst. He came further into the room and sat on the armchair. As soon as his bottom hit the cushion, he shifted himself to the side and reached underneath himself to pull out the PlayStation control he had just sat on. He dropped it on the floor next to the First World War book.

"As long as we're clear," said Barrington. "Did you speak to Wauluds?"

Pankhurst nodded. "I called him on his mobile. I told him I had been rash asking him to resign like that, when he could so clearly be an asset to the party. I told him I understood he'd been working on something that would be a game changer when it comes to the issue of perceivers and I would like to hear more about it."

"He bought that?" said Barrington.

"Of course he bought it," said Pankhurst. "He's a politician with ambition and his party leader has offered him the possibility of redemption. He'll be here."

Pankhurst's gaze drifted across the room and fell on Michael for the first time. He maintained his stare as if to show he was not afraid, but he couldn't shield his mind from the discomfort at being in the same room as a perceiver.

"I still don't understand why he has to be here," said Pankhurst.

"Because we need a perceiver to make sure Wauluds is telling you the truth and find out anything that he's not telling you," said Barrington. "Wauluds is a perceiver too, remember, and we need Michael to stop him getting into your mind and discovering the real reason you asked him here."

"Yes, well." Pankhurst averted his eyes. "I find it very unfortunate that it's necessary."

Barrington's doorbell put an end to the discussion and the security chief went to answer it.

He returned moments later with an intrigued, excited and somewhat wary Peter Wauluds. Michael threw a perception block around both Pankhurst and Barrington. It would be a strain to keep it up through the course of the meeting, but a necessary measure.

As Wauluds brushed his wispy hair over his bald patch, he saw Michael sitting there and suspicion filled his mind. Wauluds erected his own barrier around his thoughts, but it was weak and Michael could easily break through if he tried.

"I thought you were going to cure him," said Wauluds, turning to Pankhurst.

"After this meeting, I'm sure I will," said Pankhurst.

Michael shuddered as he perceived that it was no lie.

"I'm happy to talk to you, John," said Wauluds. "But I'm not happy to be spied upon by a perceiver."

"He's here because I need an expert in perceivers to evaluate what you're telling me. Why, Peter? Is there something you want to hide?"

"No, Prime Minister."

Michael focussed his perception and tore a hole in Wauluds's barrier. If there was something he was concealing, then asking him about it was the very moment that he would reveal himself.

Wauluds glared at Michael, flapping away the intrusion like a person flaps away a fly during a picnic. But the more Wauluds tried to push him out, the more Michael pushed in. And he was stronger than Wauluds.

Wauluds looked away again and dropped his barriers in surrender. *Look into my mind, Michael, if you must, but you won't find anything,* he thought.

"Okay," said Wauluds out loud to Pankhurst. "But I want my objection to him being here on record."

"Noted," said Pankhurst. "Although you do realise this is an off-the-record conversation?"

"Fine," said Wauluds. He walked over to the only remaining seat left in the room — the one on the sofa next to Michael — and sat on it at such an angle that he purposely turned his back on him.

Barrington leant against the closed living room door behind him and folded his arms.

"So," said Pankhurst. "Tell me your solution to the perceiver issue."

Michael could not see Wauluds's smile with his back to him, but he perceived his sense of superiority as he prepared to relay the information that he thought only he knew. "A serum," he said.

"Like the one that caused the Russian soldier to shoot himself in front of the most powerful people in the world?"

"Not like that," said Wauluds. "This is different. It's been refined so it doesn't have any of those unpleasant side effects. This is a serum that we can inject into any British agent anywhere in the world and they will be able to read the minds of whoever they encounter. If you want to use it domestically, then no problem. Inject it into the bloodstream of a police officer and he will be able to read the minds of all his suspects and know instantly who are the murderers, who are the rapists and who are the terrorists."

"This is a technology to make Britain 'great' again, is it?"

"Exactly," said Wauluds, his mind full of excitement.

"You wouldn't be planning to sell this technology to foreign nations and pocket the profits through the defence companies you have links to?" said Pankhurst.

"No!" said Wauluds.

The lie was so easy to detect that Michael didn't have to try. "He's lying," he said.

"What I meant was," said Wauluds, scrambling to regain his credibility. "Not right away. But you've got to understand that something this powerful cannot be kept secret indefinitely. The Americans ended the Second World War by inventing the atomic bomb, but it wasn't long before the Russians had one. The Americans, back then, lost their exclusive rights to the technology because it was stolen from them. Britain shouldn't be allowed to make the same mistake with the perceiver serum. If we keep the development and manufacture in this country, we can sell it to the rest of the world. Then we will control the supply and we can collect the profits."

"By 'we', you mean the country and yourself?"

"An entrepreneur should be rewarded for his hard work."

Barrington unfolded his arms and pushed himself away from the door so that he seemed to physically enter the space of the conversation. "Sounds very calculating," he said. "That sort of calculating, money-grabbing approach wouldn't make you look very good if it were made public, would it?"

Wauluds looked up at him and a strand of wispy grey hair fell across his eye. He pushed it back again as he returned his attention to the Prime Minister. "Are you going to let your security chief talk to me like that?"

"I don't see why not," said Pankhurst. "It seems to me he has a very good point."

"In fact," continued Barrington, "it would look even worse if someone found out that you were planning to push through such a plan by using your influence in Parliament."

"You have no proof of that," said Wauluds.

"Neither did Sian Jones," said Barrington, "but she was close to getting it, wasn't she? Is that why you had her killed?"

A wave of guilt washed over the MP and dampened his thoughts with shame. "I'm not a murderer," he said.

Michael perceived that he may not have pulled the trigger, but the blood was on his hands. "Don't try to lie in front of a perceiver as strong as me," said Michael. "The law still says you're a murderer even if you paid someone else to do it."

Wauluds got up off the sofa and backed away from Michael as panicked thoughts rushed into his head in an attempt to find a way out of the hole he had dug himself into. "You can't use anything he says in a court of law." He pointed an accusing finger at Michael. "Perceiver evidence isn't admissible."

Pankhurst stood up slowly. Calmly. Methodically. "I'm not concerned about the journalist," he said.

Michael perceived he was telling the truth. He really didn't care that an innocent woman had died.

"But I am interested in your serum," said Pankhurst. "I mean, it's perfect, isn't it? I can continue to cure every perceiver in the country, satisfy the public desire to keep their private thoughts private, and still keep the perceiver card up my sleeve. Assuming this serum stuff does what you say it does."

"Which is why I brought it to show you."

Wauluds reached into his jacket pocket and pulled out a syringe. One that was full of a clear liquid and had a plastic cap to protect the needle.

Michael hadn't seen that coming. With all his perception powers, he had missed it. He had been concerned with the knowledge Wauluds had about the serum and Sian Jones, while keeping his protective barrier around Pankhurst's and Barrington's minds.

Pankhurst backed up: only half a step in the small living room before the back of his legs touched the chair he had been sitting in. "What are you planning to do with that?" he said, staring at the syringe.

"Show you," said Wauluds. "I would inject it into myself, but I'm already a perceiver — not a strong one, maybe, but I read minds good enough when I need to — so I was thinking I would find a norm and inject them. That will show you how effective and safe it is."

He turned to Barrington.

Barrington's passive enjoyment at the unravelling of Wauluds's deception suddenly turned into a trepidation that bled all over Michael's perception. "No, wait …"

"Now, Peter …" said Pankhurst. Even his emotions revealed he was unsure.

"It's only temporary," said Wauluds. "Its effects should wear off after a few days."

He pulled the plastic cap from the needle and dropped it to the floor.

"No, absolutely not," said Barrington. "I refuse. I resign. I won't be anyone's guinea pig."

Michael leapt from his seat as he perceived Wauluds wasn't going to take no for an answer. But the MP had stepped over to Barrington before Michael could get to him.

Barrington dodged the hypodermic needle as if it were a knife and followed up with a sharp punch in Wauluds's face.

Wauluds spun with the force from Barrington's fist; sending a spray of blood from his nose across the far wall as he collapsed onto Pankhurst.

The two men fell backwards. Pankhurst's head struck the collection of hand weights in the corner with an ugly thump that was barely softened by the folded gym clothes on top of them.

Pankhurst groaned. He was dazed, but not unconscious.

Wauluds raised the syringe in his hand and plunged the needle straight into Pankhurst's arm.

Everyone in the room saw what was happening, but was powerless to stop it. No sooner had the idea entered Wauluds's thoughts than he had injected the Prime Minister.

Pankhurst cried out. But the serum was already in his bloodstream and his heart was pumping it into his brain.

Barrington pulled Wauluds off Pankhurst's sprawled body.

Michael stood and watched the horror play out in front of him.

He could perceive Pankhurst's mind changing. The mind that had belonged, so clearly, to a norm, was turning into a perceiver. Like light turns to shade when a cloud moves between the sun and the earth.

Barrington pushed Wauluds away from him and the MP crashed against the shelf of books. "What have you done?" cried Barrington.

"Shown him how powerful a norm can be when they're given perception," said Wauluds.

"Oh my God," said Pankhurst, trying to sit up from where he had crash landed. Barrington came to his aid and lifted him onto the sofa.

Pankhurst stared at his security chief with wide, manic eyes. "Christ, Barrington, you really don't like me, do you?"

"Sir, you've had a shock. Why don't you sit there? I'll get you a glass of water."

Barrington turned from him, but Pankhurst grabbed hold of his sleeve. "Did you vote for the other lot in the last election?" He concentrated; perceiving him. "You did, didn't you?"

Barrington picked Pankhurst's fingers off his sleeve and stepped back. He pulled his mobile phone from his pocket and started to dial.

"Excellent, Barrington. Call my driver."

"I'm calling an ambulance."

Wauluds composed himself, tugging down his rumpled shirt and pushing back his wayward strand of hair. "I'll call your driver," he said and got out his own mobile phone.

"Speaking as your head of security, sir, I really wouldn't advise it."

"I thought you just resigned," said Wauluds.

Pankhurst got to his feet. He wobbled a little, but Michael could perceive his head was clearing as it rushed to process all the perceptions that were being thrown at him. "You're right, Peter, this stuff is amazing!" he said. "I always wondered what it was like. If I go back to the Houses of Parliament now, will I be able to see into all the minds of the other MPs?"

"Of course," said Wauluds. "Your driver should be here any minute."

THIRTY

MICHAEL turned his back against the wind to protect Katya's baby's body from the cold. The little boy looked so fragile sleeping wrapped up the blanket that Pauline had bought for him, that Michael couldn't help but cuddle him close. Especially now that the DNA had proved he was the boy's father. Biologically speaking, at least.

Pauline and Katya emerged from the visitors' centre and the wind caught their hair, sending it flapping around their faces in little strands. Pauline waved as she stomped over the rough, grassy ground that surrounded Beacon Hill, the natural monument that rose ahead of them into the grey and white clouds. Michael didn't wave back for fear of dropping his sleeping son. Rather, he stood patiently waiting for the two women to catch him up.

"All set?" he said.

Pauline opened the carrier bag in her hand and revealed three bottles of water and a collection of chocolate bars in the bottom. "All set," she said.

Katya reached over for her baby and Michael carefully relinquished the bundle. The little boy stirred awake at the movement and Michael perceived his tiny little mind as it reached consciousness and smelled the chilly air around him. It was so strange to perceive a baby. It had no thoughts at all, not like an adult, just the feelings of its own body and basic emotions that told him he was safe or hungry or tired. His ability to perceive, which he seemed to have temporarily transferred to Katya in the womb, was gone. He probably wouldn't develop it properly until he became a teenager.

"Come on, Oliver," said Katya, as she wrapped her arms around him and the child snuggled back to sleep.

"Don't let Otis know you called your baby after him," said Michael.

"It is not after him," said Katya. "I called him Oliver because it is a nice name. An English name. Would you prefer I call him something Russian, like Mikhail?"

"Heavens, no!" said Pauline. "One Michael is enough, thank you!"

They looked up to the top of the hill. It was going to be a long climb, but others had already started the ascent. By the look of their silhouettes against the sky, they were teenagers and young adults, most of whom would have been born to mothers who had unwittingly taken one of Ransom's perceiver vitamin pills.

Michael, Pauline and Katya began the walk to join them. The air was fresh, but it was dry. The weather, Michael could tell, was going to be kind to them.

"I used to run up hills when I was in the university running club," said Michael. "It's good for building strength and stamina."

"I bet you couldn't do it now," said Pauline.

"I'm not so out of condition," he said.

"Race you?"

"You're on."

Pauline broke into a run and was one stride ahead of Michael before they'd even started. He chased after her.

Within minutes, the exhilaration he used to feel when he was training on the streets of Nottingham was back in his blood. Despite everything, he found himself laughing as he caught up with Pauline and overtook her.

But the hill was steep and the terrain uneven and he soon slowed down to declare himself the winner.

Pauline joined him as they stood and waited for Katya. Her cheeks were flushed with the exertion and she was breathing deeply enough for her breath to turn to vapour against the diffused light coming through the clouds. It was surprisingly beautiful.

"What are we going to do, Michael?" said Pauline.

"We'll survive," he said.

Pankhurst's reign as prime minister was over. Michael's call to Andy the cameraman had seen to that, along with an exclusive report on the television news and a vote of no confidence in him from his party. His fellow politicians had been happy for him to stand up in public and decry that all perceivers would be cured, but getting himself injected with a perceiver serum, reading their minds and having it all exposed on national television was something they were supremely unhappy about.

Pankhurst's replacement, a woman called Anne Wintershall, did not step in to reverse the decision to cure perceivers. Rather, she endorsed it.

The King is dead: long live the Queen.

"I'm not sure we will survive," said Pauline. "They're bound to catch us eventually."

Michael felt the absence on his ankle where he had cut off the electronic tag. He was now officially on the run, and he had dragged the two women and little Oliver with him. "Perhaps it would be better to hand myself in," he said. "Have the cure and take my chances."

"No!" said Pauline. "We stay together, we agreed."

"But it's rough on you two and the baby."

"We should go abroad," said Pauline. "How about Spain? We could find a beach somewhere and work in a bar which serves too many drinks to British tourists who get drunk and make fools of themselves in public."

"Sounds nice," said Michael. Like a dream.

Katya arrived at the spot where they had stopped to catch their breath. "You two are crazy, you know that? Crazy!"

They continued walking to the top of the hill where other perceivers were waiting. In the space of fifteen minutes, the summit was full of people like them, all with their filters engaged so they half perceived each other and half kept their thoughts private. There had to be more than four hundred perceivers there.

It was a scene that was being repeated all over the country. Perceivers and those who supported them were gathering on hills, in parks and on street corners everywhere. All with packages from Otis.

Pauline elbowed Michael in the side. "There's Kev, look!"

Michael peered through the sea of bodies and saw the back of someone's head that could be the boy who had allowed himself to beaten up to save them at Galen House.

"Kev!" Pauline called. "Hey, Kev!" But the wind was blowing in the wrong direction and he didn't hear her.

A voice, amplified by an electronic speaker which made it sound almost robotic, drifted across the crowd: "Thank you for coming."

At the very centre of the gathering, on the highest point of the hill, stood Otis with a megaphone in his hand. A tuft of his dark blonde hair against the dark of a passing cloud made it obvious it was him, while the bright yellow puffer jacket that he wore made him visible to everyone.

"Sorry about the megaphone thing," he said through the megaphone. "I was going to project my thoughts at you and you could all perceive them, but having hundreds of people perceiving me all at once was going to feel a little weird, so I thought we'd do this the norm way."

Nervous laughter flitted around them.

"So you have probably heard," Otis continued, "that they've got this stuff that can turn norms into perceivers. A bit like many of us were turned into perceivers when our mothers took those vitamin pills. They think they're going to purify it and give it to their special agents and turn them into super spies. But they also think they're going to round us all up and cure us like taking pigs to the slaughterhouse, and I don't think that's going to happen."

He paused. "Do you think that's going to happen?"

"No!" cried Michael, Pauline and Katya and their voices joined hundreds of others in a unified cry that resonated around the hilltop.

"I got to thinking, what if this stuff wasn't given to special agents? What if this stuff was given to *all* norms? Do you know what would happen? Everyone who used to be a norm would suddenly be a perceiver. Let's see the government round up and cure more than sixty million people. Where is their support going to be to get rid of perceivers when everyone's a perceiver? Who's going to complain about someone trying to read their mind when they can all use their perceiver powers to block it?"

A group of people to the left of Michael broke into spontaneous applause which rippled around the hill.

"I asked you here today because I need your help to spread the stuff that turns norms into perceivers," said Otis. "It lives in the spores of a special moss. I need each of you to distribute the moss spores to your designated areas. We need to distribute it near centres of high population like towns and cities. After that, it's up to the moss to do the work. Some spores will land and germinate to grow more moss, while others will stay in the air where they will be breathed in. When a norm breathes in a spore, it will give them mild perceiving powers for a short while. After that, they will breathe in another spore and another and another. Eventually, no one will know what it was like to be a norm."

A hushed silence fell across the hill. But the thoughts of the assembled perceivers whispered through their minds:

Is this really going to work?… Is there enough moss?… Does this mean we won't be special anymore?

"I will hand out the moss spores in a moment," said Otis. "But I wanted to release the first set of spores in front of you, on this hill in the centre of England. With all of us joining our minds together. I wanted you all to perceive the determination we have to survive."

There was no more time for words.

Michael opened his perception as he felt everyone around him do the same. It was loud — deafening, pounding at his head like an insistent migraine.

Pauline reached out for his hand and held it tight. The physical warmth of another person grounded him.

The nervousness and excitement of the people on the hill settled down and his headache cleared. So many people with only one mind. Such focus. Such strength. Such power.

Otis lifted his hand into the air. In it, he held a white plastic pot. He tipped the pot sideways and a stream of red dust drifted off into the wind and the tiny perceiver-inducing particles became invisible in the air they breathed.

They savoured the moment. Hundreds of minds all connected in that one moment as, across the country, other perceivers were also joining together in the same cause.

Eventually, their minds broke free of each other and an untidy queue formed to collect their own pots of red dust to take home to where they lived.

Michael, Pauline and Katya collected a pot each.

Michael caught Otis's eye and he came over to greet them.

"Hey, Michael," he said. "I heard you were on the run. It was a brave thing for you to come here. If news of the meeting had been leaked, the police could have found you."

"I thought it was worth the risk," said Michael. "Do you really think this is going to work?"

"My dad says it will." Otis glanced over to where Doctor Smith was handing out the few remaining pots of moss spores. "The moss is virulent and doesn't care that it's winter, which is a blessing. I just hope it spreads quick enough to stop the mass cure programme."

Little Oliver started to cry and Katya bounced him gently in her arms and left their side to walk around a bit. Another woman with a little girl a few months older than Oliver came over to investigate and the two women ended up talking. Michael took the liberty of perceiving them and confirmed that they were Otis's daughter and the woman he called his wife.

"My dad would have loved to be here," said Michael, watching the collection of perceivers drift off down the hill in ones and twos with their little plastic pots.

"It wouldn't have been possible without him," said Otis. "He's the one who got the moss out of Clairone Labs. My dad just propagated a few more and separated out the spores."

"He'll finally get his wish of turning everyone into a perceiver," said Michael. "Not as if I think it'll mean the human race will finally understand each other. There will always be people willing to hurt other people."

Katya and Otis's wife came back over. "The children are getting cold," said Katya. "We should go."

They said their goodbyes and all shook hands because it was the grown-up thing to do.

Then they opened their minds and exchanged *good luck* thoughts because it was the perceiver thing to do.

Michael, Pauline and Katya, with little Oliver in her arms, walked back down the hill and drank the water and ate the chocolate that Pauline had bought from the visitors' centre.

They took a convoluted journey back to the youth hostel in Birmingham where they had booked two rooms under a false name and spread their spores in Rugby, Coventry and Solihull. Each sent out a little plume of red dust, like hundreds and thousands of other plumes of red dust being dispersed across Britain.

In those towns and cities, norms who had once clamoured for perceivers to be cured took a breath and became perceivers themselves. While, at their feet, moss spores took hold in cracks in the pavement and began to grow into plants which would, in turn, release more spores for people to breathe in.

IN the sagging double bed of the stark room in the youth hostel, Michael and Pauline lay together and talked about running away to Spain. Maybe they could escape the cure after all until it was safe to return to Britain.

"I don't think it's right to make Katya keep running with us," said Pauline, as she rested her head on Michael's chest. "But I'm worried about leaving her here with the baby."

"She'll be fine," said Michael. "She's a norm and by the time her son develops his perceiver power, hopefully the threat of the cure will be gone."

"He's your son too," she reminded him.

"Genetically speaking. But a little boy doesn't want to be saddled with the label of being Brian Ransom's grandchild. I'd like to stay and watch him grow up, but I think Katya will be better off without me. And, anyway, I perceive Katya wants to make her own life with her baby."

"I perceived that from her too."

"Maybe one day I'll have babies of my own," said Michael. "The traditional way, I mean, not created in a Russian laboratory."

"I can't think about babies now," said Pauline. "If we have babies together, they'll probably be really strong perceivers. I don't know if it's right to bring a child into the world like that."

"Not this world," said Michael. "Maybe the world of the future will be different."

~ END ~

A note from the author…

Thank you for reading *Mind Power*. To find details of all my novels, please visit my website.

While you're there, don't forget to sign up to my newsletter to make sure you never miss out on new releases, as well as special reader discounts and even *free* stuff!

Come and join in at:

janekillick.com

Acknowledgements

I would like to thank Valentina Kingsolver for translating the Russian dialogue for me.

As always, a big thank you to July Daly for her help and encouragement with this novel and the whole *Perceivers* series.

The Perceivers series

Mind Secrets
Mind Control
Mind Evolution
Mind Power